SHADES
OF
DARKNESS

...DES OF DARKNESS

A. R. Kahler

RAVENBORN BOOK ONE

SIMON PULSE

New York   London   Toronto   Sydney   New Delhi

SIMON PULSE

An imprint of Simon & Schuster Children's Publishing Division
1230 Avenue of the Americas, New York, New York 10020
First Simon Pulse hardcover edition March 2016
Text copyright © 2016 by A. R. Kahler
Jacket photograph copyright © 2016 by Stina Persson
All rights reserved, including the right of reproduction in whole or in part in any form.
SIMON PULSE and colophon are registered trademarks of Simon & Schuster, Inc.
For information about special discounts for bulk purchases, please contact
Simon & Schuster Special Sales at 1-866-506-1949 or business@simonandschuster.com.
The Simon & Schuster Speakers Bureau can bring authors to your live event.
For more information or to book an event contact the Simon & Schuster
Speakers Bureau at 1-866-248-3049 or visit our website at www.simonspeakers.com.
Jacket designed by Regina Flath
Interior designed by Steve Scott
The text of this book was set in Janson.
Manufactured in the United States of America
2 4 6 8 10 9 7 5 3 1
Library of Congress Cataloging-in-Publication Data
Kahler, A. R.
Shades of darkness / A. R. Kahler. —First Simon Pulse hardcover edition.
pages cm. —(Ravenborn ; book 1)
Summary: As she discovers the truth about her past, Kaira, a senior at a boarding school
for aspiring musicians and artists, discovers that vengeful gods are threatening humanity.
ISBN 978-1-4814-3257-3 (hc)
[1. Gods—Fiction. 2. Occultism—Fiction. 3. Boarding schools—Fiction.
4. Schools—Fiction. 5. Artists—Fiction.] I. Title.
PZ7.K1229Sh 2016
[Fic]—dc23
2015013390
ISBN 978-1-4814-3259-7 (eBook)

To my mother,
for opening up the world

KAIRA

CHAPTER ONE

I used to think that drawing studio would be my favorite way to start the school day. Then we started doing nudes, and I realized—after spending an hour and a half staring at an old dude's junk—that no amount of coffee or optimism could get me through the full two-hour class. Especially not today. Not after a month of drawing the *same* guy in the *same* chair with the *same* expression to the point where I had nightmares about his draping skin. And definitely not after pulling an all-nighter just to finish the still-life homework.

"Looking lively, Winters," came a voice behind me.

I nearly jumped.

"Why do you think I'm in line, Davis?" I asked as I turned.

Ethan stood in the short outdoor line for Islington's saving grace: the Dark Note Café. He was the type of boy any self-respecting mother would love to have her daughter date. He was gorgeous in that sharp-angled, European model sort of way. He even dressed nice—when he had to—though today he was wearing a holey cable-knit sweater and had a beanie squashed down over his mousey-brown hair. He'd totally read you poetry by the lakeside and bring you flowers for no reason at all other than that they made him think of you. Any mother's dream.

Which was a shame because, like pretty much every other gorgeous, sensitive, artistic boy I knew, he was gayer than a rainbow-shitting unicorn.

"Let me guess," he said, sidling up to me and hooking his arm through mine, prom style. "You didn't do the drawing homework last week either? You look like you haven't slept in ages."

I reached over and gently rubbed a spot of charcoal from his cheek. It only made it worse, which, again in the typically unfair fashion, just made him even more attractive, in that brooding-artist sort of way.

"You know me well," I replied. But being up until two a.m. drawing eggs didn't account for my insomnia or the dreams that followed. Ethan just didn't need to know about that right now. Before I could wonder if that counted as lying, the violinist in front of me walked off with her coffee and it was my turn to order. "Quad-shot mocha with caramel and hazelnut, *por favor*."

"Make that two," Ethan said. He squeezed my arm. "I love it when you're buying."

I pulled his hat down over his eyes, but I didn't refute.

"Yeah, well, we always knew I'd be your sugar momma."

He pulled off his hat and tried to fix his hair while I paid the barista. I didn't know of too many boarding schools that had a private espresso bar on campus, but then again, with four hundred artists locked away in the middle of Michigan's woods, an espresso bar was about the only thing keeping us from mutiny or a sexual revolution. That and homework.

"I'm still banking on Oliver," Ethan said, sliding his hat back over his mop of hair and adjusting it so it looked just disheveled enough. His eyes took on that lovesick dreamy cast while he mused about his boyfriend. "He's gonna be the next Mozart."

"Bank away. Just remember the little people when you two are honeymooning in Aruba."

Ethan just laughed.

The barista leaned out the window and handed me the drinks. He was in his thirties, with long black hair and a goatee that made him look like either a performer at a Renn Faire or some heavy-metal guitarist. The tag on his T-shirt read MICHAEL, but he'd crossed it out and written IKE over it.

"How's The Hierophant coming, Kaira?" he asked.

"Oh, it's coming," I muttered, taking a sip from both drinks, just to screw with Ethan. "Thanks again for modeling."

Yeah, I know, a little creepy that I asked the barista to model for me, but seeing as I'd just taken a photo of him sitting on a bar stool for reference, it wasn't that big of a deal. It's not like I invited him back to my room.

"Not a problem," he said. "Good luck in class. Your model just ordered a triple espresso, so I doubt he'll be sitting still."

Another thing about Islington I loved and hated, depending on the moment: Everyone knew everyone else's shit.

"Thanks for the heads-up," I said, and threw an extra dollar in his jar for tips.

5

Ethan snatched his drink from my hand as we walked toward the visual arts building. There weren't many kids out and I couldn't blame them; the morning sky was the usual overcast gray that Michigan seemed to favor and tourists detested. I kind of loved it, though—it made the fir trees stretching up between the school buildings a little greener, the snow a little whiter, as though everything was pushed to the edge of living and stillness, caught in the perfection of its prime. We wandered down the winding path, the hem of my patchwork coat trailing in the dusted snow at our feet, while I tried to figure out how I'd best capture the shade of brown of the cafeteria's log staircase. Probably a mix of umber and yellow, with a definite need for sharp white and black framing to make it pop. . . .

"I'll take that as a yes, then," Ethan said, nudging me nearly into a snowdrift.

"Hm?"

"That when we're both old and decrepit we'll never force high school students to draw our private bits."

I chuckled and said, "You're already kind of decrepit."

"And you're already kind of old," he retorted, flashing me a winning grin.

"Touché, young'un, touché."

Ethan was only four months younger than me. Apparently that meant I was a geriatric.

"Ugh," Ethan muttered into his cup. "You really *are* old. You say things like 'young'un.'"

I punched him in the side, gently—can't mar my delicate flower—and said nothing.

We wandered down the long asphalt drive, the academics concourse stretched out to our right and rows of house-like dorms on our left. Even with all the windows closed, I could hear someone blaring pop music from Graham (all the dorms were named after famous artists, which was often unfortunate, seeing as artists rarely had happy endings—case in point, the other female dorm: Plath) and someone else practicing tuba in the basement practice rooms of Rembrandt. Everything on campus was the same rustic style, all bare wood and raw stone, which meant it all looked like one big Christmas card when covered in snow. And, being in northern Michigan, it almost always was.

The arts building loomed at the end of the road. Nearly every wall was made of glass, including large chunks of the ceiling. It still had the rustic log-cabin charm, but with a little more Frank Lloyd Wright mixed in, complete with odd-angled corners and a second story that sat atop the first like a slightly offset block.

"How do you think they got the name?" Ethan asked as we walked.

"What?" I asked.

He nudged my shoulder and gestured up, to the power line laden with crows.

"A murder," he replied. "I mean, a flock makes sense. Or even a clutch. But a murder of crows? I don't get it."

I took another long drink of coffee, suddenly colder from all those beady black eyes staring at me.

"No clue," I replied. "Maybe it's symbolic or something."

"Speaking of," Ethan said, "how's your project *really* going?"

"Well, it hasn't killed me yet."

"Yet?"

"Yet."

He didn't inquire further as I opened the great glass door to the arts building for him. The moment that first draft of warm air embraced me, I felt at home. The floor was slate slats and the walls flat white. Yesterday the walls had been blank. Now, the foyer was filled with black-and-white photographs. I slid off my coat and wandered up to the nearest photo.

"Beauty," Ethan muttered, and took a sip of his coffee.

And he was right. The photo was slightly surreal, clearly a double exposure and some darkroom manipulation, showing an abandoned clapboard house with a figure floating in front of it, but the figure—a small child holding a balloon—was upside-down, as though she was floating and the balloon held her to the Earth. Below it was a small piece of cardboard with the piece's title and artist.

"*Untitled thirteen*," Ethan said. "How original. I dread to read the artist's statement."

I shrugged. Truth be told, I hated the whole "untitled" thing too . . . but then again, I still hadn't settled on a title for my own upcoming exhibition. *Untitled* was becoming a strong contestant.

"Kai never was one for words," I replied. "Come on, we're going to be late."

Which was a lie. We had a good ten minutes before class. I just didn't want to stand out here, staring at another senior's thesis. Kai had applied to many of the same colleges I had, albeit for a different department, and I hated comparing my work to his. Especially since my paintings would soon be dotting this very hall. Ethan didn't protest as we walked away. Probably because he, too, was facing an upcoming exhibition and, like me, was entirely unprepared. At least he had a month to finish; his thesis went up two weeks after mine.

We headed down the maze of a hall toward the back of the building. A few other seniors had their final projects on display deeper in—Tina had her funky silver-and-found-object rings scattered about on a few pedestals; Jeremy displayed a collection of rather tasteless line drawings that almost but not quite resembled genitalia; Kah-Yee showcased a textile exhibit that involved one large crocheted web over the ceiling, bits of found objects dangling from it like old memories—which just made the usually comforting walk more stressful than it should have been. My time was ticking. Soon, too soon, I'd have to compete with the big guys. And I couldn't convince myself I'd pull this one out of my hat. Not even the scent of oil paints drifting down the corridor could help. We took a stairway off to the side and headed toward the top level.

"We should go fishing tonight," Ethan said when we reached the big black door leading to the drawing studio. He pushed it open and gestured grandly for me to enter. "If, you know, you aren't terribly busy."

"You're the one with the boyfriend," I said, giving him a half curtsy as I walked past.

"I know," he replied. "And yet I'm choosing to spend my Friday night with you. Feel the love, Winters. Feel the love."

I blew him a kiss and let my brain switch over to class mode.

The drawing studio was probably my fourth favorite place

9

on campus. Only one of the walls in here was glass, but since it was on the second story and overlooked the forest, that was okay. The other three walls were white and as pristine as a giant studio can be when said room hosts charcoal drawing classes. Easels and stools were set up in a half circle around an overstuffed armchair. Thankfully, the armchair was empty; our model stood in the corner by our instructor's desk, still fully robed. It always felt awkward walking in when he was already naked.

Ethan and I settled onto our respective stools. I flipped to the first clean sheet of paper on my easel and took one last sip of my short-lived mocha. The Dark Note seriously needed to invest in thirty-two-ounce cups.

The rest of the class—twelve of us in all—was already there and settling in. Another reason why I hated being even a fraction of a second late.

Jane sat down beside me. Her family was Korean, though she'd lived in the States for so much of her childhood, her accent was flawless. She was also seriously the only painter I knew who didn't have at least one splotch of paint on every article of clothing she owned. I glanced down to my own ensemble: faded skinny jeans covered in patches and hand-drawn runes (not my doing), pink long-sleeve shirt covered in ink smears (admittedly my doing), studded black vest with some alchemical wheel drawn on the back (again, not my doing). Paired with the magenta streaks in my hair (definitely not my doing—Ethan demanded I let only him touch my hair) and the burgundy eye shadow and Eye of Horus spiral I'd drawn under my right eye, I definitely bordered on the edge of "trying too hard."

But hell, if growing up in the Midwest taught me anything, it was that people stared at me no matter what. Probably because I was some unknown blend of Native American bloodlines. Makeup was my mask; it gave people a reason to stare for nonracist reasons.

"How was the still life?" Jane asked the moment she settled in.

Despite the coffee, the very thought of last night's last-minute homework made me yawn.

"Same," Jane said, smiling. "I feel bad for Cassie. She's the one who really suffers when I'm up till two drawing eggs."

"No wonder she and Elisa are friends," I said. "They always have something to commiserate over."

Well, I'm sure there were many more reasons Cassie and my roommate, Elisa (pronounced *ah-LEE-zah*, because she said it made her sound refined), got along, but having visual artist roommates definitely gave them cause to bond. The girl beside Jane asked her something, so I turned back to Ethan.

"Are we really on tonight?" I asked. I didn't want to get my hopes up in case he changed his mind last minute to hang out with Oliver. It was Friday night, not that it meant anything (because yes, our school ran Tuesday to Saturday—don't ask, I swear they only did it to be different), but Oliver often took Ethan to the movies on Fridays so they could pretend they were a normal high school couple. But I could really use getting off campus, even if only for an hour.

"Totally," he said. He rubbed a hand across his nose and left a charcoal smear. I said nothing—it just added to the charm.

"Oliver's roommate's *finally* out of town, so I'm staying at his place tomorrow night."

My jaw dropped.

"No way. How did . . . ?"

"I'm old guard, Winters," he said with a wink. "Four years here and you can get away with murder."

Before I could ask how Ethan managed to score a sleepover at his boyfriend's, our instructor, Andy, came forward. He was in jeans and a blazer, dapper as always, but there was something about him that seemed a little off. Maybe it was because he was in his sixties and still tried too hard to connect with his students. I mean, all teachers at Islington tried to connect, and most of them succeeded because we're all a little batshit. But something about Andy just made him feel like a doddering uncle. Potentially because he kind of smelled like cabbage.

Our model, Mr. G., took his place on the chair and carefully arranged his red bathrobe to cover his delicate bits. Give him a pipe and a library and he'd look like the perfect English gentleman: thinning white hair in a cunning combover, wispy eyebrows, and skin that didn't appear to have seen sunlight since birth.

"Good morning, everyone," Andy said. "It's Mr. G.'s last day with us, so we're going to hit the ground running. After break we'll bring out your assignments for critique. Sound good?" My classmates gave a couple of half hearted nods. I couldn't help that skin-crawly feeling I got whenever Andy spoke to us. He just made every interaction so *awkward*.

Without any further forced preamble, Andy nodded to Mr. G. and went back to his desk.

At that, Mr. G. disrobed completely and the work began. Our warmup was simple and familiar: minute-long sketches in charcoal to capture overall shape and tension. I grabbed a piece of willow charcoal and began to sketch, my arm and wrist arcing across the tablet of paper, black lines blooming under my fingertips like curving road maps. I looked over to Ethan only once; beyond that glance, I was lost in the flow of the line.

The figures that formed were simple and clean: Mr. G. adopting *The Thinker* pose, him standing on one leg, him reclining with legs crossed. Figure drawing had always come easily to me, which was a good chunk of the reason I'd sent myself off to Islington in the first place. Not many kids my age cared to go to an arts school that promised an extra two hours of daily class time, extended summer hours, required after-class studios, and double the workload. But I did. I couldn't stand public school, with its stupid cliques and braindead jocks. I couldn't even fit in with the goths or the geeks or the band nerds. I wasn't dark enough or gamer-y enough or into obscure music. Though, if I wanted to be perfectly honest, that was only a small part of the reason I came here. Home was filled with ghosts. And here, hundreds of miles away, their cries were silenced. At least, in theory.

You just need to get out and relax a little, I convinced myself as I drew. *You're just stressed. Too much work and too little sleep. That would make anyone a little nostalgic and a little . . . sensitive.*

After the warmup, we did a few ten-minute poses and worked our way down in time until we ended in twenty five-second traces, each in a different color of oil pastel but occupying the same space. My hands were greasy and looked like a rainbow had vomited all over them, but the resulting explosion of color on the page was fantastic. Andy paused behind my stool and put a hand on my shoulder.

"Nice work, Kaira. Really nice work. It almost looks angelic."

He moved on and said something to Jane that I didn't really catch because I was too busy trying not to laugh over Ethan mouthing "akwaaaaaaaard" when Andy's back was turned. I tried to focus on the sketch instead. The center of the page had a dark outline of Mr. G. from where his parts had overlapped, but there were strands of color arcing off—arms and legs and arching torsos, so it almost looked like he was sprouting rainbow wings.

"Show-off," Ethan muttered in my ear. I jerked and looked back. He was standing right behind me, his lukewarm coffee in hand (he wasn't a pro coffee drinker like me). I swatted him in the chest, leaving a light blue smear on his now multicolored sweater.

"Come on," I said, standing up to stretch. We had a five-minute break before the next set of sketches. "I need to pee, and you need to gossip."

"Hopefully, not all at once," he said. I just shook my head and led him from the studio by the cuff of his sleeve.

Ethan waited for me outside the bathroom, leaning against a cardboard Roman pillar. My little sanity anchor. My reminder that the past was the past and this was the present, and the present was pretty fucking great. He was doodling something on his wrist with a Biro pen and leaning beside one student's collage rendition of a Monet, looking like he was waiting for someone to snap his Polaroid and label it *Too Hip for Hipsters*.

I'd known Ethan since I came to Islington. We were given peer mentors before the start of term to help us newbies acclimate to the school's quirks, and Ethan had been mine. He'd attended Islington since his freshman year and knew the place inside and out. During our first meeting, while our group lounged on the leather sofas in the Writers' House with the electric fireplace going despite the late-summer heat, Ethan had presented us with a particular dilemma: Each of the mentor groups had been given a stipend to spend for group activities, and he wasn't interested in doing the usual tie-dyed shirt and movie night thing. He recommended we use the money to fund a weekly café trip in hopes of finding hot men. He affectionately called the project *Fishing for Dick*. Then and there, my love for him was affirmed.

"Come on," I said. "Spill it." I nudged up beside him and looked down at the notes on his skinny wrist. Sadly, they were just reminders of upcoming assignments and project ideas. Nothing juicy.

"What?" he said. He glanced around as though we were already discussing his sex life, cheeks blushing. Save for a few girls chatting as they went into the bathroom, the hall was empty.

I grabbed the pen from his hand, grasped his wrist with the other, and wrote in my hastiest cursive: "will u fuk?"

When he looked at what I wrote, he went an even brighter shade of crimson and tried to scrub it off. He didn't succeed.

"You're classy, you know that?" he said. Then he looked up

at me, and a stupid little grin perked up the corner of his mouth. "And yes, probably. Maybe. Definitely. Gods I hope so."

I sniffed and wiped an invisible tear from my eye. "My little boy's all grown up," I said, making my voice crack.

"Yeah, well . . ." But he didn't say anything else because the girls came out from the bathroom then and it was clear our short break was up. He cleared his throat. "Did you want to go fishing or not?" he asked. Even though the mentor group eventually disbanded, Ethan and I had kept up the good fight: Nearly every Friday we went to the same teahouse, though it had become more a ritual for finishing homework before the weekend than finding men. Especially since Ethan had found Oliver at the beginning of this year.

"Of course," I said. I'd never miss out on these tea dates. Ever. Even if we did have to shuffle them around a bit now that a romance was in the picture.

"Good. If you're nice, I'll tell you more about my planned seduction. Casanova's got nothing on me."

"There's still lunch," I offered, because we didn't have any more classes together today.

"And my boyfriend still sits with us," Ethan said.

"Then you can tell me on the way there. You know I hate waiting."

Ethan just rolled his eyes.

"I swear to Paula Deen, if Andy assigns us one more still life this term I'm going to scream."

I snorted into my hot chocolate. We sat in the far corner

16

of the cafeteria, nestled between a wall of past students' art and a window overlooking the frozen lake. A flock of crows circled lazily in the sky. Sorry, a *murder.*

"Did you really just swear to Paula Deen?" I asked Ethan.

He nodded and crossed himself, holding a packet of butter in his hand as he did so.

"I don't think praying's going to help," I muttered, looking out at the lunch crowd. "Andy does love making us sketch the most exciting of subjects."

There was a groan, and then a thud, and when I looked over Ethan had his head on the table in defeat. I reached over and rustled his hat. His hand snatched up and caught my arm.

"Watch the hair," he mumbled from the tabletop, not budging an inch.

"I am," I said. "I'm giving you that hot disheveled look."

"He's already hot and disheveled," came a voice behind me.

Oliver stepped around to the other side of the table, setting his tray beside Ethan's. Ethan immediately sat up, grinning at his boyfriend.

"Hey babe," Ethan chirped. Oliver grinned, leaned over, and gave Ethan a quick peck on the lips.

"Afternoon gorgeous," Oliver replied, then sat down.

Oliver was, as my mother would say, a tall glass of water—not that I'd ever say such a thing to his face. Six foot two, gorgeous coffee-color skin, and brown eyes to match, he looked like he should be playing bass in some smoky jazz club in Paris. His penchant for wearing button-downs and vests—and the fact that he actually *did* play bass—only made the image more tantalizing.

"How you doing, Kaira?" he asked. He reached over and took my hand, raising it up to kiss the backs of my fingers.

"Better now that my Prince Charming is here," I said with a grin.

His smile could have lit a cave.

"You look tired," he said, studying my face. "Have you been sleeping okay?"

"Okay, seriously, I'm starting to consider plastering my face with foundation. I thought gay boys were supposed to be good for a girl's self-esteem?"

Ethan laughed. "I don't know where you got that idea."

"Fine," I said, shaking my head and readdressing Oliver, who hadn't stopped grinning at me. "I was up all night working on homework last minute, just like you said I would be, oh prophetic one."

"Sometimes I hate being right." The smile said quite the opposite.

I went back to eating my veggie lasagna. *Oh heavenly carbs, at least you'll never betray me.*

"Anyway," Oliver continued, unfolding a napkin onto his lap, "I need you to make sure this one gets his work done. I worry I'm distracting him too much."

"You know my babysitting rates double on weekends."

"I'll pay. Pretty certain being your friend is paying my dues."

I chuckled. "Most of the time. But yeah, I'll make sure he doesn't slack off."

Ethan leaned across the table and waved his hands. "Um, guys? Still here. Can hear every word you're saying."

"Of course," Oliver said, completely ignoring his boyfriend, "this goes both ways. You only get paid if you both have your theses finished."

My hands shot to my heart. "Lo! I am slain!"

Ethan slugged Oliver on the shoulder. "I told you never to mention that word to her."

"What? Finished?"

"Thesis," Ethan gasped. "The word of death."

As expected, Oliver just chuckled to himself and went back to eating. Ethan shot me a glance, one that read both *I'm sorry he said anything* and *Oh gods, we really do need to finish these soon.* "Thesis" was one of those words that carried the same sort of weight between me and Ethan as "juxtaposed" or "post modern." We simply didn't use it—ever—out of mutual respect for each other's feelings. Oliver knew this, but it didn't carry the same punch for him. He thought it was funny, the way we squirmed around like he'd just asked which of us he should behead first.

Trouble was, he had a point. Ethan and I needed to get our shit together. Otherwise we'd both be showcasing Post-it notes of stick figures for our senior theses. And we couldn't copy Jeremy.

"Fine," I relented. "We'll do it. Prepare your kidneys, Ethan. We're about to consume more coffee than any mortal has before."

CHAPTER TWO

Islington wasn't like most high schools. Actually, that's sort of an understatement. I'm pretty certain the original founders had a meeting and said, "Let's take everything they do at public schools and reverse it." Like most boarding schools, we had things like evening sign-in and curfews and ridiculous lights-out rules that no one actually followed. Boys and girls were only allowed to mingle in public spaces or—if you got permission and kept the door open—in dorm rooms during specific hours. Unlike most boarding schools, we didn't have a uniform or a dress code beyond "try not to expose too much skin because, after all, most of the school year is covered in snow." We also didn't have any sports teams steeped in glory, unless you counted ultimate Frisbee. And no one really did. Not even the team members.

Islington was an entity unto itself—a bastion of learning and creativity. Or so the admissions guide proclaimed. Four hundred teenage artists from every discipline, gathered in one place in the middle of nowhere, each aspiring to be the Next Big Thing.

No parents. Extreme workloads and stress. Raging hormones. Endless days of isolation and dark winter skies.

As one could expect, it was a reality TV show waiting to happen.

After leaving the cafeteria, I headed toward Myth and Folklore. Being a lit course, it was one of the few academic classes I had to take to graduate, though unlike the other options—like Russian Literature and Postmodern Poetry—I was actually interested in the subject. Not that it prevented me from spending the majority of class doodling in the edges of my notebook and passing witty notes back and forth with Elisa. I had to be careful and look like I was paying attention, though—the instructor was Mr. Almblad (aka Jonathan), my faculty adviser. Screwing up with him could screw up the rest of my year.

Elisa passed me a tightly folded note while Jonathan scribbled the names of Norse gods and their associations on the whiteboard.

"Wild party tonight?" the note read.

I grinned and nodded. Elisa and I had been roommates from the get-go, and we had our own little code. In nerdy art-school land, "wild party" translated to "soda and bad movies night."

Like me, she was in her senior year. And, like me, she'd sent herself here her junior year, much to her parents' dismay. That's pretty much where the similarities ended.

Elisa was a figure painter's wet dream. She was a theatre student, which meant that, unlike most of the kids in my own department, she cared about her looks. Her long brown hair was always perfectly wavy, even today when it flowed from under her knit hat like a waterfall. Delicate, almost Nordic-elf features, bright blue eyes, dimples. She did yoga and modern dance and could hold a modeling pose for hours. And, since she was my roommate, she often got roped into being my subject.

"Out with Ethan. After sign-in? What are we going to watch?" I wrote on the other side of the note. I folded it into a crane and tossed it to Elisa when Jonathan was turned around.

Last year, people were positive she and I were a lesbian couple. After all, we walked hand-in-hand to and from dinner, and spent most of our free time (well, the time I wasn't with Ethan, which wasn't too often) working together. Neither of us refuted the rumors, mostly because we didn't care—Elisa was bi, and I was definitely not dating. We probably wouldn't have ever clarified anything, but our hall counselor asked outright because having couples room together was against school policy.

Now she was dating a dance major named Kyle who, we were both pretty certain, also played both sides of the field. And I, as planned, was still resolutely single. I preferred the term "off-limits." Ethan preferred the term "future crazy cat lady."

I watched Elisa bite the tip of her pen in consideration of what movie to stream, but before she could write it down, Jonathan turned back around and addressed the class.

"As we've read time and time again," he said, standing behind his desk, "the worshipers of pagan gods didn't see their deities as untouchable creatures. The gods were living, breathing things, able to interact with mere mortals and disrupt their affairs. From the Celts to the Greeks to the Egyptians, the old pantheons were notoriously interactive with their mortal subjects. The Norse were no different in that worship—to them, Loki and Thor and Freyja were as real as their own kin. The gods were allies, albeit feared ones. It was the gods who blessed you with good crops, and it was the gods who took the innocent away."

Jonathan had been my adviser for only a few months—my old adviser left to do a photo residency in Brazil after fall term— but we'd gotten on immediately. Like my drawing instructor, Jonathan had a penchant for wearing jeans and blazers. Unlike Andy, Jonathan actually pulled them off. He had curly brown hair and a short beard and wire-rim glasses. His blazers were often tweed with leather elbow patches. Some even had pocket squares. And he was maybe in his early thirties.

All of this paired quite well with the fact that he was covered in tattoos from the jaw down. I'd never seen most of them, just the bits that poked up from his collar and cuffs (birds up the neck, clouds and vines and figures on the forearms), but I'd asked him once what the grayscale tattoo was. He said it was a scene from Ragnarök.

Gotta love the hipster professors. I was pretty sure 90 percent of the male and female student body wanted to jump his sexy-intelligent bones. I just wanted to be him, tattoos and nonchalant air and all.

"Over the next three weeks we will be shifting focus from Celtic folklore to Scandinavian mythos. As you'll quickly learn, there is a great amount of crossover between the two pantheons and modes of worship. And, as I'm sure you expected, that will be the topic for your next research project."

There was a collective moan throughout the class, which just made him smile. I wasn't one of the kids whining, however. This sort of shit was right up my alley. Besides, any excuse to look up mythology could only help my painting thesis.

"We're going to start by examining how the Norse viewed the worlds of men and gods. If you'd open up to the chapter titled 'Yggdrasil' and follow along?"

The name was a shot of adrenaline to my chest as I turned to the chapter. The print of a tree, black and stretched between the realms of man and gods, stared back at me. A stain. Ink on paper, blood on concrete. . . . I squeezed my eyes shut and took a deep breath.

Something landed on my desk, and I opened my eyes with a jolt. I glanced at Elisa, who had flung the note my way while Jonathan was rooting in his desk. I tried to grin as I spread open the paper over the chapter header, quickly covering up the woodblock print of *Yggdrasil, the World Tree*.

"*Let's watch something bloody,*" the note said. "*Also, give Ethan my love.*"

The last few hours of my day were spent in silversmithing, my throwaway arts course. I spent so much time staring at canvas or paper that doing something that involved getting hands-on and dirty—and I mean *really* dirty, like wearing goggles and leather aprons and lighting things on fire dirty—was a nice switch. The studio was in the back of the arts building, near the loading dock. It was one of the few areas in the entire building that didn't provide some stunning view of the grounds, mainly because the only window looked out on the outdoor welding and soldering area, which was only picturesque if you liked the industrial motif.

By the class's end at five, my stomach was rumbling and the coffee from this morning had long since worn off. I put away my saw blades and sandpaper and put on the ring I just made for myself—a tiny silver band with little birds cut out. Technically speaking I should have been working on a collection of brooches for my final project, but the instructor, Ginny, didn't mind. It was one of the few year-long classes at Islington, and by now she'd learned that I always got my shit done on time. Always. So long as I was working on new techniques in class, she wasn't too bothered if it wasn't strictly for the project.

After all, how would we learn our own style if we weren't allowed to play?

"Nice work," Chris said as I admired the ring.

I tried to hide my blush at the sound of his voice, hoping the extra five seconds it took me to put on my coat was enough to let the rouge fade.

"Thanks," I replied. And then I did what I'd been training myself not to do this entire school year. I looked him in the eyes and smiled.

There were a few rules in my life that I followed to a T. One: Never ignore an omen. Two: Never pass up a new opportunity unless, you know, you'll die from it. And three: Never fall in love.

They were all tried and true rules, but Rule Three was the most important. Love was for getting hurt. Badly. Or hurting someone else in the process. It wasn't safe, in direct violation of Rule Two.

Chris made me want to ignore the rules in spite of all that. And that's why I had to keep him at arm's length.

Every time I saw him, I imagined him darting through the woods like an elf. His usual earthy, hand-accented attire only helped that image. He was a senior, like me, with a brown floppy undercut that was almost a mohawk and a goatee. His hazel eyes had that really unnerving habit of not looking away when you were talking to him.

Like they were doing just now.

"How's your thesis going?" he asked. Again, he didn't look away, and I know I said it was unnerving, but it wasn't creepy. It was actually really charming. The unnerving part came from the gravity it created. The pull I'd been fighting from day one. Chris was gorgeous and talented, albeit a few inches shorter than me, and the first two points were definite reasons we couldn't date. Never, ever trust the pretty ones with your heart. Unless, of course, they're gay.

"It's going," I replied. It took me a moment to realize him saying "thesis" didn't cause the same violent reaction it usually did. Probably because I was already so focused on not looking into those eyes. "I should be ready though. How about you?"

He ran a hand through his hair and looked over to his shelf in the corner. Jesus, that boy's jawline. His face was basically the embodiment of aquiline. My fingers itched to sketch him, but that was an alley I was *not* going down. Getting him alone to stare at him for a few hours? *Danger, Will Robinson, danger.*

"It's going," he repeated, and chuckled to himself. "Who'd

have thought doing a dozen different surrealist landscapes would be tiresome?"

"I could have told you that one," I said. "Though the idea is rockin'."

He laughed again and slung his canvas messenger bag over his shoulder. "Did you really just use the word 'rockin"?"

"I did. Is there a problem?"

"Not at all. And thanks. I was worried it was pretentious."

I shrugged and held open the door for him. The hall outside was mostly empty as the school filtered toward dinner, which I would be skipping to go fishing. My stomach rumbled again, and I mentally assured it there would be plenty of dolmas and hummus to keep it from mutiny.

"You heading to dinner?" he asked.

Okay, what was going on? Was I just overthinking things, or was it honestly unusual for him to have lingered after class to chat when we hadn't exchanged more than a passing hello all year?

"Actually, no, I'm heading out with a friend."

"Oooh, is it a date?"

My imagination, or did his smile slip just a little?

"Definitely," I said. "Though his boyfriend will always have dibs on him."

He raised an eyebrow and I realized where that mental train was going. Oh Islington, where sexuality was as fluid as the blood in our horny little veins.

"I mean, no. He's gay. Like, really really gay. It was a joke."

"Got it," he said.

We walked in silence for a bit, passing the works of other

27

students and pausing to stare on occasion. I pretended Chris was Oliver. Cool, confident, sexually uninterested Oliver. It made the whole interaction much easier.

"I can't believe it's in two weeks," I muttered, staring at a student's impeccable self-portrait. Two more weeks to finish my thesis and tie up my entire high school career in one neat little package.

"Lucky. You're getting it over with. I've got another four."

"More time to prepare?" Of course. His show was going up with Ethan's—it would mean I couldn't skip the opening.

"More time to panic, in all honesty."

When we resumed walking, I couldn't help but notice that he kept glancing over to me, like he wanted to ask me something. It just made me walk a little faster. Thankfully, Jane was coming down the stairs from the painting studio. She bounced over to us as she zipped up her downy aquamarine coat and grinned.

"Hey guys," she said. "Mind if I walk with you?"

"Not at all," I said. Maybe a little too quickly. I didn't want to be alone with Chris, and I couldn't tell if it was because I didn't trust him or myself. *Don't be so nervous, you can trust me.* I shoved down the voice before it could get louder, jabbing my finger with my room key to stay grounded.

"How's it going?" Chris asked Jane. If he was upset by someone else joining in, he didn't show it. Maybe he *was* just being cordial.

"Great," she replied. "Just trying to get tomorrow's homework finished up." She nudged me. "Though Little Miss Amazing over here's already done."

I shrugged and tried to fight down my second blush in five minutes. My heart was racing from the words that had bubbled up from the depths. I clearly needed sleep. And out of this situation. Where was Ethan? I needed his snark to keep me in balance.

"It's what happens when you don't have a social life," I said, looking everywhere but at Chris. "Work comes easier."

It was only a partial lie. The truth was, I could spend days painting and not notice the time. I'd finished the assignment two days early not because I was trying to be efficient, but because I'd seriously lost myself to the process. I almost missed sign-in because of it. There were reasons I set alarms when I went in to paint on my own.

"So says the girl who's ditching us for an off-campus fling," Chris said.

"Let me guess—Ethan?"

"*She* gets me," I said, gesturing to Jane.

We reached the end of the hall. Chris opened the door for us and bowed as we exited. Five o'clock and the sky was already dark as death. Most kids complained about it, but I actually really enjoyed the short days. It wasn't an emo thing; I just wasn't cut out for sun or heat. Another reason I sent myself to boarding school in the northern wilds.

"Anyway," I said, wrapping my burgundy scarf around my neck. Chris buttoned the last few buttons of his tan duster and Jane pulled on a knit hat. It felt like it was going to snow. We already had two feet on the ground, but I seriously hoped for another flurry. The woods felt most alive in the silence and snow. "This is where I must bid you adieu."

Chris shook his head.

"Don't say that. Adieu is sort of a permanent farewell. It pretty much means 'to God.'"

How fitting, I thought, and shoved it back down with the rest of my past.

"Oh well then," I said, struggling to keep my wit in check, "since I don't plan on overdosing on tea, I shall say . . . catch you later, alligators?"

Jane laughed and gave me a quick hug. Chris just stood there awkwardly. "In a while, crocodile," he fumbled.

"Nice try, champ. Better luck next time." Then I slapped him on the shoulder (holy crap, what was I becoming, a bro?) and turned before that itchy gravity between us could connect. I didn't look back to watch them head toward the cafeteria. I kept my eyes on the road, but I had no doubt that the murder of crows on the power lines weren't the only ones watching me depart.

Get a hold of yourself, Kaira, I thought as I walked. *You just need to sleep.*

Yeah. Tell that to my dreams.

I shook my head and focused on the chill air, the way it made my nostrils freeze. *This is what's important. Where you are, not where you've been. Your past can't hurt you unless you let it.* I'd learned a lot in the last few years at Islington. The most important, though, was how to keep moving forward.

There was something about winter dusk that made Islington look like an entirely different beast. Color seemed to seep from the landscape, and everything sharpened in shades of steel and snow, save for the warm lights flooding from the practice rooms and dorms. Kids wandering around in parkas and gloves held hands and threw snowballs and sang show tunes (*drama kids*). It looked like the cover for an admissions packet. Every single place on campus was an invitation to come inside and get warm and have some hot cocoa. I glanced behind me to where the Writers' House beckoned at the lane's end, a great A-frame lodge created just for the writing classes, and one of the many buildings I wished I could convert into my personal living space. And ahead, the five dorms housing all of Islington's four hundred students waited.

I trudged past the boys' dorms and up the front steps into Graham. As expected, Ethan was already waiting at the front desk, perched on a stool with Oliver at his side, chatting with Maria. The rest of the waiting area was empty—no one checking their cubby mailboxes or watching TV in the lounge behind the front desk. Everyone was at dinner. My stomach growled again. One of the drawbacks of boarding school's food schedule: It turned you into a geriatric in a week. Dinner by five? Please.

"Hey boys," I called.

Maria—my hall's RA, with red pin-up hair and a penchant for polka dots—looked past Ethan's shoulder and raised one perfectly painted eyebrow.

"And bombshell babe," I corrected. "How was the rest of the day?"

"Droll," Ethan said lethargically. Oliver nudged him.

"Ignore him. He's channeling angsty art student hardcore today." Oliver walked over and gave me a hug while Ethan slouched deeper onto his stool. "Poor boy says he's dying of cabin fever."

"I can fix that," I said. "You coming with?"

It was hard to keep my question smooth. Oliver had never, ever come to one of our tea dates. It's not that he wasn't allowed, it's just that . . . it was kind of Ethan's and my time.

"Nope," he said. "I need to practice for the concert tomorrow. You coming?"

"Of course she is," Ethan called from his seat. He sat up a little straighter. "She's my date."

"Speaking of, I'm starving." I looked to Maria. "We all set?"

Normally I'd have to sign out to be off campus, but it was rare that I actually signed anything. Ethan had probably already told Maria we were heading out and filed the necessary paperwork even before I'd left class. They were tight like that.

"Yup," she said. "Provided you bring me back a scone."

"Done." I kissed Ethan on the forehead. "You ready, hot stuff?"

"And eager."

He slid off the seat and took Oliver's and my hands, then led us out the front door. The three of us walked together toward the parking lot behind the cafeteria. Somehow it had gotten even darker in the half second we were inside. The streetlamps along the lane came on, casting their fierce white light over everything. A crow, startled by the sudden light, took off with an angry caw down the lane and into the woods by the lake.

"So what's on the agenda for tonight?" Oliver asked. "We still on the hunt for the man who'll melt Kaira's icy heart? Or woman, I guess."

I nearly skidded on a patch of ice. "Um, homo say what?"

"Smooth," Ethan said, and I wasn't certain if he was talking about my horrible comeback or Oliver's question. They both knew that dating wasn't in the cards for me. But Oliver seemed to forget that at times. "And no, tonight we're going to escape the meaningless cycle of art and academic industry."

"By working on homework," Oliver said.

Ethan pointed to his boyfriend. "That . . . is accurate. But we're working off campus, so it doesn't count."

"What's gotten into you today?" I asked, eager to turn the conversation back to him and away from talk of potential boyfriends. "You're more broody than usual. Did you watch *The Breakfast Club* again?"

Oliver snorted and flashed me a grin. Ethan's lack of a laugh told me I'd hit somewhere close to home. Woops.

"I got a C on my American Civ paper," he muttered.

In Ethan's world, that was pretty much the equivalent of being shot in the kneecap. It had taken me a few months to understand that his perfectionism wasn't just a facade—he really *did* need to be the best at everything he tried. Otherwise, he took it as a personal failure.

"I'll take some credit for that," Oliver said, letting go of Ethan's hand to wrap an arm over his shoulder. Ethan, being a good eight inches shorter than Oliver, leaned in to the embrace. "I feel like I've been distracting you too much, now that college apps are over."

Ethan just shrugged. "I don't mind the distraction. Just need to get better at time management."

Oliver gave him a squeeze. And I knew, then, that Ethan wasn't just upset about the grade. He was upset about *why* he'd gotten the grade. In a few weeks we'd be hearing back from colleges, and once that happened, the happy little dream of the three of us living in this Eden together would shatter. I knew Ethan was trying to make the most of the time he had with Oliver. And I knew it killed him that he couldn't have the boyfriend and the best friend and still keep his grades up.

Priorities, man. For some reason, art school fucked with them.

We parted ways at the steps leading to the cafeteria. Oliver gave Ethan another quick kiss and pecked me on the forehead. Then, with a backward glance and wave and "Make sure you get her at least one number!" he bounced up the stairs and into the bustling dining room. From the smell that wafted out, it was Chinese night. Definitely a good reason to eat off campus. Islington couldn't do fried rice to save its life, and the smell of soy sauce and General Tso's stuck to you for days.

"Sorry about that," Ethan muttered as we walked down the drive to the parking lot.

"What?" I asked, looking away from the crow perched above the cafeteria door.

"Being grumpy. Oliver being . . . Oliver."

"It's why I love him," I said. Chris's face flashed through my mind. *Someone to melt my heart?* No way in hell; my heart was perfectly fine on its own, thanks. I stuffed the thought down into the shadows. "And it's why I love you. Tea will make everything better."

"You're so British it hurts," he said, and opened the passenger

34

door of his old Lincoln town car for me. "But thankfully not with the teeth."

He was the only person I knew under sixty who had those beaded seat covers. The rest of the interior was, like him, a study in presented chaos: Papers and art supplies were strewn over the backseat, though there wasn't any rubbish in the footwells or wrappers on the cushions. I'd spent so much time in this car that it felt like a second home, to the point where I kept a chunk of my art materials in here, just for occasions such as this. He sank into the driver's seat and turned the ignition on, cranking up the frozen heat. Some whiny indie band came on, a "local favorite" as he liked to say, which just meant they played banjo and hadn't had a tour outside of the state.

"Shall we?" he asked.

I nodded, and we pulled out of the lot and onto the narrow road leading into town. The birds in the branches watched us the entire way, and I couldn't fight down the shadowy mantra in my mind, no matter how loud he blared his music.

A murder of crows. A murder of crows. And the dream, like a stain in the night air—the face of my ex watching me through the bleeding boughs.

Never ignore an omen.

CHAPTER THREE

The teahouse was at the edge of the nearby town, down a small side street between a secondhand store and the organic supermarket. Fairy lights swayed back and forth above the alley like mutinous stars ready to fall. It was a good twenty-minute drive, seeing as Islington was settled far outside of civilization. I don't know how Ethan had found out about this place, but I was glad he did; T'Chai Nanni was a second sanctuary, a more urban Islington. The café itself was a small house stuck in the side of a shopping center. A wooden porch stretched out front, covered by more fairy lights and a tin roof laden with snow. Empty chairs and cushions were arranged in circles on the patio, braziers and wine barrels in between. On warmer nights, they had live acoustic bands out here, or poetry readings, and the chairs would be swamped with hipsters smoking hand-rolled cigarettes and hippies smelling like patchouli and weed. Like I said, a more urban Islington, hipsters and pot smoke and all.

By the time we pulled up, the first of the flurries had begun drifting down from the sky. I smiled as I stepped out of the car, tilting back my head and sticking out my tongue. I didn't catch any flakes. Ethan trudged over to my side and held my hand and did the same. Silently. We stood there for a good minute or so, waiting for snow to drop and dissolve. The air was sharp and metallic and smelled of cumin and cold, a strange balance of ice and warmth from T'Chai Nanni. No matter what, the first moments of snowfall always made me feel like a little kid, like anything was possible and everything was beautiful.

Lately, it seemed, I needed that reminder more and more often.

After a while, Ethan squeezed my hand and stepped aside to grab our portfolios from the back of his car. I opened my eyes and stared up at the crows darting about like black comets. *Dark omens. Shut up, Kaira, you're being ridiculous.* Then Ethan handed me my portfolio and began walking toward the café, and I followed, trying to push down the scent of blood lingering in my nostrils.

T'Chai Nanni was warm and humid and smelled like cardamom and cloves, which immediately brought my brain back to reality. The birds were just birds, and everything else was my tired imagination trying to fill in the blanks. Chalk one up to the artist's brain: always creating, and especially great at creating problems.

Plinky guitar music drifted from the speakers. It felt like being in some hippie hobbit hole: The walls were all rustic wood, the ceiling exposed rafters and prayer flags; bronze elephant statues and paintings from local artists made up the eclectic decor. And—

the first real blessing of the day—all the mismatched chairs and tables were empty. The coming snow must have scared people off.

"Score," Ethan said.

The back curtain opened and Veronica stepped out. She was maybe forty, with light blond hair and green eyes and a willowy frame. As the owner, she also knew tea better than anyone else. On many occasions, Ethan and I had plotted how to steal her away to be our Tea Mistress in our future bungalow.

"Evening, Veronica," I said, hanging my coat on one of the cast brass fingers sticking out from the entry. An electric heater hummed below it.

"Nice night, eh?" she asked.

"Lovely," Ethan said.

"Hungry?"

We both nodded. "Hungry" was an understatement.

"On it." She disappeared into the small back kitchen and Ethan and I took up our usual space in the far corner. The two sofas here were plush red velvet, the arms and cushions faded and threadbare. Ethan chucked off his sweater and threw it over the back, then unzipped his portfolio and began rooting through projects. I shuffled around in my own bag and pulled out a couple of papers, spreading them on the Tarot-card-mod-podge table in front of us.

Veronica came by a few minutes later bearing a tray with two handmade teapots and thick mugs. There were also two bowls of soup and a steaming loaf of fresh bread.

"You're an angel," Ethan said when she set the pot of faerie's blood tea in front of him.

"And you're a fabulous brown-noser," Veronica replied, reaching over to hand me my pot of spiced lemongrass chai. Our orders were predictable, but since she hand-blended the teas each time we came in, the taste was always just a little bit different.

"What's on the agenda for tonight?" I asked her. I poured a stream of milky tea from the pot; the scent was almost heavenly enough to make me forget my looming thesis. Almost.

Veronica reached into one of her apron pockets and pulled out a novel with a half-naked man on the cover and a woman kneeling in front of him, hands on his chest.

"The classics," she said with a wry smile. Veronica had once admitted to doing a PhD in English literature; it had been enough to turn her away from reading "good" books for life. It also earned her another point in my eternal devotion department. That and her wicked-good chai.

"Can I borrow it after you?" Ethan asked, rooting around in his bag.

"Not until you give me back the other ten I've lent you."

"Nine," Ethan said. "The tenth was a gift. You said so yourself."

Veronica just laughed and ruffled his hair before going over to a loveseat by the kitchen curtain to read.

With that, we settled in to working on our theses. Neither of us said anything for the first half hour or so. The music faded into the background and mingled with the occasional rumble of wind and the door didn't open once to admit new customers. The warmth of chai sank into my bones as the electric caffeine buzz heated my veins. This was familiar. This was what I needed.

Work was always the best answer for putting the past behind you. And yes, I realized what sort of complex that would create in my future years. It worked for now.

My project both terrified and exhilarated me, which was how I knew I was doing the right thing. I was going to be presenting with two other artists, and I had an entire thirty-foot stretch of hallway to fill. It was supposed to be thematic, to showcase the culmination of my work at Islington. Two years of practice and prep, two years of late nights and frustrated tears and way too much caffeine. Two years to sum up in a single, week-long showcase.

And I was making Tarot cards.

Well, paintings of Tarot cards. The eventual goal was to scan them and package them as a deck, but for right now I had a series of eighteen-by-twenty-four-inch paintings depicting most of the Major and some of the Minor Arcana. Tonight's project was finishing up The Hierophant. I pulled out the canvas and the photo of Barista Ike and a few magazines. This card was all about ritual and formality, the sort of guidance that comes through process and strict mysticism. At least, in my view. Which meant a painting of Ike on a golden collage throne, holding a cross and a horned moon and sitting in a temple I'd constructed of photos of Stonehenge and Ethiopian mystics and anything else I could find in *National Geographic* or travel magazines. It was still in that "hot mess" phase of creation, where nothing really fit together quite yet. But it was getting there. Slowly.

As I scoured magazines, I kept glancing up at Ethan, a knot slowly forming in my gut. He reclined on the sofa with *Great*

Expectations propped open in one hand, his eyebrows furrowed and his lips occasionally dancing along with his reading. We'd been performing this ritual weekly for the last year and a half, and even now, in the depths of February, there was something about this that seemed hopeful, like together we were on the verge of discovering something greater about ourselves. And there were only a few months left until we graduated. How many more times would we sit in this same location and worry about homework and art while the rest of the world slumbered on?

He glanced up at me and gave me a cocky little grin.

"Planning on drawing me like one of your French girls?" he asked.

I blushed, but I didn't look away. Winter always made me think of firsts and lasts.

"I'm going to miss you," I said. I gestured to the café. "All this."

The smile dropped off in a heartbeat, his face softening.

"What are you talking about?" he asked.

I sighed. My life seemed like one giant timeline right now: College applications were in, which meant two weeks until my thesis, one or two months until I heard back from colleges, then another month or two before graduation and then . . . I had no idea.

"You, me," I said. He and I had always had a joking relationship. Banter was how we showed we cared.

He nodded slowly. We'd each applied to four colleges, and only two overlapped. For me, they were both *reach* schools. My grades were good. My art was good. But I wasn't certain they were good enough. And, judging from how many panic attacks

41

Ethan had while applying (often remedied by me buying him ice cream and walking through the snowy woods or by the lake together), I knew he felt the same.

"We're going to be fine, you know," he said. He looked into my eyes when he said it, which was kind of unusual for him when being serious—he had that way of glancing off into the distance dreamily, like he was choosing his words from the ether. This new gaze reminded me of Chris. "Even if we don't get in together, we'll still be in touch. I mean, c'mon, we're practically married. You're stuck with me for life, whether you want to be or not."

I laughed.

"Truth. You are like glitter."

His smile came back.

"Exactly. I'm serious though, I have good feelings about this. You're my bestie. You're not going anywhere." He leaned in closer. "Are you sure you're okay?"

I glanced away. "Just tired."

"Let me guess. Not all homework related?"

I took a sip of tea. His next words were almost a whisper.

"Are they back?"

It took all my self-control not to let the teacup spill.

"You can tell me, you know," he said. I slowly set the teacup down, careful not to let it shake too much. "It helped, last time."

Well, *he* thought it helped. The fact is, I don't know if telling him about the dreams of my ex had done any good.

"It's nothing," I said. "Just a bad dream. I'm sure it's just stress."

He nodded.

Ethan and I were besties. We would be together till the very end. But that friendship, it only really went forward. I didn't tell him much of my past and he didn't press the subject. He knew I had a boyfriend before coming here. He knew it went south. He knew that because of what happened with Brad, I wasn't interested in dating. And that sometimes I had nightmares about my ex. Ethan knew it, and he respected it. And that's all he would ever know.

He wouldn't look at me the same way if I told him the rest.

"You know I'm always here for you," he said.

"Thanks love," I said. *But you wouldn't be. Not if you knew.*

"Any time doll," he replied. "Now get back to work. You've been promising to do my card for weeks. It'd better be making its debut in your show."

"Working on it," I lied. Because I wasn't entirely certain how I was going to do the Knight of Cups, though I knew it was his card. Emotional depth, steadfastness, poetic nature . . . Ethan to a T. Especially since, reversed, it indicated a severe narcissistic douchebag. A side of Ethan I'd seen only on occasion.

He went back to reading and I went back to looking at photos of Egyptian tombs, trying to find the perfect statue for the interior of The Hierophant's chamber. But I couldn't stop looking up at Ethan, wondering just how many times we'd be here, how many more weeks or days or hours we actually had together. I'd felt the clock ticking ever since January, when we stood in the mailroom and sent out our applications and portfolios. We'd started some celestial clockwork that morning. It was a tick I seriously wished I could slow.

Like I said, winter always made me think of beginnings

and endings. This year, especially with Brad's image once more haunting my dreams, it felt like less of a beginning and more of an end.

We left the teahouse around eight. The Hierophant was closer to completion and Ethan, to quote, "might vomit if [he] read any more Dickens." Plus the tea had gone cold and we'd eaten all of our baklava.

The roads were slick and the sky a blur of flecked white, and I think Ethan drove all of fifteen miles an hour the entire way back, which just meant we made it through an entire album, rather than half, like usual. We didn't talk. Didn't need to. I leaned against the window and watched the town and the trees flutter by like ravens in the snow, while he hummed along to the music and tapped out rhythms on the steering wheel. It was monotonous and familiar and lovely, and every single mile reminded me that soon, this too would be a *last*.

It wasn't like me to get nostalgic. I'd had more than enough *lasts* in my life to get me over a fascination with the past. Which was probably why the night felt so unearthly, like I was watching Ethan and myself through a lens. And why I kept noticing the little inconsistencies in the white-and-black landscape: a broken tree, a flickering porch light, two crows on a mailbox. I needed something to cement this moment, to make it mine. To make it worth remembering.

Campus was sleepy by the time we arrived. A few vis art students wandered back to their dorms from the studio; musicians carried their heavy cases back to warmth. Every window was golden and electric, the common rooms in every dorm crowded with kids trying to cram in a few more minutes of socializing before sign-in and lights-out and an early morning of classes. Thank the gods I got to sleep in—no early morning art class spent staring at wrinkled bits.

Ethan and I parted ways in front of his dorm—Rembrandt—and I made my way down the quiet lane toward Graham. A few flecks of snow still fell from the sky, drifting down to fade out on my coat. There was a quietness here I didn't think I could live without. There were reasons I'd applied only to tiny art colleges in the backwoods of New England. I needed the snow and the silence. They helped me think. And somehow, the expanse of it all helped calm the other thoughts, froze them into stillness. Something about the darkness always made me feel at peace.

I heard the door of the academics concourse open, and paused when someone called out my name. When I turned, Jane was already halfway toward me, a huge grin on her face and one hand waving. I was surprised she didn't slip as she jogged; I'd nearly faceplanted twice already.

"Kaira, wait up!" she called. I stopped and waited with my hands deep in the pockets of my coat, watching her dance in and out of puddles of light. When she reached me, she *did* slide, but I caught her last minute and helped her steady.

"Heya," I said when she was stable.

"Sorry, didn't want to miss you. You'll never guess who I was just talking with."

"Um . . ."

"Chris!" she exclaimed, and she actually did a little bounce. I kept ahold of her arm, just in case.

"Oh yeah?" I asked. I grinned. "Does someone have a crush?"

"I'd say so," she said. "He couldn't stop talking about you."

"Wait, what?"

I was honestly asking about *her*. Chris couldn't have a crush on me. I mean, we had two classes together and we barely ever spoke. It was ludicrous. My stomach twisted as Brad's face drifted to mind.

"Yeah," she said. "We went back to the studio to finish up the still life, and he kept asking me questions about you."

"What sort of questions?" I asked slowly.

"Like, I dunno, general sorts of stuff. How I knew you. How long you'd been here. If you had a boyfriend or girlfriend."

"Please tell me you lied," I said. I glanced over to the boys' dorms, fully expecting Chris to emerge and look over and wave. He didn't, of course. There were maybe five minutes until we were late for sign-in, so he was probably back in his room or in the lounge chatting with his dormmates.

"What? No. I told him we'd had a few classes together and that you were an awesome painter and came here last year. And that you were most definitely single."

"And keeping it that way," I said. Maybe a little too forcefully. Jane was one of those satellite friends—someone I knew and hung out with on occasion and joked with in studio. She didn't know the finer details of my life, and my distinct aversion to the "dating" word. Her smile dropped the moment I spoke. "I mean, sorry. I guess I'm just trying not to get too attached right now, is all. End of term, college. Kind of bad timing."

46

She nodded. "Still, though. He's really cute. And talented. And he seemed pretty genuine, so I think he's not one of those pervy creepers like in the drama department."

It was well known that spring term last year, she dated a guy named Justin for a few weeks before learning that he was dating three other girls at the same time, one per department. Pretty certain the slap he received from her had been heard across campus.

The portrait she did of him and hung on the "works in progress" board in the vis arts hallway had been icing on the cake. It was in the style of those convicted felon posters, with the title *Terrible Kisser*.

For Jane, it was a vicious move. I'd always thought it was kind of endearing. I'd even asked her to make one for me, which had just made her blush and had garnered no definitive response. I was still waiting. I wanted my title to be *Unfashionable Fashionista*.

"Well, I guess we'll just have to wait and see," I said, seriously hoping we never would. "He hasn't mentioned anything to me."

"Mhm. I think that's because he's nervous you'll reject him. He asked if you were single a *lot*."

I shook my head. There was a hopeful glint in her eyes that told me A) there was no talking her out of this, and B) no point trying to convince her I was totally okay being single. Better than okay. Brilliant. "Anyway, we're almost late."

"Right! Well, I'll see you tomorrow. Can't wait to see your painting."

"Thanks." My stomach dropped a few inches. I'd always looked forward to Advanced Painting; it was my one chance to really zone out and focus on my work. But knowing Chris was interested in something beyond friendship? It made my stomach twist. How was I going to focus *now*? Especially since tomorrow was crits.

I gave her a quick hug and jogged up the steps to my dorm. The lobby was filled with girls in pajamas and sweaters and slippers, some with tea, others with books and soda. A few of them glanced at me and smiled or said hello, but to be completely honest, I didn't really get along with anyone in the dorm save for Elisa. Okay, that sounds harsh—it wasn't that I didn't get along with them, more that I just never really gave anyone the opportunity to test out the waters. When I wasn't with Ethan or Elisa, I was pretty much a hermit.

Which wasn't a problem at Islington, really. Everyone here was a hermit in some way, even the theatre kids. We just liked to call it "focused."

After initialing next to my name on the sign-in sheet, I went upstairs to my hall. For all the appearance of Islington being quaint and rustic, there was something almost clinical about the dorm halls—harsh fluorescent lighting, generic blue carpet, cinderblock walls, and wooden doors. But even in here the arts had pushed their roots through the cracks. No matter how many times they vacuumed, there were still traces of glitter in the carpet from the epic glitter fight we'd had the second week of term (and nearly all gotten detention for); every door was plastered with posters and pictures and magazine cutouts, and a few of the lights were decorated with (fireproof) plastic flowers and wilting balloons. My door was halfway down the hall, overlooking the woods that engulfed all sides of campus.

Elisa was already in her pjs, holding a bowl of popcorn that filled the room with the deliciously intoxicating scent of butter.

"I was wondering when you'd get back," she said.

"Sorry," I replied, slinging my coat over my chair. "Got a bit carried away with thesis work."

"It's okay. I found a really terrible zombie flick online involving pterodactyls. It is queued and ready." Terrible horror movies were Elisa's forte—she relished them as eagerly and excitedly as other people experienced five-course meals.

"Gimme a moment to clean up and I'm all yours, baby."

She patted the bed beside her and blew me a kiss.

Yeah, I stopped wondering why people thought she and I were lesbian lovers a *long* time ago.

I remember when I first stepped foot in a dorm room here, thinking they were huge. But I think that's just the freshness of new things—everything is vast and impressive at first glance. The moment Elisa and I had really started unpacking and settling in, listening to boy bands and singing at the top of our lungs in what would be the first of many such afternoons, I realized just how compact the space actually was. The rectangular room was split down the middle, a mirror image of itself with a twin bed on either side, shelving underneath, and two desks opposite each other. The only break in the symmetry was the hall leading in, which had a closet on one side and a door to our tiny bathroom and shower on the other. The one perk of dorm life here: Every room had its own bathroom. No foot fungus for us classy artists.

I wiped off my makeup and washed my face before heading

in to slip into pjs. Technically speaking, lights-out was in an hour, but our RA barely checked. The last time Maria came in to break up our late-night movie, she ended up staying to watch the rest of *Vampire Hedgehogs* and ate all our popcorn.

"How was your night?" Elisa asked when I flopped down on the bed beside her.

"All right," I said. I snuggled deeper into the covers and grabbed her plush oversize piece of toast, aptly named Toastie. My mind was still spinning with what Jane had said about Chris. But it wasn't just that; I kept thinking over all my interactions with him—his side glances, his appraisal in crits. I'd always just thought he was being nice, in that *stranger I'll never connect with* sort of way. Now, I couldn't help but look at it in an entirely different light. "Got some work done."

"Nice. You have no idea how ready I am for this movie. We've been blocking for *Marat/Sade* all night and I want to scream."

"I can't wait to see it," I said.

"And I can't wait for it to be over."

Which we both knew was a lie. She had one other performance before the end of the year, and that was a scene in the Senior Showcase. Like me, she was holding on to every experience she could. It was just easier to verbally try and convince ourselves otherwise.

She curled up against her pillows and I curled against her. As always, she smelled like flowery perfume and tea, something soft and antique. The scent would forever remind me of nights like this, of watching stupid movies on her laptop and eating junk food and waking up the next morning feeling more exhausted than not. I hated to admit just how much I loved this. How alien and perfect it felt. I wasn't used to this sort of friendship. If I had been, certain things in my life would have gone much, much differently, and I probably wouldn't have sent myself to Islington in the first place. There was a reason my side of the room was covered in sketches while her side was filled with family portraits. Thankfully, she never really asked what those reasons were— another point in her favor.

Without further ado, she hit play on the computer and I hit pause on my inner thought process. Or at least, I tried to. My thoughts were notoriously hard to silence. Tonight, I knew, not even sleep would still them.

CHAPTER FOUR

Dark dreams.

Shadow

Feather

Root and Bone

The gods created you for this.

And I sit in the gnarled roots of the World Tree while the
horned god Cernunnos speaks from his knotted pulpit:
"The gods demand blood. They have always demanded blood.
To speak with divinity, you must pay in pain."
He turns, but he is now Odin, the Allfather, the ravens Hugin
and Munin perched on each shoulder. His suit is coal, his cowl
crow feathers, his staff a root from the Tree itself.
"When Yggdrasil burns, god and man shall dance."
And I turn in the classroom of glass students and see a girl. Her
dark hair drips down pale skin, hides violet eyes.
"I know you."
I say. She says.

My reflection wavers. Glass cracks.

Snow burns outside the window. Ravens scream.

"Of course you know me," she says. "For we are the same."

She steps forward, reaches out, touches my face. Only it isn't her hand, it is my hand, and I stare back at my face through her eyes.

"When the battle comes, you will be mine," she says. "Together we will fight the Aesir. Together, we will earn the mortals' worship."

I step back. "I don't want to fight."

"But you will. You were born for this." She smiles. Violet eyes glow. "You were born to be mine."

Her skin touches mine. Ravens scream as blood burns and the World Tree cries as the battlefield stretches before us, blood dripping, blood on fire, boughs brimming with blood and ravens. And in my hand—our hand—a dagger, and at my feet, a body. His golden body.

I scream. Ravens fly.

"Why are you hiding from me?"

Her words crack. She cries blood.

"Why are you hiding from me, Kaira?" Brad asks, his hands on my cheek, lips on my neck. His words dripping down my throat.

"Why are you hiding from what you've done?"

And I scream as raven feathers fill my lungs, as Brad bites my collar, presses hips to mine as Munin buries himself into my chest.

CHAPTER FIVE

I woke up feeling like I hadn't slept in weeks. Fragments of my dreams filtered between my fingers as I pushed myself up to a sitting position. My alarm buzzed on the shelf above my bed, playing *Carmina Burana* because I liked pretending my mornings were epic, rather than just me dragging myself from a stupor into a caffeine-induced high. Elisa, as usual, was already up and showering in the bathroom. Despite this, the room was quiet and dark in the heavy winter dawn. Definitely not inviting. Why had I forgotten to turn off the alarm before passing out? I silenced the music and tried to curl up tighter into the covers. Sleep drifted back, slowly.

At least until Elisa came back in and threw Toastie at my head.

"No oversleeping," she said in her most cheery yet demanding voice. "You know how grouchy you get when you miss breakfast."

I sighed and opened my eyes, sticking out my tongue at her while her back was turned. I must have passed out longer than

I thought—her hair was already dry and she was just slipping into a fluffy Icelandic sweater I envied (and had stolen on many occasions, which accounted for the small ink stain on the sleeve).

"Fine," I muttered. "But I blame this all on you. You never told me *Prehistoric Zombies* was two hours long."

"You never asked," she replied. "Besides, you started snoring halfway through. If anyone gets to be sleepy today, it's me."

"I don't snore," I lied.

"Breakfast's over in thirty," she said. She slid into her parka and grabbed her book bag. She was one of those girls who set out everything she'd need for the following day the night before. How she and I managed to live together in harmony was anyone's guess. "Last minute" was often the name of my game. "I'll save you a cinnamon roll."

I moaned. Saturday mornings were always cinnamon roll mornings. It made going to school on a technical weekend bearable, which is probably why they did it. I also guessed they put drugs in the frosting. To keep us pliable.

She left a moment later, leaving me to drag myself out of bed. Today was definitely not a makeup day—the world could just rejoice in me putting on clothes. I slid into a pair of jeans crusted with ceramics and paint, and a T-shirt in roughly the same condition. Painting Studio later today basically meant "dressing up" was an exercise in futility.

Last night's dream scratched at the corners of my memory, but I couldn't quite place it. When I was dressed and had the day's stuff together, I took a cursory glance out the window, just to see if it had snowed any more during the night. Sure enough, a fine dusting coated everything, turning the pine branches into lace and the ground to cotton.

And there, on the snowy windowsill, was a set of bird prints.

My stomach gave a little twist as I remembered pieces of my dream, of a raven piercing my chest. *Not just any raven—Munin. Why the hell is he back?*

The worst part about learning how to read omens wasn't knowing that bad things would happen; that was just a part of life. It was the fact that you never knew what the omen entailed, exactly, or when the event would strike. Or how disastrous it would actually be.

But if Munin was involved, it couldn't be good.

Today was going to be a *great* day.

The morning dragged by in that expectant blur I'd grown far too accustomed to—waiting for Painting Studio was almost like waiting for Christmas, but today was different. Because today, I'd be spending half of that four-hour chunk in critique, which I was pretty certain was a special level of Hell. Depending on the moment, I was both excited and terrified to be back in that room in a semicircle of easels, staring at a still life and trying not to look too hard at Chris.

Ethan joined me at lunch. I spied Oliver in line, waiting to get his macaroni and cheese and fake chicken nuggets. Oh yes, Saturdays were always good days, food-wise at least. Lunchtime was also an excellent people-watching opportunity.

Even though there weren't any real cliques in the bitchy sense, the kids of Islington definitely filtered into their own groups. It made sense; I mean, you spend a good chunk of your day talking ceramics with a group of people and you'll naturally be drawn to spending your social time with them as well. It was ridiculously easy to pick out who focused in what: the dancers were all shapes and sizes, but they had a definite poise when they walked that singled them out from the rest of us clunky movers; the drama kids were—just like at public high—the loudest and most outgoing and prone to fits of overbearing laughter; the musicians were reserved and generally had that air of *I spend a lot of time staring at sheet music and that's what I'm thinking about now*; the writers just looked depressed most of the time; and the visual artists? Well, we were the ones who looked like we didn't shower very often and had gotten all of our clothes from a more bohemian Cirque du Soleil. Myself included.

"Ready for the gauntlet?" Ethan asked, bringing my attention back to the present.

"Never," I muttered.

"It won't be that bad," Ethan said. "I mean, the scene couldn't be that open to interpretation. Right?"

"Um, really? Have you already forgotten the last one?"

Ethan buried his head in his hands, running his fingers through his hair in defeat. "I'm trying," he mumbled. "I never knew doing a painting of flowers could release so much emotional trauma."

"Yeah, well, symbolism and shit."

"I'll never look at a lily the same way again. If I hadn't known I was gay before, I would have after that piece of . . . art."

"I'll just be happy if Tamora didn't do this one naked. Her poor roommate. I don't think I can stand to critique another piece of work done via ladybits."

57

Ethan shivered.

"Can we please talk about something else?" he implored. "Something not about genitalia?"

"I catch you guys at the strangest moments," Oliver said, sitting beside Ethan. Ethan reached over and stole a chicken nugget from Oliver's tray before the boy's butt even hit the seat. "What's this about genitalia?"

"Art talk," I muttered. "You wouldn't get it. Rather, you wouldn't *want* to get it."

"I think you may be right about that one." Oliver managed to intercept another grab from Ethan. "You have your own!"

"But stolen food always tastes better," Ethan said with a grin.

Oliver shook his head. "I don't understand why I love him."

"Neither do I," I responded. Then stole one of Oliver's chicken nuggets.

"I'm cute?" Ethan ventured. "And crafty. Definitely crafty."

"Speaking of cute," Oliver said, and gestured with his chin to my left. And there, lo and behold, was Chris, bee-lining toward us with a tray heaped with food.

"You've got to be kidding me," I muttered. Ethan raised an eyebrow, but before I could answer or tell him to keep his stupid mouth shut, Chris was standing beside us. Beside *me*. It took a great deal of self-control not to scoot over, even though the other half of the round table was free.

"Hey guys," he said. There was a tentativeness to his voice that was cute. I mean, cute if I could actually care about that. "Mind if I sit with you?"

And I won't lie, I almost told him we were just about to leave, but that was stupid seeing as Oliver's tray was still full and mine was only half picked over. Ugh, what was I becoming? He was just a guy and I wasn't interested in dating and there wasn't any more to it.

"Not at all," I said, sliding out the chair. Playing nonchalant was my best way out of this becoming awkward. In theory.

The next ten seconds of silence were potentially the most cringe-worthy of my life. Especially because Ethan was leaning forward with his hands clasped before him, a slight grin on his face, like he was about to do a job interview. Thankfully, Oliver came to the rescue.

"You ready for the Russian Lit quiz Tuesday?" he asked, popping a nugget in his mouth.

Chris's face lit up at the bone Oliver threw him.

"Not really," he said. "I still have to finish the last fifty pages of Tolstoy."

"Ugh, have fun," Oliver replied. "At least it's not Nabokov anymore. Guy made me want to shoot myself."

"Isn't that the whole point of Russian literature?" Chris asked innocently.

I chuckled. "Well played, sir. Well played."

"Speaking of shooting ourselves, we were just talking about Painting Studio," Ethan said. "And how excited we are for Tamora's piece."

Chris laughed—it was one of those laughs that was too loud for the situation, which just made it even funnier.

"I nearly lost it last time," he said. "I just hope she wasn't using oil paints. Those can damage you."

I tried to filter out the boys' banter and focus on food. Faux nuggets and macaroni was easily my favorite meal in the known universe, and if I let myself pay attention to the boy sitting a foot to my right, I'd lose my appetite entirely. That would be a grave disservice to the gods of food.

It worked. Right up to the point where Ethan threw a nugget at my head.

"Earth to Kaira," he said when I jumped back in my seat. "You still there?"

"What? Sorry, zoning out."

"We noticed," Ethan replied. "Chris just asked what we were doing tonight."

"We?"

"You were coming to my concert, right?" Oliver asked.

I nodded, then caught the drift.

"What our eloquent friend is trying to say," Ethan intervened, "is that you're more than welcome to join us. Kaira and I were going to meet in the Writers' House at six thirty to grab some hot cocoa before braving our way to the auditorium. Sound good?"

"Perfect," Chris replied. A pause. "You don't really think Tamora painted with her nether regions again, do you?"

It took a moment for my brain to start working and connect the dots, as it had begun to spin on *he's going to a concert with you, he's going to a concert with you.* It made my pulse race, and not in a good way.

"I hope not," Ethan said. "But as they say, 'God hates the gays.' This would just be another fitting form of punishment."

Oliver chuckled and kissed Ethan on the cheek. I glanced to Chris, who was grinning and picking at his food. When his brown eyes darted to mine, I was immediately grateful for that previous stuffing of my face. My heart leaped into my throat, and any chance of food getting past the obstruction was lost.

I know it was stupid, but something in that smile reminded me of Brad.

"You were totally smooth," Ethan said as we left the cafeteria. "I mean, like, Oscar-worthy performance in there. I nearly cried."

"Shut up." I rammed my elbow into him, maybe a little harder than necessary. I wasn't pissed, really, but the fact that Chris made me think of my ex had me on edge. "If I remember correctly, you weren't nearly as eloquent when you first met Oliver."

"Girl has a point," Oliver said, grabbing my free arm. "She led that conversation. In fact, she nearly took our first kiss from you."

"I hate you both," Ethan muttered.

"Anyway, Chris is cute. And intelligent, at least from what I've seen in class."

If Oliver hadn't been holding my arm, I might have smacked him, too.

"And talented, which we know is a necessity for you," Ethan said. "I think he might be just your type, Winters."

"I don't have a type, Davis," I replied. There were only two times we used each other's last names: when we were jovial and when we were being deadly serious. I was hoping Ethan could tell it was the latter. "You know that."

"Uh huh. That's why you jerked when Oliver mentioned him. Someone has a crush."

Just the word "crush" made me sick to my stomach. *Love is for getting hurt.* "He's cute," I admitted, because Ethan was incredibly good at spotting a lie. "But in that distant, untouchable sort of way."

"She's already talking about touching him," Oliver said with a chuckle.

"Can it," I warned him.

"Let me guess," Ethan mused. "This is another topic we add to our no-no list."

"Your what?" Oliver asked.

"The list of things we don't talk about. It's a very short list, to be fair."

Eager to change the subject, I jumped on the topic.

"Like 'thesis,' which you still haven't seemed to grasp." I made sure to direct that last bit at Oliver, who just shrugged and kicked a bit of snow to the curb.

"And tiny insects that burrow under your skin," Ethan added with a shiver. "I hate parasites."

"And . . . actually, that's about it. Not much else is off topic."

"So Chris is definitely going on the list?"

"Definitely," I said. "Call me cat lady all you like. I will never crush on an Islington boy. Or girl," I added, before either could beat me to the punch.

"If you say so," Ethan said. "Though we'll see if you change your tune after the concert." He chuckled to himself. "See what I did there? It was a pun. You know, a music pun. Because I said 'tune' and we're going to a concert and—ow!"

The last part was compliments of Oliver and the snowball he launched at his boyfriend's face.

"And now we know why you aren't in the writing program," Oliver said. Ethan just dusted off the snow from his peacoat and glowered.

I parted ways with the boys outside my dorm and headed inside to gather my things and my wits for the last run of the day. There was another half hour before class began, which was *just* enough time to check e-mail and all that other social media junk. And apply some makeup, because even though Chris just saw me without, I needed my warpaint to tackle an intensive four hours of playing eye avoidance with him. Yes yes, it was a complete one-eighty from my stance this morning, but I was allowed to be fickle on some things when I had to be rigorous about everything else.

Out of habit, I checked my cubby for mail. A little blue slip sat inside, which was pretty much like discovering a hidden twenty in your pocket. It meant I got a package, and seeing as I hadn't ordered anything, it meant a care package from home.

Which meant cookies.

Elisa would be pleased. Our weekend was just made.

I took the slip over to the front desk and handed it to Jessica, another RA.

"Score," she said when she handed the large package over.

"Are these more of your mother's delicious baked confections?"

Like Maria, Jessica was fresh out of college and sweeter than honey. Which was kind of funny, seeing as she usually wore black and had a tongue piercing from her "wild days."

"Looks like it," I said, giving the box a cursory shake. It was very obvious this was from home and not from a shipping department: There were heart and star stickers all over it, and the return address said *MOM* with her address in tiny parentheses below. *"Don't worry, I'll save you some."*

"You're a gem," she said with a wink. "And you just got a week's pass on room inspection."

That didn't mean much, seeing as the RAs only glanced into seniors' rooms to make sure we weren't living under garbage. But it still made me grin.

Elisa wasn't up in the room, which was kind of a relief. I always felt awkward opening presents when she was around. Not that she didn't get her fair share—her side was practically littered with photographs and mementos sent from home—it was just . . . something about this was insanely precious to me. A moment to be savored. It still blew my mind that Mom was willing to spend twenty bucks on shipping just to send a box of cookies and some handwritten notes. I definitely cried the first time she'd sent me a package, a month into my first year here. And Elisa had definitely been sitting there, pretending not to watch while she typed on her computer. She never asked a question.

I sat down on my bed and glanced around. Yeah, her side of the room was more homey, with silk scarves draped from the shelves and a plethora of photos of her and her family on vacations. There were even a couple of shots of her and Jane on their West Coast trip—a collage of them in the car, standing by a large concrete troll, the Space Needle, a forest. My side was a little more bare, though I'd been trying to make it a nest this year. Mostly, it was sketches either Ethan or I had done. I had a few photos taped to the wall of Ethan and me at the mall in one of those photo kiosks, as well as some shots from when I had visited him in Chicago last summer. Mom knew I was lacking in the personal decor department; I'm pretty certain she'd made it her secret mission to fill my room with knickknacks without my knowing.

I took a deep breath, trying to preserve the moment of anticipation, and then opened the box.

Purple and blue tissue paper rustled inside, hiding the contents, and I carefully dug through it. Mom often hid little notes and letters between the layers, and I didn't want to miss a thing.

Sure enough, between one fold and the next, I found glitter stars and sequins and intricately folded lines of poetry. Each one made me miss her just a little bit more.

Farther in was a plastic container of chocolate-chip cookies, probably three dozen. There was also a handful of parcels wrapped in starry paper (Each of Mom's boxes had a theme, I'd learned. This one apparently was the cosmos. The last had been dinosaurs; Ethan had stolen all the stickers, though, the tool.), and some bags of miscellaneous candy. And yes, even the candy was moderately star-themed, right down to the jelly alien eggs.

I unwrapped the smaller packages one by one, a stupid grin plastered on my face. The first gift was a photograph of her and

Dad and me at a picnic, all of us smiling. Mom and her black hair and pale skin and curvy frame, Dad and his pencil-thin stature and short graying hair and skin as dark as mine. And me, not quite as crazily dressed as I was now, with a smile on my face and a spark of hesitation in my eyes.

The next was a miniature constellation globe, the stars inked in silver and linked to show the major formations. She tacked a note on the bottom, her curving script so perfect and familiar: *So you can always find your way home.*

There were a few more toys—a plushie star, an egg of glowing cosmic goo, glow-in-the-dark star stickers—and some staples she sent in every box: sachets of homemade tea, gemstones, a feather that made her think of me. I placed each of the items on my shelf, one at a time, and hid the tea in my drawer and the mystic items on my makeshift shelf altar. And then there was the small box with a note attached saying *"Open Last."*

Which, of course, I did.

It was one of those boxes that lockets came in, roughly three inches by three inches, and a note was folded up inside.

Kaira-Love,

The winds tell me you're having troubled dreams.

This should help keep the dark ones at bay.

The tea is chamomile and mugwort—it will ease you into a more peaceful sleep.

Remember, where there is the deepest darkness,

close by lies the greatest light. You are my Star.
Much love,
Mom

Inside the box, covered in thin velvet, was a piece of clear quartz wrapped in silver wire, smaller lapis lazuli stones threaded over it in an intricate cobweb. It reminded me of stars spiraling around a galactic nexus. The stone was warm in my hand and gave a faint electric buzz. Resting beneath it was a Tarot card. The Star. *Guidance, hope, a beacon in the dark.*

Another reason I preferred being alone when opening gifts from home: Mom was pagan and the high priestess in her local coven, which meant many of her gifts deviated from the norm. I suppose most kids would have felt awkward about that, but it was one of the many things she and I clicked on. But it did lend a sort of privacy to these gifts—magic was often meant to be kept secret, and although Elisa never prodded too far, there were certain things I didn't want to try to explain.

Like my Mom's uncanny timing. Did she know what I'd been dreaming? Or just that I needed to be shielded from the shadows in my own mind?

I kissed the quartz and visualized her face, whispered *thank you* before hiding it beneath my pillow. I could only remember fragments from last night's dream, which was probably for the best. Every time I tried to summon it, I felt like I was choking. I just knew it had to do with Brad, and ravens, and that was more than enough reason to want to forget it had ever happened.

I placed the card on the windowsill. Outside, another set of bird prints lingered like a curse.

It made me want to call Mom now, ask her to do a reading or something, but I didn't want to worry her. Whatever this was, I could handle it. I had before. I would again.

I just had to get through critiques first.

CHAPTER SIX

Advanced Painting Studio was my bastion of sanity, save for the few painful hours when we had critiques. Sure, I loved my other art classes—who didn't like making jewelry or getting dirty in ceramics?—but painting was my heart's calling. The moment I opened the ginormous black wooden door leading to the studio space, the moment the scent of oil and ether and paint washed over me, I felt like I was finding Zen. The classroom only had two white walls; the other two were floor-to-ceiling windows, overlooking Islington's forested backyard and letting in what little winter light we got. We even had skylights. Massive red and white pines stretched out into the distance, dotted with small wooden cabins used in the summer for camps. Being in here always made me feel like I was sitting on the edge of a fairytale, an adventure waiting for its heroine to take the stage.

I wandered over to my easel, which was arranged with the others in a semicircle around a table laden with a variety of oddities: broken porcelain jester dolls and papier-mâché masks, silver candlesticks and plastic fruit. It was a completely different still life from last week, but damn if I wasn't getting sick of inanimate objects.

Ethan wandered in a few seconds later. He set up his paper on an easel and scattered tubes of paint on the small table between us.

"I'm starting to think she was lying when she said we'd be painting figures soon," he muttered.

"Me too." I paused. "I still can't believe you invited him along."

"What?" he asked. He looked over to me. "Oh right. Well, listen. It's nothing. It's the three of us going to a school production. Not a date." He shrugged. "Chris just really looked like he wanted a reason to hang out. I couldn't leave him in the dust."

"Sometimes I think you're too nice for your own good."

He pressed a hand to his heart.

"It's my cross to bear. And I do so willingly."

"You aren't setting us up," I whispered.

"I know," he replied. "But you have to admit, there are worse candidates to spend your Saturday night with."

"I know. I'm already spending it with you."

"I'm still cuter," he said.

I didn't have the chance to refute him, as Chris came in then and I busied myself with looking through my bag for absolutely no reason beyond avoiding eye contact.

"I hate you," I made sure to mutter to Ethan.

"You're welcome," he responded.

The rest of the class came in and began setting up in silence. There were only eight of us in the class; you had to submit a portfolio to be considered, which meant I was either a cut above the rest or no one applied and they needed to fill a seat. I was kind of hoping it was the former, but the other classmates were leagues above me. Except for maybe Tamora. Her vag paintings were definitely one extreme of the bell curve—I hoped she didn't actually do them naked and just lied so we'd take her seriously, but I also wouldn't put it past her.

Art kids are weird. And no, I'm not an exception to the rule.

Chris sat at his easel across from me. I half expected him to come over and make some awkward small talk, but he didn't. Just nodded and smiled when our gazes caught and went back to focusing on setting up his paints. First minor crisis averted.

I took out a pencil and scribbled on the cover of my drawing pad, angling it toward Ethan, You owe me for this.

Ethan looked over, smiled, and wrote on his own pad, CALL ME CUPID.

I glared, but didn't have any time to bitch him out. Helen came in, a thermos in one hand and a canvas shopping bag in the other. Everything about her just screamed "painter." Today she was wearing blue overalls liberally splattered with multicolored paint, a faded teal rock T-shirt underneath, and at least a dozen bracelets and malas on her left wrist. Her long, dirty-blond hair was pulled back in a ponytail. As usual, she wasn't wearing any makeup, which in my humble opinion made her look more attractive than the painted-up dolls that tended to haunt the drama department. Not that I could say much, seeing as I'd drawn three lines under my left eye and applied a terrifyingly vibrant purple lipstick.

"Afternoon, guys," she said. She was one of those teachers who insisted you call her by her first name and didn't believe in letter grades. I'd had her for an introductory painting class last term; the entirety of my final critique had been us sitting in her office, drinking espresso and chatting about Renaissance influences in postmodern art. It was the only time I could say "postmodern" without flinching, which just shows the sort of relationship she and I'd forged.

She set her thermos on her book-laden desk and leaned against it, addressing us. "As you can probably guess, we're doing another still life this afternoon. You'll have the first two hours of class to start, and the rest of the weekend to finish. And before you start groaning, because I know how much you all love drawing inanimate objects, I found a way to spice things up a bit."

She held up the canvas bag.

"Within this bag is a collection of paints. You will pick two tubes, and you will only use these two colors, along with white and black, to finish the piece. Blending will be key, and you will be graded on proper shading and gradation. Think of it as a grayscale on LSD."

Ethan raised his eyebrow, perfectly conveying both *she's insane* and *this might be fun*. Ethan was a master of eyebrow-raising. He practiced often and to great effect.

Helen began wandering around the easels, letting us blindly choose our colors.

"No peeking, Kaira," she said when she got to me.

I closed my eyes and pulled out two tubes. She chuckled when she saw what I drew.

"I'd hoped you'd get one of those."

No question what she meant by that: One of the tubes was purple sparkle paint. The other was neon orange. Well, at least they were close to complementary colors.

Ethan eyed my tubes. He'd drawn pthalo blue and a particularly nasty brown. Another eyebrow raise, this one of envy and displeasure. He wanted my sparkle paint.

"Okay," Helen said. She walked back at her desk and tapped at her laptop. "Two hours on the clock. Let loose the hounds!" On cue, AC/DC blared through the classroom speakers.

I glanced at Ethan, who was already mixing colors on his glass palette. Then, after a flicker of a glance toward Chris, I picked up my paints and began preparing my colors. I didn't look up again, but judging from the occasional chills I felt, I could guess that Chris wasn't so good about keeping his eyes to himself.

Critiques weren't nearly as painful as I'd feared; Tamora had not, in fact, painted her still life with her ladybits, and Chris wasn't too obvious in his glances at me when critiquing my piece. I did find myself a little tongue-tied when talking about his painting (which was stupid because it was a picture of plants—nothing remotely romantic there), but it could have been much worse. I made sure to linger after class, slowly covering up my carefully mixed paints and ensuring nothing in my painting would drip or smudge. Mostly though, I just wanted to make it awkward for Chris to wait around for me, which worked—he left with Jane and gave me a little wave on the way out. She grinned like a madwoman, in an *I told you so* sort of way.

"I'm pretty certain it's not going to run away," Ethan grumbled from his stool beside me. He was fully dressed to enter the Michigan night, his beanie scrunched up in his hands. "Though my stomach might, if you don't get your ass in gear."

"I'm stalling," I muttered. I counted slowly in my head, imagining Chris and Jane walking down the hall, potentially lingering to look at the senior theses. "Because *someone* invited *someone else* to come to a concert tonight, and now she has to fend off all the awkward interactions before then."

"*Someone* needs to stop talking in third person," he said as I slid on my coat. "Seriously, girl, what's your problem? The boy's cute and interested. You've worked hard. Don't you deserve a little senior fling?"

I knew he was trying to be funny, and I knew he had my best intentions in mind, but his words pissed me off more than he knew.

"I told you," I said slowly, trying so hard not to grit my teeth. "I'm not dating. I'm not sleeping around. I am off limits. And I would appreciate you respecting that and not trying to set me up with a stranger."

He actually leaned back a little.

"Sorry," he said. "I just . . . I don't know, I'm sorry. I thought it might be fun for you to have someone. Because, you know, I'm always with Oliver now and I feel bad making you be the third wheel."

I shook my head. "I don't mind. I love Oliver. And I love your stupid face. I don't need anyone else."

And I don't want anyone else. I don't want to be hurt again.

I pushed those thoughts away, suddenly reminded of the crystal on my altar. Mom had always been spot on in her premonitions. Why hadn't she been more on target that night? Why hadn't I? My anger ebbed, replaced with a numbness I'd spent years cultivating. *You deserved what happened, that's why. And that's why you don't deserve to date.*

"Fair enough," he said, breaking through my inner diatribe. "Still friends?" He held out his arm and I took it, slinging my bag over my other shoulder. I hated the fact that it reminded me of taking Brad's arm. I hated that it almost made me miss him.

"Till the end," I replied.

Together, we wandered down the hall, my feet dragging and Ethan practically pulling me along. He did, however, let me stop near Tina's display of rings. I'd passed by it every day this week without actually giving it any pause. Then again, I *had* spent the last few weeks putting up with her crazy K-pop music in the studio while she frantically hammered and sawed and drilled her rings to perfection. We weren't in silversmithing together—she was in the advanced class, and I was just in intro—but I'd seen her in the studio during open hours. Her work was good. Really good.

"She's improved a lot this term," I said, almost but not quite touching one of the rings carved into an ornate teacup and adorned with tiny ruby swallows. "I mean, did you see what she was putting out before?"

Ethan shrugged, glancing both ways. The hall was empty and open, the sky outside so dark it was impossible to tell the time. I knew he didn't like critiquing work out in the open, and I felt the vibe too—it was almost sacrilegious, in a way, especially in here.

"It *is* pretty impressive," he said. Which was an understatement. Last term, the girl could barely solder copper. Now she was blending fine silver and even gold into her pieces, both of which were notoriously temperamental to work with.

I looked over to one of the more intricate rings, which was a delicate lace of silver wire.

"Jesus H. is she using diamonds?" I asked. Because there, in a nest of filigree, was a stunningly cut stone as clear as ice.

"Probably not," he replied. "Even here, I can't imagine her leaving anything that expensive out in the open."

Islington didn't have a theft problem. I mean, really, where would students run? Lost computers always showed up the next day, either exactly where they were abandoned or at the student's door with a note saying, "You left this in the library." But still, all this silver and gold in the open was kind of . . . well, asking for it. Which wasn't a phrase I used lightly.

Ethan glanced at his watch. "We should get moving. Oliver's going to be pissed if we miss the concert for anything."

"Fair," I said, and let him guide me down the hall. As we walked, I paid a little closer attention to the seniors' work lining the halls. My own would be up there in two weeks. Some of the kids had put up a good fight (and gone down swinging) while a few others were just stunning. Would I be one of the stars like Tina? Or would I be like Jeremy's crappy line drawings?

My stomach flipped at the thought of all the students walking down this very hall and judging my culminated work in judgey-judgey silence.

Despite the stupid descriptor, I still felt inferior.

"We're finishing our theses this weekend," I said, squeezing Ethan's arm. "And then we're going to critique the shit out of each other so we have time to polish."

"Done," he replied. "Though I don't know what sort of brain state I'll be in after tonight."

"Tonight?" I asked, glancing at him.

"Tonight," he said, and wiggled his eyebrows surreptitiously.

"Oh! Sleepover," I said. "Yes, well, get *some* sleep, please. I need you at peak brain capacity."

"No promises."

He opened the door for me. Outside, the air was static and dry, a cold snap waiting to shatter. The sky was crystal clear, stars shining brighter than I'd ever seen them in the city. It was one of those nights that felt like possibility could sweep down at any moment, everything clear and pristine and on the edge of perfection. Even the nerves of my upcoming thesis got sucked out into the ether.

At least, until a shadow dipped down from one of the streetlamps, flashing obsidian in the pool of light before vanishing into the forest beyond. Too big to be a crow.

"Was that a raven?" Ethan asked.

I just nodded, something from my dreams clawing into

consciousness, dragging shards of my past with it. *It was just a bird,* I tried to convince myself.

It didn't work.

Ethan and I ate dinner with Jane and Elisa and Jane's roommate, Cassie. Oliver had already vanished to get ready for the concert and Chris was nowhere to be seen. I tuned out most of the conversation. For the life of me, I couldn't get the damned raven out of my mind. Just thinking of it made me feel colder than the snow ever could. *Black on white, ink on concrete, blood on snow. . . .*

I couldn't shake the mantra. Nor could I forget the images it conjured.

When we finally left the cafeteria and headed to the Writers' House for hot cocoa and Chris, I felt like my brain was about to melt. Thinking of the boy just made it worse. *You aren't falling for him and he isn't falling for you, okay? It's just a little boredom crush. You're both in your senior year and getting cabin fever. It will all be over soon.* The trouble was, I couldn't tell if I was actually happy about that fact, which didn't make any sense. Romance wasn't in my cards—quite literally—and I wasn't about to entertain the notion otherwise. Brad had pretty much killed any notion of being in love again.

So why did I think of him every time I looked at Chris?

"You okay?" Ethan asked as we trudged up the drive. The Writers' House was at the far end of campus, peacefully removed from any and all distractions. An oasis of sorts. It also meant getting there in the winter was an ordeal. Well, if you could call walking two blocks an ordeal, which we often did seeing as everything else was in a few-hundred-foot radius.

"Just distracted," I said. Which was true, for the most part. I just didn't want to tell him *why*. And I probably, hopefully, never would.

He grunted, but didn't press further, which was probably why we got along so well. He knew when to back off and let my mind ruminate. Perk of being around artists: They understood silence.

A few minutes later we approached the wraparound patio of the House. All the buildings on campus looked like lodges, but this one exemplified the architecture. It was two stories tall, overlooking a field that, when not covered in two feet of snow, was used for soccer and Frisbee games. It looked like an alpine ski lodge, with a sharp A-frame roof and raw log walls and picture windows on every side. There was even a small second-story patio overlooking the road, where Ethan and I would perch (no matter the season) to watch the passersby in secrecy.

Even though we weren't in the creative writing department, the House had become a second home on campus. And since it was fairly removed from the hub, it was usually empty. Judging from the view from out here, we were in luck once more.

The interior was seriously like what I wanted my future house to be, except maybe with less angsty teenage writers hanging about. A huge fireplace crackled on the far side of the open atrium; it was two levels, but the second story balcony encircled the room, all open and airy and allowing writers to look over the wooden banister and throw folded haikus at the kids below. Or whatever writers did here. A few kids were settled on the overstuffed sofas by the fire, deep in their books or journals.

Even from here I could feel the literary gears turning. There was a warmth that wasn't in any other building on campus—this place felt lived-in, infused with words and stories.

I slid out of my coat and wandered to the open-floorplan kitchen to the left of the foyer. The place was stocked with the necessities of literature: a water kettle, a microwave, a coffee maker, and a plethora of teas and coffees and cocoas. I filled the kettle and set it to boil while Ethan rummaged in the cabinet for mugs and chocolate.

A part of me hoped Chris wouldn't show. Maybe he'd remember a ten-page essay due in the morning. Maybe he'd get eaten up by his own stomach butterflies and bail.

The kettle hadn't even begun to boil when those vain hopes were dashed at the sound of him opening the front door.

"Damn," he said the moment he was inside, "it's freezing out there."

"Kaira will warm you up," Ethan said. He caught my glare. "With cocoa. You *do* like cocoa, right?"

"Obviously," he replied, and sat down on one of the stools behind the bar.

"Milk or dark?"

"How is that even a question?" Chris scoffed. "Dark. I'm not five."

He was wearing his duster and fedora again. I had to give it to the boy—for a straight guy, he knew how to dress. The coat fit him perfectly in the shoulders and was trim to the waist. Even the fedora, which I'd usually make fun of, accented the angles of his face and the color of his scruff. Maybe because his facial hair matched the brassy falcon feather poking up the side.

I dragged my eyes away from him and set about mixing the hot cocoa. I could feel him watching me, but thankfully, Chris didn't let the silence go on for too long.

"So, question time," Chris said. I handed him a mug, which he took in both hands. He didn't look away from my eyes, however. "Why'd you send yourselves to the middle of the woods?"

"Well, I came here as a freshman," Ethan said. "So it was partly me and partly my parents. I applied in photography and got in. Couldn't stand public school and I had a feeling I'd fit in even less once I came out."

"You knew as a kid?" Chris asked.

"I've known for ages," Ethan said. "Just never had a word for it until someone called me a faggot on the playground." He winked and took a sip of his cocoa. "Kid was right. But hey, I'm here and he's back in suburbia. I think I'm winning."

"What about you?" Chris asked. Again, those eyes, pinning me into place. I forced down the nerves and told my voice not to stammer.

"It's a long story," I said. I could feel Ethan leaning in. I'd never told him this tale either. And I wasn't about to. "Basically, I didn't want to stay in public high anymore, so I sent myself here."

"It's kind of funny, isn't it?" Chris asked, completely ignoring that I hadn't given him a real answer. "The fact that we really came here to escape the real world? It doesn't seem like anyone comes here just because they want to study art."

"Of course not," Ethan replied. "We're all running from something. Islington just gives us a place to produce the greatest alchemy."

"Oh yeah?" Chris asked.

"He means turning pain into art," I said. "Don't give him too much credit for his pretty words. It's still a cliché."

"Truths usually are, just like the old 'love finds you when you aren't looking for it' adage," Ethan replied, and went back to sipping his drink. I wanted to slap him.

That night passed by in a blur. I managed to make Ethan sit between Chris and me at the concert, which I could tell unnerved Chris a little bit, but whatever; I wasn't about to give the impression that I was actually open to dating. After, we met with Oliver and snagged frozen yogurt at the Dark Note and walked in the woods while talking about art and music and what we were going to do after Islington. Oddly enough, college never came up in conversation—it was always the big plans, the dreams so lofty they seemed to rise from our lips in the cold night air to become apparitions, entities in and of themselves. I made Ethan walk me home. I didn't want Chris to think there was going to be a goodnight kiss.

Elisa and I stayed up a few hours after sign-in, chatting back and forth as we did our homework. For her, it meant reading Sylvia Plath and trying to emulate the style in a series of sonnets. For me, it meant beginning research for my folklore essay. Every now and again I'd make little notes in the margin of my book—not for the essay, but for my thesis. Those Norse had a lot of stuff to draw from. Trouble was, most of it was bloody, and I did *not* need my brain going in that direction tonight.

When my brain couldn't take any more talk of Eddas or the Futhark, I closed my book and glanced over to see Elisa already sound asleep on top of her bed, her poetry notebook open beside her and Sylvia Plath plastered over her face. I chuckled to myself and grabbed the book and notebook and slid them into her drawer.

"Night doofus," I whispered to her, and turned off the light.

My hand brushed against something warm under my pillow when I curled up in bed.

Right. Mom's crystal. I'd spent the last few years of my life intentionally keeping my dreams in check. It had been working. For a time. But as I lay there in the dark, watching shadows of birds and branches flit past the window, memories of last night's dream inked into consciousness. My chest constricted at the sudden image of a raven penetrating my ribs, Munin's dead white eyes piercing my vision as Brad watched and laughed.

How long had it been since Munin had invaded my dreams? Rather, how long had it been since I remembered? If he was getting vocal again. . . .

"No," I whispered into the darkness. "I'm not going back."

I closed my eyes and curled into my comforter, clutched the warm stone tight in my fist. And while sleep slowly washed in, I prayed the raven and the ghost of my ex would stay far, far away.

The weekend was the usual Islington fare: lots of homework, socializing in brief spurts, and then panicking about the work you hadn't gotten done and going back to study. I seriously thought I was going to have a complex by the time I left this place; if I wasn't busy working on something, I was fighting off stomach ulcers from worrying I'd forgotten a Very Important Project. About the only perk to this high-level stress and creative output was the fact that I didn't have to interact with Chris. In fact, after the concert, I'd been doing my best to give him the cold shoulder. I felt bad about it, sure. He was a sweet guy and he deserved someone great. The trouble was, I couldn't be that "someone great," and the sooner he realized it the happier he'd be. Thus, I'd kept my headphones on while working in the painting studio, even when he glanced over with a look that clearly said he wanted to talk. I preferred not to think of it as rude, but as *focused*. And, hell, if I'm being honest, *thoughtful*. He didn't want to get to know me. It would be better if he went for someone who was actually sweet and charming and emotionally available. Like Jane. He and Jane would be a very cute couple.

Long story short, by the time Monday night rolled around, Ethan and I needed out. And seeing as there weren't too many places to go around here—least of all on a Monday—we used our usual escape tactic. It was maybe seven, and we were sitting in the back corner of T'Chai Nanni surrounded by hipsters discussing Kierkegaard and Dostoevsky, or whatever hipsters discussed. Ethan and I were too deep into our work to really notice. Even with the tea—a simple peppermint this time—my stomach was in knots, and I couldn't tell if it was the stress of the work or the stress of waiting for the other shoe to drop. Even though my dreams were blank, I still had a gnawing feeling that shit was about to get real. Too many memories of Brad drifting to the surface. Too many black birds waiting for me in the snow. I told myself over and over it was my tired, overactive imagination, that I was being ridiculous. So far, even drowning in work, I was unable to really convince myself of it.

I was just about to put academic work away to focus on sketches for my upcoming silversmithing project—anything to do with *chains*—when Ethan's phone buzzed on the table. He gave it a cursory glance and let it ring out.

That was the unspoken rule of fishing: Phones only told the time. Nothing more.

I don't know why it reminded me of the raven, as though the vibration on the table mirrored the guttural call that had been following me every time I left the dorm. My stomach clenched into a clove hitch. *Never ignore an omen. Never ignore an omen.* I sketched wedding rings joined by a thick iron chain. Work was the answer. It was always the answer.

When his phone rang again, I looked from the phone to Ethan, who was contorted back on the sofa with an arm behind his leg and his worn copy of *Great Expectations* held in one hand.

"You should probably answer that," I said. I don't know why I said it; normally I'd recommend he turn it off. But I didn't think my stomach could take any more nervous twinges.

"I don't want to be rude."

I didn't say anything, just gave him a look. He dog-eared his page and picked up the phone.

"Hey babe," he said. "What's up?"

Ethan's brow furrowed. His next response was slow.

"Are you serious?"

My phone started to ring then, and I snatched it up without

waiting for the second buzz. Unknown number, but Michigan area code.

"Hello?"

"Kaira?" The voice on the other end was familiar.

"Yeah."

"This is Maria, your RA. Where are you right now?"

I told her. Ethan was still on the phone with Oliver, and he looked even worse. I heard him say, "Who?"

"We need you to come back to campus now. Please. Both of you."

"What? What's going on?"

A long silence.

"Just come back please. And head straight to your dorm. We'll be making an announcement later."

Maria hung up then, leaving me flabbergasted and staring at Ethan with my mouth open. He said good-bye to Oliver a moment later. He was pale. Paler than usual.

"What was that all about?" I asked.

"They didn't tell you?"

"No. Just said to come home."

He took a deep, shaky breath.

"Someone's dead." He looked at the floor while he said it.

My phone clattered to the table. Inside my head, I heard the raven caw.

CHAPTER SEVEN

Neither Ethan nor I spoke the entire ride home. We'd paid Veronica and left her the rest as a tip—we were out the door before she even had time to count the change. The entire ride back, all I could think was, *Not Elisa, not Elisa, please not Elisa*. I'd tried calling her cell phone, but whether it was shitty backwoods reception or her not being by her phone or worse, she never picked up. My stomach was acid; I nearly screamed at Ethan to drive faster, but kept the frustration in check.

Is that what this was about? I whispered inside my head. Munin didn't answer. The silence was deeper than death. I felt like I was on the other side of a tidal wave, the calm emptiness following the executioner's ax. Even though I still had no clue what was going on, a part of me knew this was the worst. And, horrible as it made me feel to think it, the worst was over.

For now.

Campus was swarming with cops when we arrived, their lights cutting through the snow in scratches of red and blue on white. It felt like rolling into a dream, only I knew I wouldn't wake up when it was over. I watched the lights shift with morbid fascination as Ethan pulled to a stop outside my dorm. It wasn't until he spoke that I realized I was, in fact, still there in my body and needing to act.

"Call me if you need anything, okay?" he asked.

"Of course. Likewise."

I leaned over and kissed him on the cheek before running inside.

I guess I expected chaos—after all, isn't that what we're taught to expect? Sobbing friends, cops demanding order while a white-clothed body is rolled out, a familiar hand slipping from obscurity? But there wasn't anyone milling about in the foyer or lounge area. Everything was empty, silent, save for the distant sound of crying and the lone figure at the desk.

"Kaira," Maria said, standing like she was going to say something else. The words seemed to get stuck behind her lips; we stared at each other for a long moment.

"Who was it?" I asked, my voice rough. I didn't mean for it to sound so harsh, so clinical—Islington was a small school, barely topping four hundred students, so there was no way this wouldn't be personal. *Please not Elisa.*

Maria walked around the desk and gave me a hug without saying a word. My heart dropped.

"Mandy," she finally said. She hugged me tighter. "I'm so sorry."

My breath caught in my lungs. How was that possible? I knew Mandy, vaguely. She was a ceramicist. And yeah, she kept to herself most of the time, but I'd never had any warning signs with her; isolation was just the nature of being in the ceramics studio.

"What happened?"

"We don't know yet. They're releasing more information later tonight. For now, it's mandatory sign-in. You should get up to your room—Elisa's already up there."

Elisa was sitting on her bed with her knees curled to her chest when I opened the door. She looked a little shell-shocked, but I'd seen her in far worse states.

"Hey," she said. She slipped from the bed and wrapped me in a tight hug. "You okay?"

I nodded.

"Yeah, I think so. I mean . . . did they tell you what happened?"

"Just that Mandy killed herself," she replied. She took a half step back and looked me in the eyes. "You're sure you're okay? I mean, were you guys close?"

"I knew her. Last I saw she was preparing her thesis for tomorrow."

Hell, I'd spent a few minutes with her this weekend in the ceramics studio. Her project was one hundred ceramic origami cranes. She joked that it was the most frustrating meditation ever: folding pieces of paper into cranes, dipping them in slip (a sort of runny clay mixture), drying them, and then praying the shape held when firing in the kiln. She'd been working on it for the better part of a month.

"It doesn't make sense," Elisa said. "She was in my physics class. She didn't seem like the sort to take her own life."

"Maybe she was just good at hiding the stress," I muttered. Elisa and I had shared mostly everything, but this still wasn't a conversation I wanted to have with her. With anyone, really. It struck too close to home. "What with her thesis and colleges and other work . . . who knows what sort of pressure she was under?"

There was a look in Elisa's eyes that made me uncomfortable. Like she was examining more than my words. Damned actors and their damned training—she could analyze me better than anyone I'd ever met, often because I gave myself away with the flick of a finger or dart of an eye. Thankfully, she had tact with her observations. I had a feeling that if Ethan had her skill, he and I wouldn't be friends.

"Please tell me that if you ever get that stressed, you'll talk to someone, okay?" Her words were quiet and serious and somehow incredibly tender. "Even if it's not me. I don't want to lose you."

Walls shifted inside of me. A crack in the barriers I'd built up over the last two years.

Back in the bathroom, everything orange and white and red and black, colors seeping into shadow, fluids draining into air. Pain fading into nothing. Ravens shifting from shadows . . .

Elisa's grip tightened, and our dorm room came into focus. Not without consequence—there were tears in the corners of my eyes and a shake building inside of me I couldn't force down.

"Please," she said. "Promise me?"

I tried to still my jaw and keep my words from trembling. I didn't trust myself. I could only nod and hope that she thought I was emotional because of Mandy. She pulled me in for another hug. The fissure in my composure cracked deeper. I squeezed her

90

tight and carefully rewrapped the wounds that scratched their way to light. Now was not the time. Now was *definitely* not the time.

This moment was about Mandy.

Not me.

I opened my eyes and looked over Elisa's shoulder. There, on the windowsill, silhouetted in lamplight, was a crow. He cocked his head when my eyes met his. Then, before I could blink, he flapped and disappeared in a fluff of snow.

A few hours and one terrible movie later, Elisa curled under her covers and fell asleep almost before her head hit the pillow. For that, I was a little jealous. I had a feeling tonight wouldn't be a night of restful sleep.

It was nearly ten. Supposedly lights-out, but no one was coming around to enforce it.

I turned from Elisa's bed and stared out our window, both hoping and dreading to see the crow again. The woods beyond were dark, lit only by a single streetlamp a few yards away. The light wavered in the snow, glittering against branches and falling like confetti in some silent celebration. I couldn't begin to count how many nights I'd sat here for hours after lights-out, watching the trees sway and the darkness change shape.

And then, as expected, a shadow flew across the window. I followed its arc to where it alighted in a nearby fir. I couldn't see it, swathed in shades of darkness, but I knew what it was. A raven. Sitting on the branches of a fir tree. Watching me as I tried to find it.

I felt like I should say something, some prayer for Mandy's peaceful transition. But as I watched the shadows shift, I knew the wish was unnecessary. Mandy was gone. Prayers for the dead were never really meant for the dead—they were meant for the ones left behind.

I was used to being left behind. I didn't need any more praying in that department.

Is this why you've been following me? I wanted to ask. But I didn't want the answer; Munin didn't show up for something this simple. He was an omen reserved for more . . . apocalyptic . . . events. I'd learned that one firsthand, and two days too late. *So what are you trying to tell me?*

The raven said nothing. Just like last time.

Finally, after a few more minutes of staring at shadows and convincing myself I wasn't going insane, I pushed myself from the bed and ducked into the bathroom.

I didn't turn on the light when I locked the door behind me; I knew the corners of this place like the curves of my own body. I slid out of my clothes and turned on the shower, pushed the heat to almost-scalding. Then, in the pitch blackness, I stepped under the spray. In here, I could pretend I was anywhere else. The darkness could be a cave, the cosmos, the water some magical liquid washing me clean inside and out. I slid to the wall of the shower, sinking down to rest on the floor of the cubicle. And it was then I let the last week crash in. It was too much, all too much. Mandy's death. Memories of blood in the bathroom. Even Chris's presence, touching on wounds I didn't want to feel. Too many wounds. Too many aches. Too many reasons I shouldn't even be here. I pressed my palms to my eyes and prayed into the spray, *wash me clean, wash me clean*. But I knew I couldn't get clean, couldn't run fast enough—nothing would cleanse me, not the water or my tears. I didn't deserve to be clean, to mourn. Mandy was dead. Dead. And even though I'd heard Munin's warnings, I hadn't known enough to stop it.

Cold wrapped around me in spite of the burning heat. The darkness wasn't a comfort. Not now. I wrapped my arms around my knees and pulled them close to my chest. I felt Brad behind me, wrapping his arms around me, kissing the back of my neck. Whispering that it should have been me.

After the shower I felt empty, but that was better than the alternative. I didn't look in the mirror after drying off. I didn't want to see Brad there, staring back. My moment of weakness was over. Now wasn't about me. Now I would focus on Mandy and those who knew her. My phone blinked with a dozen texts from Ethan and Oliver, all asking if I was okay, though Ethan's escalated from Are you okay to Please tell me you're not dead to if you are dead, please don't text back, I don't want to behead a zombie-kaira to holy shit if you don't text back I'm going to sneak from my dorm room and find you and you know I live on the second story and can't climb. My paralysis is on your shoulders.

I sent him a text first. I'm fine. And I hope you're not in the bushes outside Rembrandt with a broken spine.

A second later he texted back. Moderate paralysis. I expect cookies.

I chuckled softly, careful not to wake Elisa. The room was lit by my little desk lamp, and I settled onto my papasan chair with a blanket over my legs. For some reason, Ethan's humor didn't feel sacrilegious or an affront to Mandy's memory. It was a reminder that my support network was still there, that life was still moving forward.

Despite what Brad had told me years ago, there were people who cared.

Oliver's texts were much more his calming style: I heard about Mandy. I hope you're okay. and Call if you need anything. Any time.

I thanked him, then set my phone to silent and leaned back, staring at my cluttered desk and wondering what to do with this insomnia. I didn't want to sleep. Even with Mom's crystal, I didn't want to risk the shadows.

Mason jars with charcoal sticks and colored pencils and fine-tip markers lined one corner of the desk, while a stack of papers and folders was piled haphazardly in the other. My bulletin board was covered in snippets of paintings and inspirational quotes, pressed leaves and feathers, and a few photo-kiosk strips of Ethan and me at the mall.

I sighed and tore my eyes away. There was no way I was going to try to do work tonight, so I quietly slid out the drawer under my bed and grabbed a tiny cloth bundle. My Tarot deck.

The cards were warm and soft as I slid them from the bag. Four years of nearly constant use had worn the edges smooth and the cardstock supple, almost velveteen. The deck was the traditional Rider-Waite, with the primary-color images and geometric sky-blue card backs. Not my favorite style of art, but there was something to be said for the simplicity, the easy symbolism. It had been a gift from my mom the first day of freshman year. *Because the gods know a young girl needs more guidance than her mother can give.* Those had been her words when she handed it over, and a similar quote was written on a tiny notecard inside the bag, her handwriting perfect and looping in black ink. I envied my mother many things, but her handwriting was among the top.

I wasn't too worried about being quiet—Elisa had long grown used to me shuffling in the dead of night. The familiar whir between my fingers was calming, rhythmic, almost more soothing than the guidance I was seeking.

I'd nearly thrown them out sophomore year. Almost. The idea of being connected to the occult after . . . well, it felt like a dangerous line to walk. But the idea of trashing something my mom had given me caused too much guilt, so the cards stayed.

"What's going on?" I whispered, images floating through my mind to make the question solid: Mandy's smile, cop cars in the snow, Ethan's words ringing like omens: *Someone died.*

A card flipped out mid-shuffle, landing on the desk.

"Ten of Swords," I muttered, staring at the man stabbed by his own blades. Obvious enough—defeat, destruction, death. "Tell me something I didn't know."

I kept shuffling.

Minutes seemed to drag by. The cards shuffled quietly, none dislodging. I couldn't think of anything else—no other question seemed pertinent. Then, after my eyes began to droop and my shuffling faded, a new image flashed through my mind: Jonathan, standing before our folklore class, a raven on his shoulder. *It was the gods who took the innocent away.*

I jerked awake as two cards spilled from my hand, landing on the floor, one crossed over the other.

The bottom was The World, inverted. And above it, The Tower.

"Shit," I muttered. Chills ran down my neck. I reached down and slid the cards back into the deck, passing it off as an accident. I was too tired to be doing this.

But when I slid into bed and turned off the light, my cards tucked beneath my pillow, all I could see behind my closed eyes were those two cards. The inverted World: a woman twined in fabric, falling upside down. The Tower: a great obelisk destroyed by lightning, figures leaping from its heights. Apart, they were important, almost cosmic—great shifts, catastrophic turns of events. Together, in that combination, they felt like a curse.

The world on fire. The world crumbling like the tower. Everything falling like feathers in the snow, like blood on the tiles.

The gods walk, something inside me whispered. And hell if it didn't sound like Brad.

CHAPTER EIGHT

Elisa was, unsurprisingly, up before me. She plodded silently to the bathroom, but that slight rustle of covers was enough to wake me. I blinked and rolled over, glaring at the alarm clock on her shelf. Six thirty. I closed my eyes. I really, really didn't want to be awake. I didn't want to face whatever was going to happen today. Surely, we'd have some sort of assembly. Classes would be canceled, and I hated to admit that that would be one of the worst parts of all this—work always helped me get through things. If we just had a day to sit around and think about what happened, I'd go insane.

Ethan found me at breakfast. I was sitting at the far end of the cafeteria, by the windows overlooking the woods and the iced-over lake. The mood of the room was as gray and heavy as the world outside. No one seemed to be talking, and if they were, it was in muted tones. He saw me, saw the look on my face, and immediately slipped into a side of himself I saw only in dire circumstances.

"How are you?" he asked, setting his tray beside mine. There was only a banana and half-filled bowl of oatmeal. Looked like I wasn't the only one without an appetite.

"I . . ." I was about to lie, to say I was okay. But Ethan's eyes were on mine and right then, I didn't want to pretend anymore. Not with him. I'd been pretending with Elisa all morning. "I'm feeling pretty fucked up."

He gave me a half grin, the sad, consoling sort, and put a hand on my arm.

"Do you want to talk about it?"

"I don't know if I can."

He nodded like he understood. And maybe he did understand, at least partly. He'd once admitted it took him two years to come out to his parents. Some secrets were hard to hide, and even harder to share. His, at least, had nothing to do with blood or ex-boyfriends.

"Well, I'm here when you're ready," he said, breaking me from my thoughts of the past. Tears welled up at the corners of my eyes. I knew he meant it. I just didn't know if he'd still mean it if I told him the truth.

We ate our breakfast in silence, the cafeteria's mood getting both of us down. Elisa sat beside us a while later. She didn't even bother with the facade of food: She had a mug of coffee and a handful of grapes. I couldn't blame her for losing her usually voracious appetite.

"We're having an assembly at nine," she said. "Maria told me when I left."

Ethan and I both sighed, staring down at our plates. There

really wasn't anything to say to that. Even when Oliver—usually the bright spot in any conversation—came over and sat down, the mood didn't shift from morose. It felt wrong to even try to be cheery. Mandy had killed herself, and none of us had done anything to prevent it. We hadn't even known there was a problem. *You knew something would happen*, whispered Brad. *But you were too scared to do anything about it.* I shook my head and shoved down his voice and focused on getting what little food I had down. I felt like I was floating, not really there. And everyone else in the cafeteria had the same dissociated air. No laughter, no loud chatter. Everyone moved and spoke like they were in a daydream, one they were terrified of rupturing. Some small part of me hoped I'd wake up to a morning that didn't involve old nightmares and a dead classmate. Brad's whispers told me that wouldn't be the case.

Outside, it began to snow again.

"Do you guys want to go for a walk?" Elisa asked quietly, when it was clear everyone was done picking at their breakfast.

I nodded. There was still an hour before the assembly, and sitting inside seemed like a terrible idea. We stood and left like a funeral procession.

Islington was a nature lover's paradise. You almost had to enjoy nature when you studied here—there wasn't anything else. We didn't walk any of the short trails along the lakeside, though. No time, not with the looming assembly. Instead, we sat on one of the benches by the shore and stared out at the frozen lake. Fishermen's huts dotted the snowy ice, and a line of fir trees on the horizon marked the shore. I'd sat out here so many nights, daydreaming about what went on in those houses: people having dinner or watching TV or fighting. People not worrying about art or college or trying to make their mark on the world. In my imagination, they all had simple, happy lives. Lives my own convoluted mess could never imitate.

The things we didn't talk about far outweighed the things we did. For the most part, we sat in silence, watching a few figures roam the lake and the clouds churn above. Ethan asked Elisa about her play. Elisa asked Oliver about his concert.

We didn't mention Mandy. We didn't wonder aloud why she'd done it or what would happen next. We didn't need to. Those questions perched on our shoulders, heavy and laden with oily feathers and sharp beaks.

For my part, I could barely concentrate on their small talk. Ethan leaned against me on one side and Elisa rested her head on my other shoulder, but I hardly felt them. Their weight felt worlds away, unable to tether me to the Earth. I watched the crows circle above the snow, flecks of black dodging between a sky as pale and solemn as the ice spread out below.

Why are you back? I wanted to ask. I didn't know if I was asking the birds or Brad, or if it even made any difference. *Why are you following me?*

Mandy had killed herself on her own volition. I had barely known her. This had nothing to do with me. So why did it feel like I was the center of all of this, like the crows above were circling around *me* like some cosmic nexus? *I had nothing to do with this*, I wanted to scream.

Only because you did nothing to stop it, Brad whispered back. *A trait you've gotten quite good at. How long do you think you can run away, Kaira? How long until they find out what you did?*

"It's time," Elisa said, snapping me from my reverie. Her voice seemed swallowed by the lake, her words small and insubstantial.

We slid off the bench and wandered to the black box theatre where the assembly was taking place. It didn't take a genius to figure out why they chose it over the actual auditorium: This was more intimate, a conversation rather than a lecture.

We followed the line of students leaving their dorms up the asphalt drive that led to the performing arts complex. My entire body felt numb as we walked down the hall and into the cozy theatre which, as the name implied, was just one large black box with a row of risers and chairs on three sides. Ethan and Oliver and I sat near the back, while Elisa took a spot up front with Cassie. The place was filling fast.

I closed my eyes. I didn't think I was empathic, but being in large crowds always drained me. It might be part of the reason I gravitated toward painting. Right now, I felt like I was suffocating in other people's muck. I leaned my head against Ethan's shoulder and nearly whimpered when he wrapped his arm around me.

"Is this seat reserved?"

I quirked my eye open.

Chris stood in the aisle, in a green plaid shirt and black jeans, looking down at me a little uncertainly.

"What? No," I said. Ethan was staying resolutely silent.

Chris gave me a slight smile and sat down. If one could fidget while sitting, he did so. He stared straight ahead, hands clasped in his lap, his foot tapping nervously.

"How are you doing?" I asked. I knew Chris knew Mandy—everyone in the art department knew everyone. It's just how things worked.

"I'm okay," he said. Definitely a lie. "What about you?"

"Okay," I replied. I could lie just as well as he could.

He nodded. For some reason, I wanted to apologize for the distance the night of the concert. Pushing people away right now seemed like a bad idea, even if it really was in his best self-interest. I didn't say anything though. Words seemed too difficult.

The theatre filled up silently. Some students and staff were even standing along the walls, since this place wasn't meant for four hundred bodies. If anyone cared about the cramped conditions, they didn't voice it.

Ms. Kenton, our president, stepped into the middle of the stage and the room hushed in a moment. She wore a somber black suit, which just made the room seem even heavier. She was normally full of life and color, putting the rest of us and our faux-hippie attire to shame. Seeing her was like the final hammer.

Mandy was dead.

And we were here to mourn her.

"As many of you know," she said, her usually strong voice a little weaker, a little shakier, "we lost one of our own last night. A senior, Ms. Mandy Rivers, took her life. This is a dark time for us. Islington is a community, and we here are dedicated to supporting each and every one of you. In light of this, we will have a guidance counselor at hand twenty-four hours a day, should you need to chat. About anything. I myself will have open office hours should you wish to speak with me. We are here for you. For all of you. You are our family, and we grieve as a whole when one of our flock is taken."

She paused and swallowed.

"I now wish to open the floor to you. I know your hearts are burdened, so let us be here to share that heaviness. If you wish to speak, please stand. It may be about Mandy, fond memories or words you remember, or it may be your own questions for me. Remember: Healing may only occur when one is open to the pain. We are ready. We support you."

She went silent then and I had a terrible image of no one standing up. Of Ms. Kenton standing there in the dim spotlight, watching us, waiting for someone to share their heart like she shared hers. Then a girl—Laura, another ceramicist—stood in the front row.

"Mandy was my friend," she said. "She was always so happy, even when she was bogged down with work." Laura sniffed, and it sounded like a laugh. "I remember, this one time right before finals, she dragged me out of my room to go make snow angels. I nearly got frostbite but she got me hot chocolate from the caf. She always did nice things like that—little notes saying hi, or a flower she found, or a painting she loved. She was so full of love. I just . . . I don't know why. . . ."

Laura broke down. Ms. Kenton was there in a moment, wrapping her in a hug. Other girls stood from the front row and joined the embrace.

For the next half hour, classmates I knew as friends or acquaintances bared their souls to the rest of the room. It seemed like Mandy had touched everyone, somehow, whether it was a smile in the hall or sitting beside a loner at lunch. I'd never realized how much of a saint she was before this.

I didn't stand and speak my part. Maybe I should have. Maybe it was a dishonor not to share my experiences of a girl I considered an acquaintance. I couldn't do it. Not out of fear of speaking, but because I knew it wouldn't be honest. I should have known the signs. I should have tried to help her. But all I'd done in our last interaction was bitch about how stressed I was over my own thesis, rather than tell her how amazing hers would be.

It made me feel guilty. Munin had warned me something bad was coming. And just like last time, I hadn't listened.

Unlike last time, though, it was someone else who'd been hurt.

And you know what that means, Brad whispered. *You should have known better. You should have tried to stop it. Since you didn't, you as good as killed her.*

There was a deep silence when the memorial was over. Ms. Kenton stayed onstage, talking one-on-one to students and staff. No one made for the door. Not at first. No one wanted to break the bubble of this place. We all knew that once that door opened, life would push forward again. Yes, we had two days off for mourning and no, nothing would ever be the same, but the spirit of Islington, the drive to create and strive, never stopped. No one wanted to be the first to let the outside world back in. It was almost like, in being here, we'd somehow managed to capture Mandy's ghost, to bring it back to life through story and tears. Leaving meant letting her go once more. For the final time.

I, however, was suffocating. Not literally, but emotion was thick in the room, sticking to my throat and filling my lungs with despair. Chris put a tentative hand on my shoulder.

"Are you okay?" he asked. I glanced to him, probably harsher than I meant, because he withdrew his hand immediately. He looked down to his feet. "You just looked like you could use some air."

I nodded.

"Yeah," I said, standing. "Yeah, I could."

I didn't expect Chris to follow me out the door, but he did, along with Ethan and Oliver. We weren't the first out but were damn well near it. The buildings were dark, empty, and the snow had already begun covering the tracks of those who came into the theatre. Taking the first step out here felt wrong, in a way, like we were staining a slate that nature wanted desperately to clean. I wandered back down to the lake and didn't stop by the bench. I kept going, heading toward one of the forest trails that snaked off in a wide loop. No one would be out there, not with the snow growing thicker by the minute. I shoved my hands deeper into my coat pockets and didn't look back. I could hear the boys walking behind me, their feet shuffling in the snow, muted over the wind that kept rustling my coat like wings.

Maybe five minutes later, once the firs had closed around us and the forest was quiet in that all-consuming way, I stopped. I tilted my head back and stared at the gray seeping through the boughs, everything dulled green and silver.

Ethan knew what was up. He stepped up beside me and slid

his hand into my pocket, wrapping his fingers around mine. Oliver was at his side.

Chris stepped beside us. I could tell from his hesitation he was confused, but I wasn't going to explain it. *Sometimes you just need to face the void.*

Then, without preamble, I screamed. Ethan and Oliver followed suit. And a second later, so did Chris.

It wasn't a scream of hatred or anger. It was primal. It was seeing death and staring at the gods and screaming your defiance, your fear, your shame. It was knowing you were worthless and worthy of a voice, important and smaller than the tiniest microbe on a grain of sand.

It was knowing this, all of this, and holding someone's hand and praying you'd keep moving on.

We screamed for a while. Maybe a full minute. I was the one who broke off first, my yell exploding into giggles, laughter that hiccuped into tears. Ethan went quiet and sobbed beside me, not letting go of my hand. Chris and Oliver just fell silent.

For a while we stood there, saying nothing and trying to calm our breathing. I kept my eyes closed. It was easier to imagine it was all a dream that way. Easier to pretend that I'd wake up and it would be Saturday again—time for class and critiques and a night at T'Chai Nanni. No birds, no Brad, no death hanging from my shoulders like broken wings.

Gods, I needed to get out of here.

The click of a lighter brought me back to Earth. I opened my eyes and looked over. Chris had a hand-rolled cigarette in his mouth, cupping the flame of his silver lighter against the wind.

"You smoke?" I asked. No one at Islington smoked. I mean, they did, but it wasn't allowed on campus grounds so it wasn't a common sight. Only, well, when in the woods.

"Just when it's bad," Chris muttered around the cigarette. It lit and he flicked the lighter closed, sliding it back in his pocket. He took a long, deep drag and then held out the cigarette.

"Sounds like a good motto," I replied. I took the cigarette and let the burn fill my lungs. I hated the taste, but it was grounding. It rooted me down, stuck me to the soil. I handed it off to Ethan, who took it without comment.

"I don't really know what to say right now," Chris said, taking back the cigarette for another drag. He handed it to me, smoke curling from his lips like dragon's breath. I hated to admit it, but there was a James Dean sort of sexiness about it. "I mean, this is all a hundred levels of fucked up. Mandy was my friend. We hung out in her lounge the other night. She would have told me if she wasn't feeling well."

I nodded and inhaled. The second drag felt like heaven, and I was all too aware that this was just touching his lips. It took a lot of control not to feel jealous over him hanging out with another girl. Which was stupid, since I spent most of my time hanging out with boys and what was I even talking about? I wasn't dating him.

I looked up into the trees. There, among the branches, was a single crow. It fluffed its wings when we made eye contact. *Go away*, I hissed inside my head. *It's over. Now leave me alone.*

The crow didn't move.

"I don't know about you guys," I said, "but I don't think I can stay here all day. This place is suffocating."

"Agreed," Ethan said. He looked to Chris and Oliver. "You guys want to come out with us?"

"I need to practice," Oliver said. He looked down to his feet as he said it. I knew he wanted to stick with us, but he set a high bar for himself—if he slipped up, he wouldn't let himself live it down.

"I'll go," Chris said. And yeah, I won't lie, I was kind of hoping he wouldn't join in. Then again, if there was ever a day to need a distraction from the thoughts writhing around in my head, it was today. Not that that excused me from the mounds of homework lingering in my room, tugging at my brain, and refusing to let me relax just yet. *Work before pleasure*, my mom always said. Little did she know what sort of complex that had given me. "But I need to get some stuff done first. Maybe lunchtime?"

"Sure," Ethan said. "I should probably do some work as well. Shall we?"

Chris nodded and snubbed out the cigarette on the heel of his boot, then slid the butt in his pocket. Without further preamble, we headed back to campus.

When we got to the main road, Chris placed a hand on my shoulder. My breath hitched; once more, it reminded me of Brad. "Do you mind if I talk to you for a moment?"

My first instinct was to say that I was busy—being alone with a straight boy wasn't a situation I wanted to be in—but there were other kids wandering aimlessly and there was a look on Chris's face that struck me as incredibly hopeful. Besides, I highly doubted he would try anything. Not in the wake of what we'd just come from.

"Sure," I relented. I looked to Ethan and Oliver. "I'll catch up with you later?"

"Sure thing," Oliver said. He and Ethan hugged me good-bye, then headed back to their dorm. Ethan gave me a gratuitously obvious look over his shoulder as he walked away. I couldn't tell if it was him seeing if I needed help or him just being smug that his plan was working.

For a moment, Chris and I stood there awkwardly. I looked everywhere but at him; I could tell from the tingle in my gut that he was trying very hard to make eye contact.

"Did I do something wrong?" he asked.

"What do you mean?" I replied. My eyes flicked toward him and yes, he looked pained.

"I mean the way you act around me. It's like I've already offended you. I mean, I know you don't owe me anything, but I just thought . . ."

I shook my head.

"You know that *it's not you, it's me* bullshit?" I asked.

He nodded.

"Exactly that. But it's not bullshit. I'm not dating anyone, Chris."

"I never said anything about dating," he replied. He actually sounded offended. "I just wanted to get to know you." He sighed and looked at his feet, scuffed the snow with a boot. "You caught my attention the first day of class, but I finally realized that if I didn't act, I'd go the entire school year without actually talking to you. And after Mandy . . . well, life's short. I don't want to miss my chance."

I didn't know if it was touching or disrespectful to mention Mandy in this context, and so soon, but his words sent my head spinning.

"You really don't want to get to know me," I said. I looked away, toward where Ethan and Oliver were throwing snowballs at each other. Some small part of me flared with want. Didn't I crave that? That easy sort of love? *It's not meant for you,* Brad whispered. *You're tainted, broken—and you'll pass that on to anyone who tries to get close.*

"That's the thing, though," he said, cutting through the words I couldn't tell were Brad's or mine. "I do want to get to know you. You're different. Even here, you stand out." I knew it was meant to be a compliment, but hearing him say it just sent my walls higher. *Different. You'll always be different. And that's why no one can love you.* He held out a hand. "Can we at least make a truce? Let me try to be your friend. I promise not to make it into anything you don't want it to be."

I looked at him, from his eyes to his fingerless-gloved hand. This was stupid. There were only a few months left in the school year and soon we'd be going to different colleges and none of this would matter. But he was right. I couldn't deny there was something that pulled me toward him, a gravity I didn't really want to escape. After today, it was difficult to justify pushing anyone away.

I closed my eyes and took his hand, trying to block out the images shuffling through my mind like Tarot cards—Brad's face as he slammed me against the wall, the report in the paper that had nothing to do with . . . *Shut up!*

Our gloved hands met. Stupid to think, but even through the fabric I swore I felt a spark. The moment his hand touched mine, the images in my head fluttered to the ground. It felt like taking a breath after nearly drowning.

"Okay then," he said. "Friends."

"Potential friends," I said. I grinned to let him know I was joking. Like I said, wit was what kept me from sinking. "Let's not get too ahead of ourselves."

Then, because I realized our hands were still clasped and that was kind of strange, I let go and slipped my hands in my pockets.

"Well," I said, once more trying to be all business and squash the butterflies raging for control, "I should probably go call home. Mom's going to want to know what's happening."

"Likewise. I need to get the okay to leave campus with you guys," he said. "Also work."

"Always work. See you soon."

"Yeah."

As I walked toward my room, I kept replaying his words in my head: *Even here, you stand out.* It was so, so close to what Brad said, the first day he talked to me. *Chris is different,* I tried to convince myself.

Overhead, perched on the power lines, a crow squawked.

"I won't let it happen again," I muttered, and hurried inside.

"Are you okay?"

Those were the first words from my mother's lips. The phone barely even rang before she picked up. Her intuition was good like that. I just wished I'd paid attention to it sooner.

"I'm fine," I said. I paused. "What have you heard?"

And no, I didn't just mean from school. My mom worked as a medium on the side—she often knew about major life events the moment I did.

"Someone passed over," she replied. Her voice didn't sound like some hack mystic—she wasn't breathy or deep. She sounded professional, like you'd imagine a woman used to leading stock meetings would sound. She was the head of a local bank, so it was a fairly apt comparison. "Tragically. I had nightmares all night."

"Pretty much," I replied. "There was a girl in my class, Mandy. She killed herself. No note or anything, but her thesis was supposed to go up today. I'm assuming stress."

"What have the crows said, dear?"

My skin prickled. I was still getting used to questions like this. I didn't think I ever fully would.

"They're . . . around."

An awkward pause as I felt the gears turning on her end.

"Well, just be careful. And remember, if you need to talk to me, I'm here for you. Always."

There was a strain to her voice I wasn't used to. She was holding back. She never held back, unless she thought it would scare me. Silence.

"Mom?"

"Sorry love, just thinking. I'm sorry you had to experience that. You know I wish I could keep you safe."

"I know."

"Keep them close," she said.

"I will," I replied.

"I love you."

"Love you too."

I looked out the window at the crow sitting on the fir branch. I didn't need to try to keep them close—they'd be there no matter what.

CHAPTER NINE

I met Ethan and Chris on the commons just before noon. The boys stood beside one of the fir trees next to the admissions building—a squat log-cabin-style hut linked to the main academics concourse—and didn't seem to notice my approach. I was still too wrapped up in what Mom had said to really register that their chatter meant they got along, which meant Ethan would most likely later try to hook Chris and me up with renewed zeal. Reaffirming my no-romance stance was the last thing on my mind, however. What was Mom holding back?

"Hey brosephs," I called as I neared. They both turned to me and smiled.

"Brosephs?" Chris asked, looking to Ethan.

"Ignore her," Ethan replied. "Sometimes she says things."

"And usually you laugh," I said. "What's *that* tell you?" I stepped up to him and wrapped an arm over his shoulder.

"That I'm a good friend," Ethan replied. "And a martyr for

the cause. Keep a careful eye on this one, Chris. She's wittier than she sounds." Chris just chuckled.

Ethan hugged my waist as we walked to his car, scratching his light stubble with his other hand. It was easy to fall into this moment, to forget Mandy's suicide and Mom's silence and the crows that seemed to be following me everywhere. *What have the crows said?* So far, nothing. But their presence was enough to set me on edge. Especially since the worst was supposed to be over.

They only appeared when I needed protection. So what was I being protected *from*? Memory flashed with the image of the crystal Mom sent. There was one way to find out. I just really, really didn't want to have to take it.

It had taken me so long to close those doors. Opening them again would be disastrous. *And that's why this is your fault*, Brad said. Just like his final words to me.

"Where are we going, anyway?" Ethan asked as we neared his car. It hadn't snowed hard since the last time we left, so blessedly we didn't have to scrape off the windshields or—even more fun—push the car from a snowbank. "I'm getting hungry and don't fancy pulling an all-day affair at Nanni's."

"Sushi?" I asked, stepping into the backseat so Chris could ride shotgun. Hey, I could be chivalrous too.

"You trust Michigan sushi?" Chris asked.

"I'm sure I can find something that will suit your West Coast sensibilities," Ethan said. He turned the keys in the ignition and began backing out. "Three-Two-Six it is."

We drove without conversation for a while, because it's hard to think of topics when you know you're just killing time . . .

which I suppose was a horrible analogy, given the circumstances. I watched the clouds and the crows roll past, but it wasn't relaxing. Brad's voice kept getting louder, and it took all my control to keep it shoved down. I really, really needed a break. Before I cracked. Finally, the music got particularly abysmal and whiny, so I leaned forward and reached between the seats to turn it down.

"So," I said, resting my elbows on the armrest and staring at Chris. "What brings you all the way from . . . well, wherever the hell you came from."

His grin never left his face, but it did seem to slip just a little bit. I knew that look; guess I wasn't the only one hiding from something. Unlike Ethan and me, Chris had transferred in just this year. A lot of people did, but I always felt like they didn't get the full experience. It sure as hell took me the first year to finally understand what this place actually was.

"Well," he said, "my parents worked in tech development back in Seattle. They were transferred out here to help set up a new branch for the company."

"But there's nothing *out* here," I said.

Chris's smile definitely slipped off then. He sighed and looked out the window.

"Yeah, well, that's the thing. They moved to Detroit. I was looking into schools in the area and found Islington. I think my parents were actually sort of relieved when I told them about it. Meant they could focus on their job. Not like that's any different from life before."

"I'm sorry to hear that," I said. "But, on the plus side, you got in. So there's that."

116

He grinned. "Yeah. I'm still just hoping they admitted me for my portfolio and not because my parents bribed them."

Ethan glanced over. "Don't worry—lots of rich celebs try to send their kids here to no avail. Money doesn't mean anything to the admissions panel, at least not on the faculty side. Though I'm sure charitable donations never go amiss."

"Thanks, I think. I believe that was comforting."

"That's Ethan," I said, patting Ethan on the shoulder. "Our man's good at emotional support."

"I thought gay men were supposed to be the comforting types," Chris said.

Ethan shook his head. "I do *not* know where you guys are getting that idea."

I just grinned and kissed Ethan on the cheek, then sat back and tightened my seatbelt again.

We didn't really talk after that, but we didn't turn the music back up, either. There was a comfortable sort of silence as we drove the rest of the way into town, watching trees thin out and become houses and gas stations and, eventually, the lakefront downtown. The lake was slate gray and stormy—it never froze, not fully, though chunks of ice floated like scattered shipwrecks. Whitecaps rode the waves, and the shore was thick with debris and tide. Above, the sky was just as tossed and frigid as the water.

"Looks like another storm," Chris muttered.

"Yeah," Ethan said. "Luckily this thing has four-wheel drive. Oh wait, it doesn't."

He parked in the lot beside the restaurant, and I was pleased to note that there weren't many cars. Wind swept around us as we made our way into the swank sushi bar.

326 was one of those upscale restaurants that charged extra because they had a lake view and giant glass windows from which to enjoy it. In the summer, apparently, the place was always crammed with tourists. During the fall and winter, though, when no one in their right mind wanted to venture to the upper wilds of Michigan for cold fish, the place was dead. Especially on a Tuesday.

"You could have warned me," Chris whispered when we stepped inside, waiting beside a perfectly pruned bonsai on a black marble stand. "I would have dressed up."

I shrugged and unzipped my coat, half-flashing him my paint-splattered T-shirt so he could see that I wasn't classy by any stretch of the imagination.

"Don't worry, they're used to us by now."

By "us" I might have meant Ethan and me, who came here practically every week, or Islington kids in general. Not many high-schoolers went out for sushi on weekday afternoons, and even less did so while covered in whatever art they'd just pried themselves away from. We were easy to tell from the crowd, especially in a place like this: long sleek leather benches and shiny black granite table tops, everything black and crisp white, from the white linens and snowy orchids on every table to the mirrorlike ebony tile floor.

Save for two couples seated near the back bar, the place was entirely empty. Looks like we were the few dumb enough to brave the upcoming blizzard.

A waiter came out from behind the back curtain, saw us, and smiled. It was Jason, a local college kid who worked here pretty much every weekday. He was gorgeous in that high fashion cover model sort of way: short brown hair slicked back, black pants and white shirt, and tight black vest. You could tell he worked out from the way his sleeves caught on his arms, and a hint of tattoos peeked out from under his cuffs.

"Hey guys," he said, stepping up to us. "How's it going? Day off?"

In normal situations, at any other restaurant beside this and T'Chai Nanni, I'd just smile and be polite and say things were great, how are you? But this was Jason. Jason, who would spend his slower days sitting at the table with us and talking about his dissertation on gender roles in comic books and, occasionally, moan about his boy troubles. Surprise surprise, backwoods Michigan wasn't teeming with gay men.

"Yeah," I said. "We . . . we lost a student this weekend. So campus is pretty much closed down."

Jason's face immediately switched from charming server to normal, concerned friend. "What do you mean? Dropped out?"

"Suicide," I whispered.

"Shit. I'm sorry, guys. I hadn't heard."

"It's okay. That's why we're here—trying to get our mind off things. Anyway," I said, shifting into a lighter tone, "this is Chris."

Jason held out his hand and introduced himself, then handed us a few menus and let us choose a table. We sat near the front windows, as far away from the other customers as possible. I didn't intend to talk about Mandy, but that didn't mean it wouldn't come

119

up on its own. Chris sat first, and I sat across from him. Ethan didn't even hesitate when sitting beside Chris; he probably didn't want the poor guy to feel like the third wheel. Jason disappeared behind the back curtain and came out a few minutes later with a ceramic pot of jasmine tea and four tiny cups.

"Just in case," he said, putting the fourth cup in the empty spot beside me. Which, I knew, translated to, *Hopefully, these other guys will leave and I can sit and drink tea with you.*

Ethan poured the aromatic tea in each of our cups, starting with me and leaving himself for last. He raised his cup between thumb and forefinger and held it out to us.

"To Mandy," he said. We all held up our teacups, clinking the black ceramics delicately.

"To Mandy," we repeated.

Outside, the snow began to fall.

The place emptied out a few minutes later, halfway through our appetizers of edamame and fried tofu and miso soup. And yeah, I felt a small note of pride at the condescending looks we got from the well-dressed patrons as they left, as if *we* were the ones intruding on *their* sacred space. Little did they know it was quite the opposite, as proved by Jason, who went over and flipped the door sign to CLOSED the moment the last table left, giving us a conspiratorial wink. When he returned, he bore eight different maki rolls, only five of which we'd actually ordered.

"I won't tell if you don't," he said as he set them down. "You guys look like you could use something positive today."

"You have no idea," I muttered. Jason smiled again, then

went to the back to grab a fresh pot of tea before returning and sitting down beside me.

I glanced to Chris, who watched the whole exchange with a strange sort of fascination, like he wasn't used to people acting like, well, *people* around him. Must have been part of coming from money.

"Thank you," Ethan said. He was trying very hard not to stare at Jason as the guy poured us tea. He'd had a crush on the waiter since day one, but had always deemed Jason "too old." I think he was just scared of putting himself out there. At least now he had Oliver to hold his attention.

"No problem," Jason replied. He poured some soy sauce in a dish and began mixing in wasabi. "Are you guys doing okay?"

I shrugged and took a sip of soup, looking out at the lake.

"We're managing," Ethan said.

"So . . . Chris, was it? What are you studying?"

"Art," Chris replied. "Painting, more specifically."

"Very cool. How'd you all meet up?"

I looked to Chris then, wondering what he'd say, but it was Ethan who answered.

"We're presenting our theses at the same time. Solidarity in insomnia, you know."

Jason chuckled. "I know that one."

Conversation drifted into the usual small talk as we ate the sushi—how were classes, how are your projects going, plans for the summer, etc. The entire time, I was acutely aware of Chris's glances over. But he was sly about it, never quite making eye contact, passing it off as looking to Jason. No one mentioned

Mandy, though it was clear from the stretch of silences that that was what everyone was thinking about. I could practically feel her, watching. Every time I looked out the window I expected to see her hovering there, translucent, begging through silent lips to—what? She'd committed suicide. That was that. There wasn't any avenging that needed to happen.

I didn't have anything to do with it.

A crow flew past, and I knew, in that moment, that I probably, somehow, did.

"Still unhappily celibate," Jason said, and I realized I had no idea what the start of the conversation had been. I glanced over while he talked to Chris. "What about you? How's the love life?"

Chris had the decency to blush. But he also had the indecency to look my way. I know Jason caught it, but he at least was able to hide most of his grin.

"Single," Chris said. He took a sip from his tea and didn't say anything else. Ethan's smile would have given the Cheshire Cat's a run for his money.

"I see," Jason said slowly. Thankfully, he didn't let the moment linger. "So what's on the agenda for the rest of the day? I can't imagine you guys just lounging around all afternoon."

"Dunno," I responded. It felt more honest than anything else I'd said today. "Maybe wander a bit. Just don't want to be back on campus."

"I don't blame you." He paused, considered his words. "Did they tell you what happened?"

I shoved down the images that flowed through my mind like

pumping blood—*red on white, blood on concrete, crows of shadow*—
and took a sip of tea. It was cold, and it tasted like raven feathers.

"No," Ethan answered for me. "Just that she . . . yeah."

"I'm sorry. I shouldn't have asked."

I stared into my teacup and my reflection stared back, ripples
distorting my face, making me pale. Wavering. Ghostly. The
room tilted.

"Are you okay?" Jason asked, putting his hand on my shoulder.
But it wasn't his voice.

I looked over as if in a dream. Blond hair, brown eyes, tan
skin, blood dripping from his lip, smeared on his hand. *Brad.*

I screamed. Legit, top-of-my-voice screamed, the teacup
falling from my grip and shattering on the floor. The moment
it hit, it was just Jason staring at me. Kind, gay Jason, his hand
quickly darting from my shoulder to his lap.

"Kaira, are you—"

"I'm fine." Too quickly. My blood pulsed the lie through my
veins. "Just . . . on edge. Sorry. I shouldn't . . . I'll be right back."

I pushed out of the chair, nearly toppling it over, and ran to
the bathroom.

"It's okay, he's gone. You're just stressed. He's gone. He's
gone. *He's gone.*" My words were a furious whisper the moment I
pressed my back to the bathroom wall and squeezed my palms to
my eyes and tried to block out his words, his laughter, the feeling
of his hand on my shoulder, the memory of the cold stall door
against my back. I couldn't stop shaking. I couldn't stop the tears.

"Kaira?" someone asked. Not Brad. Of course not Brad.
He's gone.

Ethan opened the door and stepped inside, but I didn't open my eyes. I didn't move as he walked over and slid down next to me. He didn't touch me. I could feel the static of space between us.

"Kaira?" he asked again. "Do you need to talk?"

I didn't answer. He didn't move.

The silence stretched, but no one else came to check on us. The tears stopped. Finally.

"It's just stress," I whispered finally. "I don't know. Too much at once, you know?"

"I do," he replied. His voice was grave, like he knew it all too well.

"What happened?" he asked.

I took a deep breath. It felt like coming up from drowning. When I leaned over and rested my head on his shoulder, he wrapped an arm around me. It didn't feel like Brad. Ethan never felt like Brad. Ethan felt like safety. Like home.

"Too many ghosts," I finally whispered.

He sighed.

"And in times like this, they just get louder." He squeezed me and went silent. He didn't tell me to pull myself together or that everything would be okay. He knew better than to lie.

"They're going to think I'm crazy," I finally said.

"No," he said, just as stoic. "We've always known."

I laughed, and it was almost a sob, but I nudged him in the ribs anyway. He kissed the top of my head.

"I love you, Winters," he whispered into my hair. Tears welled up again, but I forced them down. Down to where Brad waited, along with the blood and the raven feathers. Down where I shouldn't see or feel or hear them.

"I love you too, Davis," I said. "Even if you are an ass."

"So," Chris said from his seat beside me. We were in T'Chai Nanni, which was pretty much the antithesis of 326's empty interior. The teahouse was swamped with patrons, Veronica and the other waiter flitting between wicker tables and rocking chairs and sofas with trays of mismatched teapots in their hands.

"So what?" I asked. We hadn't even opened up our portfolios to work; Ethan's and my usual table was taken by hipsters talking about Foucault or something like that, so we nabbed a bench in the corner. At first I had no clue why the place was so crowded, then I saw a band starting to set up in the corner. Great. Acoustic shows always meant a crowd, even if—or *especially* if—the music sucked balls.

"So tell me about yourself, Kaira the Conundrum."

I laughed and sipped my tea—Russian caravan t'chai, which was dark and earthy and reminiscent of woodsmoke—as I peered at him over the thick cup. Ethan was on the front porch, chatting on the phone with Oliver, though I don't know how being outside in the wind and snow was quieter than being in here.

I think he just wanted Chris and me to be alone.

"I'm a conundrum, am I?" I asked. *Well, I suppose that's better than being a freak.*

"At the moment," he said. He gave me a grin, like he was totally okay waiting for my puzzle to complete itself, however long that took. Neither he nor Jason had said anything when

Ethan and I came out of the bathroom, Ethan holding my hand like he could keep all the shadows at bay. I'd felt embarrassed at first, until Jason began talking about his latest failed date that involved learning he was seeing the ex of a guy he'd almost hooked up with last year. That was the blessing of artists—everyone had their demons, and they knew not to press when yours were becoming too loud.

Being in here made me feel better. Safer. T'Chai Nanni smelled familiar. In here, surrounded by so many strangers, it was easy to drown out the words that whispered in the silence.

"Well, what do you want to know?"

"Where you're from, for one. And why you came to Islington. I'm doubting you're one of those celebrity kids Ethan mentioned."

"Wouldn't you feel like an idiot if I was? I could have my secret service off you in the bathroom."

"Are you?"

"Nope," I said. There wasn't much space on the bench, even without Ethan there. My arm and hip brushed against Chris. My gut clenched at the thought of leaning in closer, at how it would feel if he put his arm around me. Brad's face shot through my mind, that grin he used on me time and time again. *It's okay*, he'd say, *we can go slow*.

I leaned away and took another sip.

"Well," he said after a moment. He must have noticed my move; he sounded a little sad. "Where are *you* from, then?"

"Outside of Minneapolis," I said.

"Ah, is your family still back there?"

"*Adopted* family," I replied, maybe a little too quickly. "But yeah."

"Gotcha." He didn't, of course. But I appreciated the attempt at empathy. "And why did you come here?"

"I enjoy being a workaholic."

"Seriously," he pushed.

I sighed and looked at him. That was a door I wasn't going to open. Not here, not now, and not with Mandy's shade hovering over my shoulder and Brad's sneer behind my eyelids.

"Because I wanted to be here," I said. And then, because he looked like he was going to push the subject, I added something I hadn't even really told Ethan. Ethan knew when not to ask for more. "Because I couldn't stay there anymore."

"I know what you mean," he replied.

"Not to be rude, but I kind of doubt that." It came out a lot bitchier than I'd intended, but this wasn't an area I wanted to tread through right now. Not with Brad's touch still lingering on my shoulder.

"Everyone has a past, Kaira," he said. His eyes didn't waver from mine when he said it. His face was so close, I could smell the cardamom on his breath, feel a tinge of static. "You're not the only one with ghosts."

"Sorry," I said. I looked down to my cup. "It's just . . . it's been rough. This sort of thing hits a little too close to home."

"I know," he replied. "It does for me too." He paused, sipped his tea. When he spoke again, he seemed unsure. He didn't look at me at all. "Thanks for taking me in," he said.

"What do you mean?"

"Exactly what I said. I've only known you a few days, but I appreciate how kind you guys have been. Especially in light of . . . I mean, it's been really nice. I like you. Both of you."

I'd never met a straight boy who was willing to talk about emotions. It was a complete one-eighty from Brad. *Everything about him is a complete one-eighty from Brad.* And then I looked at him—really looked. The strong profile, the scruff, the hazel eyes so intently fixed on the table of chatting college kids. That, and the little things I hadn't noticed before: the slight slump to his shoulders, the way he bit the inside of his lower lip, the lithe fingers wrapped around his teacup. He wasn't stoic and distant and attractive in that self-assured way.

He's not like Brad, I realized. *And he never will be.*

I don't know why I wanted to open up then. Maybe I was too raw from the breakdown. Maybe I just wanted the idea of comfort. Or maybe Ethan was right—maybe Chris *was* my type. Maybe I just hadn't let myself see it.

"You're not too bad yourself, kid," I replied.

He laughed. His eyes darted to me, and yes, my chest felt warm as my stomach flipped and I had to look down to my cup to keep from blushing.

"You say the weirdest shit," he said.

"I know," I replied. "You'd better get used to it."

"Already am," he replied. I looked over, caught just the edge of his grin, and I knew that look—that tentative slight lean.

And I don't know why I wanted to lean in, to close that gap, to connect to the gravity. Maybe it was masochism or something else, but I felt the desire take hold, snaring me somewhere behind my heart, pulling me forward . . . at least until Ethan came over and sat down on the cask we'd reserved with his portfolio.

"It's real shitty out there," he said, either oblivious to or ignoring the way Chris and I quickly leaned back from each other. "In case you were wondering."

"How's Oliver?" I asked.

"He's all right. I mean, okay, he's panicking about his upcoming solo performance. In his words, he's 'worried he isn't interpreting the piece the way his composer expects.' Whatever that means." He sighed and picked up his mug of tea, which was still steaming. "Sometimes I swear my conversations would make more sense if I was dating another visual artist."

His eyes flickered between the two of us, not at all discreet. I could have slapped him.

"Then you gotta worry about artistic competition getting in the middle of things," I said. I couldn't tell if I was trying to snub whatever potential Chris had or what, but the situation was suddenly way too awkward for my liking. *I need to have a talk with that boy.*

"I dunno. Could be kinda hot," Ethan said with a grin. He looked at Chris. "What do you think? Date within the field or no?"

I knew Ethan was just trying to heal things the way he worked best—by making light of them. He knew I'd dated back home, knew that it had gone horribly wrong and that was why I wasn't dating anymore. And he knew that was why I had the panic attacks, the moments of sheer terror. This was his way of saying he understood and it was okay. But he didn't fully understand. I couldn't move forward—I couldn't pretend it was okay. All I could do was try to ignore it. Brad had burrowed his way deep inside me, and the memory of him wouldn't let go. Now that the strange moment between Chris and me was over, I couldn't believe I'd actually almost leaned in and tried to kiss him.

Rule number one: Never fall in love.

"I dunno," Chris said after a moment. "Guess it just depends on the situation."

Ethan nodded sagely over his cup at me.

"Love is strange," he finally said. "I hear it heals all wounds."

"That's time," I replied. "And that's also an outright lie."

He was so lucky the place was crowded. Otherwise, he'd have a bruise to explain to Oliver.

The rest of the evening was spent chatting about school and faculty and what we missed about being a normal teenager—mainly, being able to leave the house after ten, and not having your Internet shut off at eleven. And not always being stressed about homework.

It was, for all intents and purposes, a very short list.

Unsurprisingly, no work got done. We kept waiting for a table to open up but, like us, no one seemed to want to leave and head out into the storm. So we stayed there, at our little bench in the corner, chatting about normal high school things for a few hours, and it felt . . . well, it felt nice. It reminded me of the life I'd given up in coming here: afternoons gossiping and talking about teachers or students, trips to cafés that didn't involve work.

And yeah, there was something nice about sharing a bench with a boy who wasn't also interested in boys.

We headed back to campus at seven. I made sure to drop by the drugstore for cookies and popcorn and a case of cherry soda I knew Elisa would say I shouldn't have gotten because she was cutting back on sugar but would drink anyway. It was one of those days, and I had a feeling it would be *one of those days* for a very long time.

I parted ways with the boys to head back to my room. Chris lingered when I hugged Ethan good-bye, but I just patted Chris on the shoulder and told them I'd see them both at breakfast. I was too distracted to give much thought to the apparent disappointment in Chris's eyes when I walked away; I couldn't focus on anything besides the birds. Even in the snow that whipped nearly sideways, crows lined the power lines like onyx sentinels, all of them silent and still and watching. It made me shiver worse than the cold.

Having a bodyguard is one thing. Having one when you don't know why you need protecting is another.

Elisa wasn't in the room, so I left the snacks on top of her bed with a little heart scribbled on a Post-it note. As had been drilled into my head the first day here: Presentation is everything. But I didn't take off my boots or coat. There was an hour left before sign-in and the very idea of sitting in here and doing homework or staring at a wall made me claustrophobic. Going outside was worse, though. I glanced to my pillow. The crystal sat there, like a key to a large and imposing door—one that might hold a sack of gold or a vicious chimera. I knew, deep down, that I needed to take it, but the very thought made my entire body clamp up, constricted in a terrible vise. That crystal was keeping the nightmares at bay, but maybe that's precisely where I was supposed to venture.

After all, hadn't the darkness always been my second home? I'd spent the entire day trying to ignore the shadow hovering behind my shoulder. Mandy was dead. Suicide. Nothing strange beyond the fact that it was sudden and unexpected, and wasn't that how all suicides were? Always the ones you least expected—always the ones who seemed the happiest on the outside. It was human. Horrible, but human.

So why couldn't I force out Brad's image? And why were the crows so adamant about making themselves known?

I wished I could lie and convince myself I didn't already know the answer. That this was all just in my head and I was insane and that was perfectly fine. Because being insane was better than this alternative.

Munin wanted to talk.

And if he wanted to talk, I needed to listen. *Never ignore an omen.* Especially not from him.

A crow fluttered past the window then, and that was enough to tell me I needed to get out of here. I didn't want to sit around and think until Elisa came back to distract me. I didn't want to wonder if I should put the crystal on my altar so I could dream. I didn't want to be toying with these thoughts—I wanted to be normal, to be focusing on work and graduation and maybe even Chris. I didn't want to let my past catch up with me. I grabbed my coat and headed for the arts building. I'd been doing enough sitting around for one day and I wanted to see the new senior thesis show. I wanted to see if Mandy had left her mark, and if it would lend any clue as to why she'd taken her own life. Mostly, though, I just didn't want to be alone with myself. Art was a good enough distraction, even if I wasn't making it.

I wandered through the empty dorm lobby and out into the snow. In the five minutes I was inside, the weather had gotten worse. Snow whipped up the drive and turned everything an apocalyptic grayscale. The few kids who were out were huddled and running from one building to another. Everything was a shifting mass of black and white—even the buildings looked like they were moving through the flurries of snow. The only still objects were the crows on the power lines. They sat silently the entire walk up the drive to the visual arts building. When I opened the front door, they exploded out into the night in a black cloud, their caws lost to the whistle of wind and torrent of snow.

As usual, stepping into the visual arts building was like stepping back home. The warmth, the scent, the lighting . . . it made it easier to forget the crazy shit happening outside. This place was like a womb for creativity, a safe haven. It was my church. Though there was something eerie about entering it tonight. Home was haunted.

There, in the entryway and all down the hall, were Mandy's ceramic origami birds.

They hung from fishing line in beautiful clouds along the ceiling; others rested on pedestals in flocks. Some even squatted along the floor, these ones with broken wings and bits of clay shattered along the tile.

It took my breath away. Literally.

I paused in the entry and stared at the hundreds of birds and felt tears well in the corners of my eyes as my breath caught in my throat. This was beyond beautiful. And hadn't she said she was only making a hundred? How had she produced so many, and to such a beautiful extent? There had to be at least five hundred in here.

I walked slowly, examining every corner. The birds dangled and spun and stared into space, each folded wing a wish, a prayer. They seemed to whisper to one another in the emptiness, filling the space with her final thoughts, her devotion.

Whether intentional or not, she had created her own memorial. And it was more perfect than anything we could have done in her honor.

"Beautiful, isn't it?" I looked over to where Jonathan was walking out of a side hallway, holding Helen's hand. I'd never seen the two of them together, but there had been rumors they were dating. I couldn't blame them. Jonathan was hot in that young-tattooed-professor sort of way, and Helen would always be the most beautiful badass painter I knew.

"Stunning," I replied. Helen smiled sadly.

"She was a prodigy," Helen said. "It's such a shame."

"But oddly poignant," Jonathan said, staring up at the birds. "In Egyptian mythology it was believed there were three aspects to the soul: the *akh*, the *ka*, and the *ba*. The *ka* was what we'd traditionally see as a soul, but the *ba* was seen as a little bird with a human head, and it could leave the tomb and wander the world. It was the soul's messenger, in a way, but it always needed to return to the body. There's a sort of beauty to this being Mandy's last piece. Like she was creating a fleet of vessels for her own eternal flight."

"I don't know if that's the way to talk to her about this," Helen said.

Jonathan looked at me, considering. "Something tells me Kaira's not one to shy from the darker sides of life. It's healthy. It reminds us of the power of beauty and light."

"Did . . . did she finish all this herself?" I asked, gesturing to the birds. I didn't want to be caught in the middle of their lover's quarrel, and I both agreed and disagreed with Helen. It didn't seem right to talk about Mandy's suicide in terms of art, but then . . . maybe it helped place it in a larger context. Maybe it put meaning to something that seemed so terrible. Or maybe thinking about it like that was disrespectful. I didn't know her well enough to say.

"She did," Helen replied. She cast one last disapproving look at Jonathan. "Was in here all weekend working on it. I brought her coffee a few times."

"And she never mentioned anything?"

Helen shook her head. Jonathan wrapped an arm around her.

"Are you doing okay, Kaira?" he asked. His voice wasn't the reserved, aloof tone of the teachers I'd had back in public high; he sounded like he actually cared, and the look in his eyes said the same.

"Yeah. Just still in shock, I think."

"Understandable. It'll be a while before life returns to normal. Or, well, its new version of normal." He looked down at his feet, then to me. "If you need to talk, ever, you know how to find me. I don't know if us advisers are also supposed to work as counselors, but I'll always be here if you need someone to listen. And I promise not to bring up the Egyptian afterlife again."

"Thanks," I said.

"Same goes for me," Helen replied. "You know I'm always here for you, espresso machine and all. And seriously, if you need extra time to get your thesis done, don't stress, okay? You can always put it off. We understand this is a trying time."

"Thanks," I said again. The real thankful part came when they walked by me. As great as they were, I didn't want to be talking about death or homework or mythology, which felt like some strange mix of the two. I wanted to have a few moments with Mandy's work. Jonathan put a hand on my shoulder as he passed.

"I've put together a little study group," he said. "I know it's probably the last thing you want to think about right now, but I'd love for you to join. They're a good group, very supportive—you might find having a group of like-minded peers helpful in these rough times."

I looked from the cranes to him, wondering why in the world he'd mention studying right now.

"You don't need to decide now. Just think of it is a second family opening its doors. Standing offer."

Then, with one more glance to the birds, the two of them walked out into the night, hands held and coats flapping in the snow. I turned back to the display and let the rest of the world fall away.

Thoughts of Jonathan's offer vanished into clay dust. I felt like I was floating, surrounded by clouds of paper and ceramics. It didn't make sense. None of this. It was all one giant knot on the verge of unraveling, but there was nothing I could do or say to make it happen any faster. All I knew was that Mandy was dead and Munin was back and Brad wouldn't shut up and my life— so carefully constructed, so perfect in its detail—was derailing. I wasn't supposed to be falling for someone. I wasn't supposed to remember how Brad's hands felt, how the blade felt. I was supposed to be past this. I had *moved on*.

I fell to my knees.

"I'm so sorry," I whispered. I didn't know if I was talking to Mandy or myself.

The birds turned slowly. Maybe it was the breeze, maybe it was her *ba* drifting on to the land of the dead. Or maybe, like me, she was stuck here, mingling in the shadows, tethered to a past that wouldn't quite let go.

CHAPTER TEN

The rest of the week passed by in a fugue. Everything seemed muted—the colors, the conversations, the weather. It snowed fitfully every night, and every morning I'd wake up from blank dreams to bird feet imprinted on the windowsill. If Elisa ever noticed the watcher, she said nothing, though she did start closing the curtains at night. I was completely fine with that. The farther I was from the birds, the better. If only I could have gotten them to leave me alone during the day.

As for the dreams, well . . . I never took the crystal from under my pillow, and if I *did* dream, I didn't remember. It felt like staring in the other direction while a train barreled down the rails, but I was oddly okay with it. I didn't want to know when it was going to hit. I'd avoided the dreams and the shadows before. I could do it again.

I didn't have any other choice.

With my thesis closing in, I didn't hang out with Chris too often, unless he was joining me and Ethan in our work parties.

And, seeing as they were presenting at the same time, they were often neck-deep in work and too distracted to talk in the first place. I only caught glimpses of Chris's project, but I didn't try to dig too deep. I didn't have time.

It was strange, really, the way life kicked back into motion. It was like a buoy pulled from the sea: Something was missing, something had forever inextricably, immeasurably changed the fabric of life, but life just surged back in and resumed its process. Kids continued to stress. Concerts and open mics were planned. In the corner of my mind, in every class and every late-night homework session, there was a voice screaming that this wasn't right, that something—some*one*—was missing, and things should have felt more different than they did.

But they didn't. And that made everything feel like a waking dream.

Jonathan's classes weren't helping. Whether by design or by chance, we started discussing the rituals and folklore surrounding funerary rites in Nordic countries. If I never had to listen to another discussion on the Valkyries and Valhalla and Hel, I'd be happy. He hadn't mentioned the study group again, and I didn't broach the subject. I had more than enough on my plate with finishing my thesis and keeping the voices in my head from regaining control. Being normal was difficult in and of itself. I didn't need to join a group of people exploring what I so vehemently wanted to avoid.

Every day I got just a little bit closer to being finished with my thesis. The cards I was displaying were all done, save for a few minor adjustments, and I knew I could have had the whole thing finished by now if I'd wanted. But I didn't. I would lay out the cards on my bed and stare at them and panic or feel a small note of pride. I couldn't bring myself to say they were done. I couldn't do the finishing touches, and it took a lot of self-control not to throw them all out and claim that I needed to start over and put off my thesis until the very end. I kept finding things I wanted to change. I kept finding reasons to keep working.

Because I didn't want to be done. I didn't want to admit to myself that this was it. Every time I stared down at those paintings, it was like my school year was staring back. And the moment I said it was over, the moment I admitted the project was complete, the dream of Islington I'd been living in so contentedly would vanish.

I couldn't let that go. Not just yet.

Not when I still had no idea what the dream that came after would be.

It was Friday night. I was lying on my back on Ethan's bed, his head on my stomach and his stuffed bear, Dudley, under an arm. Some soft post-rock played from his computer, the light dim and drifting down from fairy lights strung in the corners of the room. Ethan's roommate was out practicing, not that Kyle ever cared when I was over. We'd spent the entire night in the studio finishing up homework and trying to get in some thesis work. I was brain-dead, Ethan was frustrated, and this little ritual of cuddling and listening to music was what had gotten me through some of my most stressful moments at Islington. Trouble was, it wasn't really working for me tonight.

I hated to admit it, but being in his room *hurt*. There was something so precious (a word I hated to use) about lying there listening to music and watching snow fall outside the window. The scent of his cologne, the heat of the radiator, the closeness of winter . . . I'd spent all week pretending that this was my life, that this was all there was, and every day I was reminded it was a lie. I was reminded that my list of lasts was growing.

"Have you talked with Chris at all?" Ethan asked.

I shook my head.

"Shame," he replied.

"Why?" I asked.

"Because he likes you. And you deserve to have someone nice like you."

I tilted my head to look at him. He shifted on my belly so our eyes met.

"What?" he asked.

"How do you know?"

"We've been hanging out. You know, when you're busy in the studio getting things ready. He's really cool. I totally approve."

"I told you I'm not dating," I said.

"Why?" he replied. He'd never pushed the subject before. Suddenly, the quiet and closeness of the room became claustrophobic.

I went silent. He sat up.

"No, seriously Kaira. I know you dated in the past and it didn't go well. I've been able to fill in the blanks. But why are you against him? He's not your ex."

"I don't want to talk about it."

"You never do. Listen, I'm not trying to start a fight or anything.

It's just . . . you've been so stressed out lately, and ever since Mandy's death all I can do is think about time and how we don't ever have enough of it in general and even less when it comes to being around the people we love, and how Islington just screws all of that up by making us focus on being artists rather than being teenagers with needs and desires and ambitions beyond being stellar creators." He took a deep breath and ran a hand through his scraggly hair. "What I'm trying to say is, I want you to be happy."

"I am happy," I said. "I have you."

"Lame," he countered. "I was happy with you, too. Then I fell in love with Oliver and it's like all my happinesses are amplified. Like, being in love with him makes it easier to love everyone else even more. And I want that for you. I really do."

"I don't *need* a boyfriend." My voice was harsher than I wanted it to be. *I don't need to be vulnerable again—that's how you get hurt.*

"No. No, of course not. Neither do I. We're all totally stable and steady adults and we don't *need* anyone or anything beyond ourselves. But I can tell you like him. I'm not stupid—I know you better than you think. You totally steal glances at him when he's not looking and he totally steals glances back. It's like watching a damned tennis match. So why not just go for it? What do you have to lose when you know he won't reject you?"

Nothing that wasn't already taken by Brad.

"Ethan . . ."

"What did he do to you?" he whispered. It wasn't an accusation; this was a question he'd clearly been dying to ask for months. There was more hurt in his words than I could bear.

And that did it. Tears formed in the corners of my eyes as Brad's smile came back, the scent of his breath as he pressed me to the wall. . . . Ethan put a hand on my wrist, anchored me down.

"You can talk to me," he whispered. "Please. I feel like you've created this persona and I don't get to see anything that everyone else doesn't already see. And I know there's more to you than that. I know you're hurting and I know you don't want me to see it. But I do. And I want to be able to support you and help you through it."

I wiped the tears and sat up, pushing myself back on the bed so I could prop myself up against the wall and pillows. He shifted and crossed his legs, looking at me head-on. His gaze didn't break from mine.

This was not the conversation I wanted to have. This was not the ideal way to wind down the weekend before my show. But he was right. A week ago, someone was ripped from my life. In a few months, Ethan would be out of my life as well. Did I really want to have secrets from him? When I grabbed my diploma and parted ways with this place, did I want to look back and wonder if things would have been different if I'd opened up?

"His name was Brad," I said. Even just saying the name was like aiming a gun at my forehead. "I met him my sophomore year . . . we were in pre-calc together. He was charming and a jock and he knew I didn't really have any friends. So I guess he knew I was an easy target."

This made Ethan's eyebrows furrow.

"Things were great at first. I mean, I thought they were great.

He took me on real dates where he'd pay for food and then take me to the movie theatre. Super respectful. I told him I wanted to take it slow and he said that was okay, he was fine not having any pressure. I wanted it to be like all the TV shows and movies, where the nerdy girl gets the guy and rules the school. Hopefully after some really cool makeover montage." My laugh was bitter.

"We were together a few months and it was . . . I don't know. It wasn't perfect, I guess, but it was all I'd known up to that point and I figured that's just how all first loves went. And yeah, I actually thought I loved him. Isn't that stupid? I wanted someone to care for me so badly, I just let myself fall for him without thinking twice. He'd buy me things and leave me notes and it made me feel wanted, you know? Like finally, someone out there really cared and saw me for who I was and wanted to be with me in spite of it. But even though I loved him, I think a part of me was always convincing myself that it was love, like I needed a reminder that this was what everyone told me I wanted. But there were times when he'd look at me, or put his hand on my shoulder, and it just felt like I was a prize to him, and I couldn't figure out why. I remember . . . he got me this necklace, right? Simple gold chain and a little heart charm. For our two month anniversary. And when he put it around my neck and kissed me it felt like he was putting on a collar. I couldn't explain it, but I thought that's just how dating was, you know? Our first kiss was terrible and I always felt a little awkward, but I was the awkward girl and he was the pretty boy and I figured it always worked out in the movies so maybe it would work out for me. He could have anyone in the school. He picked me. And that meant I was special and important and better than everyone else, which wasn't something I'd ever felt before. We did everything together—homework and dinner and movies, and not once did he make a move, even though he kept hinting that he wanted to, saying I was beautiful or sexy or whatever. But I was scared. Even though I loved him, even though I thought it was what I wanted, a part of me didn't want to trust him."

The crows didn't want me to trust him either. And they were right.

I took a deep breath. This was more than I'd told anyone, but I knew Ethan would want the full story. Not because he wanted me to be vulnerable, like Brad had, but because he wanted to share my burden. He squeezed my arm.

"Then came homecoming," I continued, my voice dropping and becoming more clinical. Apparently, that was my way of coping with shock. "Mom helped me pick out a dress. I wore the necklace Brad got me. And he picked me up in his truck and took me to a fancy dinner and held my hand whenever he could. It felt . . . honestly, it really felt nice. Like I was finally playing my part properly, you know? Except I apparently wasn't playing it good enough. We had our first dance, he started drinking. Before I knew it he had me against the wall in the bathroom with one hand on my neck and the other up my dress."

I went silent. Inside, I was numb. I stared at Brad's grin within my mind and felt absolutely nothing. I knew I should have had a reaction of some sort. I knew I should be more broken. I probably would have been, too, if things hadn't turned out the way they had.

"Jesus Kaira," he whispered. "I had no idea."

I shrugged and looked at his wall, staring at the sketches he and I had done together.

"Not many do. The sickest part was, I didn't even try to fight. I didn't scream or push him away. He kept saying I'd made him do it, that I'd held out too long and I owed him this. That's what I got for trusting someone who seemed to care about me." I shook my head and tried to get the scent of his cologne and sweat out of my memory. It might not cause a reaction, but I sure as hell didn't want him to linger on when he should have been dead to me. "When he was done, he kissed me on the forehead and said that I'd finally gotten what was coming to me. I called home and had my mom pick me up. I didn't tell her anything. I never did."

"Fuck," he muttered.

I nodded.

There were holes in the story. Many holes. But I wasn't about to tell him that Mom had warned me from the dance, had nearly forbid me to leave until my dad asked her to calm down and let me go. I didn't tell him about the crows that dive-bombed the truck on our way to the school. And I didn't tell him what happened to Brad. Not yet. Probably not ever.

There were many things Ethan could have said and done after that. He could have told me that Chris wasn't like Brad, that I couldn't let this stop me from loving forever. He could have told me that he understood. Any of those things would have pushed me out the door.

Instead, he leaned down and curled up against my shins.

"I am so, so sorry," he whispered. And that was all.

After, right before sign-in, I left out the back door and stood

146

on the fire escape, staring up at the sky. The snow had stopped and pockets of stars shone through the clouds. My breath came out in tiny wisps, the air so cold my nostrils froze the moment I inhaled.

I wanted to embrace the beauty of the moment. I wanted to feel good about finally releasing Brad's demon from my subconscious. I knew, deep down, that telling Ethan was progress, that this was good. But I couldn't ignore the omens: Crows lined the roof of the opposite dorm. All watching. All waiting. They were patient, but they weren't letting me forget.

Brad had hurt me, true. What he did was unforgivable and I wasn't the forgiving sort anyway. I knew without a shred of doubt that my hatred toward him—locked away though it was—was completely justified. But what I had done in return . . . I clenched the rusted rail of the fire escape and let the grit and ice dig into my flesh.

I would never escape the repercussions of my actions. I had run to boarding school, but it wasn't to escape Brad or the traitorous friends who'd done nothing after the attack. It wasn't to avoid the memories and malice lingering in every inch of that damned school and town. I'd run away to escape myself. Airing my past wouldn't help. Sharing the burden wouldn't ease the pain. I couldn't escape who I was or what I'd done, no matter how fast or far I ran.

The crows were just a reminder of that. They wanted back in. My past wasn't done with me. Not yet.

Coffee House was Sunday night. Normally, I would have skipped to put the finishing touches on my thesis, but Ethan forced me to put away my paints and collage materials and, as he said, be back among the living. Coffee House was Islington's version of an open mic, only the people here actually had talent so it wasn't painful like the ones I'd gone to before. So at ten to seven I met Ethan in the lobby of his dorm and we headed to one of the larger cabins dotting the edge of campus.

Kids were already crammed inside, the cabin door open and spilling light and warmth out into the snow. The orange light was a shifting triangle on the sidewalk, windows showing dozens of heads all circled around a semi-stage in the corner. And here, we were five minutes early.

Ethan and I crowded in behind some junior dancers—an easy tell, seeing as they all had annoyingly perfect posture—and waited for the show. Elisa was at rehearsal and Oliver was studying, so it was just the two of us. The two of us, until I spotted Chris's fedora over in the corner. He looked over the moment I spotted him. When he waved, I knew the duo was about to become a trio.

I hadn't seen nor spoken to Chris outside of class since telling Ethan about Brad. My gut turned when Chris began pushing through the crowd toward us. Telling Ethan had made me feel a small amount better, but the past was still way too close to the surface for comfort. Walking down that memory lane had pretty much ensured my walls were back at full height.

"How's it going?" Chris asked when he neared us. The dancers did *not* look too pleased when he brushed past them. Though they definitely did an appraising over-the-shoulder glance when he went by.

"Fine," Ethan and I replied in unison.

"Whoa, that was creepy. How much time have you been spending together?"

"Too much," Ethan said. "Thesis work."

"I hear you," he replied. But he didn't get a chance to empathize further; at that moment, the lights dimmed and the crowd hushed and Jonathan took to the stage.

The first time Jonathan hosted Coffee House, I thought it was strange it hadn't been done by a theatre faculty member. Then he started talking, and I realized that his minor in theatre (so he could retell stories more effectively) hadn't gone to waste. Tonight, he'd changed from his usual tweed blazer into a sleek ensemble of black slacks and a royal blue button-down. The sleeves were rolled up, showing even more of his tattoos than usual. I wondered if one of his goals in undergrad was to become a hot professor—he'd certainly cultivated the look.

"Evening friends," he said when the room went quiet. "Thanks for braving the weather for this month's Coffee House. We've got a full lineup tonight that I think you're going to love. As a quick reminder—no negative shout-outs, please. Keep it classy." He winked. "Without further ado, we have Kevin and Lisa."

A boy and girl went up, both of them freshmen I'd only seen at meal times. I think they were both in the theatre program, though the boy was playing guitar and the girl sang this beautiful cover of a pop song I knew I'd have stuck in my head for the next week now. Throughout it all, I was keenly aware of Chris bobbing side to side, his arm occasionally brushing mine. I knew it was just the heat and the closeness of the room, but it felt like my skin was on fire every time he touched me. Oddly enough, these brushes weren't as unwelcome as I'd expected. It was easy to remember the gravity between us in the teahouse. Just as it was easy to remember the gravity Brad had exerted at the very beginning.

About halfway through, after a surprisingly funny bit of stand-up comedy from a sophomore dance major, Jonathan stepped back onto the stage and announced Chris's name. I thought it must have been a mistake, or maybe a different Chris, but sure enough, the Chris standing beside me pushed his way through the crowd toward the podium.

"Hey everyone," Chris said. He didn't sound uncomfortable like I expected him to—like I would have if I were in his shoes. Instead, he smiled and held his shoulders back and stood up straight, owning every inch of the dim spotlight. "I'm going to sing a song I wrote. I'm afraid I don't play guitar so it's gotta be a capella. Hopefully, you can fill in the blanks."

And he closed his eyes, took a deep breath, nodded his head to some inner rhythm, and began to sing.

I expected it to be awkward. The preliminary *embarrassed for you* chills crept across my arms. But the kid was good. Really good. He sang about snow and home and the girl he never knew. At first, I thought it was about me. Then, with a flush of misplaced vanity, I realized it was actually about Mandy.

When he was done, I wasn't the only one with tears in my eyes. I glanced over to Ethan just in time to see him wipe his face with one mittened hand. He sniffed and caught my gaze, his eyebrows going wide in a *holy shit that guy can sing* expression.

Right? I mouthed through the applause. No time to get into it, though, as Chris was back the next moment with a sheepish grin on his face. The dancer girls in front of us all did the second-look appraisal this time. If he didn't walk out of here with at least one offer of a date, I'd be surprised.

"What'd you think?" he asked as he sidled up beside me. And yeah, it was kind of nice seeing those curious looks on the dancers turn to disappointment when they saw him lean in to talk to me.

"It was beautiful," I said. "I didn't know you were into music."

He shrugged. Onstage, Jonathan was announcing the next act. When Chris spoke again, he leaned in closer so his lips were inches from my ear.

"I was in a band back home," he said. "I mean, before here. Kinda gave it up to come here."

"You should get back into it," I said. "That was amazing."

He smiled and reached over, like he was about to hug me. Instead, he just squeezed my shoulder and turned to face the next act.

Our knuckles touched; electricity sparked through my veins. My hand jerked away.

"You okay?" he asked, looking at me, confused. I suppose to him it felt like I was swatting his hand.

"Sorry," I said. It wasn't an answer.

Because the moment our hands touched, I saw Brad's smile. And in the darkness of Brad's eyes, I saw the raven, bleeding.

CHAPTER ELEVEN

"Kaira, wake up." Something fluffy smacked into my face.

"Bitch," I mumbled. I rolled over and grabbed the toast plushie, nestling it to my chest. "Mine now."

She giggled. "Come on, it's almost nine. You don't want to miss brunch."

My eyes shot open. Whatever dreams were drifting around the edges of my mind vanished in the promise of ice cream and all the glorious toppings provided. Definitely a reason to wake up.

"Is it waffle or omelet day?" I asked.

"Waffle."

"Score."

Yes, I'm ruled by my stomach. Aren't all sensible people?

I hopped out of bed and slid a pair of baggy, torn jeans over my pajama pants (because it's Michigan, and one must layer to stay alive) and a sweater over my top. Brunch was the only time I felt okay dressing like I had a house I shouldn't be leaving. I pulled my hair into a short ponytail and grabbed a hat Elisa had knit for me a few months back, just in time for the first snow. It was magenta and matched the streaks in my hair perfectly.

"Ready," I said, probably all of three minutes later.

"Damn girl," Elisa replied. She was still at her computer. "That was easily your fastest yet."

"Stress makes me hungry," I replied. I glanced out the window. Two crows perched in the branches of a fir tree, and suddenly memories of last night refocused. Touching Chris's skin, the flash of a vision . . . I turned from the window and tried to convince myself it had just been stress. That the crows weren't warning me away from Chris. *Then what are they warning you away from?*

"Everything makes you hungry," she said.

"It's like you know me or something."

She grinned and shook her head, then stood and pulled on her coat. She was already in boots. I wondered if she woke up at her usual weekend-sleep-in seven a.m.

"So," she said as we wandered down to the lobby.

"So?" I knew that tone of voice. There was mischief in her eyes.

"I hear you and Chris were getting close last night."

I nearly tumbled headfirst down the steps.

"What? We were just standing next to each other."

"Yeah? Cassie said her friends said you guys were making out after Coffee House."

I snorted. Of course—the dance community was even tighter than the drama department and a whole hell of a lot cattier. None of the girls in front of us had been Cassie, but I'm sure everyone in ballet had heard some iteration of the rumor by now.

"Right. Because that's so me." I shook my head. "At least

now people might stop thinking I'm a lesbian."

She took my hand as we stepped out into the still, cold air. It was like walking into a freeze-frame of Antarctica. Pun only moderately intended.

"Don't worry," she said. "Even the people who think you're gay know you're off limits. Because you're mine!" She growled the last bit and wrapped me in an awkward hug that nearly sent both of us to the snowbank.

"Careful, crazy!" I squealed. But we caught our balance last minute. Overhead, a murder of crows flew past, cawing. I definitely had no place calling her crazy. She wasn't stressing over the appearance of common birds.

She just giggled and took my arm again and dragged me toward the cafeteria.

"When do you put up your show?" she asked.

Long ago, she learned that saying "thesis" was a no-no. Unlike Oliver.

"After brunch," I said. I already had all the mounting materials (Ethan had nearly pissed himself when I asked him to drive me to town to get stuff for mounting) and my space was assigned (front hall, right where all of Mandy's stuff was). I wasn't about to say my project was done, or even ready to admit that I was going to display it today. It felt too momentous. I wanted to tell myself it was because I was excited, that I wanted the school to see what I'd been doing with my time, that I was proud or whatever. It didn't feel like that at all, though.

It felt like admitting defeat.

My time here was almost done. Islington was nearly over.

The end was here, and it was eager to rip everything I'd worked so hard for away.

Elisa went silent for a moment.

"Who took her stuff down?" she asked. She didn't need to clarify.

"I don't know. Probably someone from the ceramics department. I heard them talking about displaying a few of them in the president's gallery." Which was the permanent art gallery here. Very few students had their work selected to be put in the president's office. It was a huge honor.

"I still can't believe . . ." she trailed off. She didn't need to finish the sentence; we were all thinking it.

It was still impossible to think that Mandy was gone, and not just on some visit home. But life shambled onward.

We didn't talk the rest of the way to the dining hall. Thankfully, once we were inside and the sugary scent of ice cream and maple syrup and warmth surrounded us, the mood lightened considerably. The actual lighting helped a great deal as well, seeing as it was still dark as dusk outside.

We didn't even bother to find a table—Ethan and Oliver would no doubt already have a space reserved for us. Mondays were sort of our family meal. I grabbed a plate and made my way to the waffle bar. Today was definitely a strawberry-chocolate-maple-whipped-cream sort of day. Also coffee. Lots and lots of coffee. Probably mixed with ice cream.

It was thesis day; I'd need all the energy I could get to make it through.

When I made my way back to the usual table in the corner,

my tray carefully loaded with carbs and sugar and caffeine, I realized the family brunch had expanded. Jane was also sitting at the table. As was Chris. There was a space right between him and Ethan, and I could tell from Ethan's grin that it had been carefully orchestrated just for me.

A small part of me wanted to spite them and sit on the opposite side.

Screw it. I wasn't going to play that game. I sat between the boys and started pouring sugar packets into my coffee.

"Damn girl," Chris said. "You could run a small country with all that sugar."

I looked to his much more sensible scrambled eggs and fruit salad.

"Don't you worry," I replied. "I'm a professional."

A few moments of silence passed while we consumed our breakfast.

"You ready for today?" Jane asked. I'd nearly forgotten that she was also putting up her work this weekend.

"I think so," I replied. "How about you?"

She nodded. "I'm feeling a lot better about it than I was a month ago, yeah. Got hit with inspiration at the last minute." She smiled. "I think it's going to blow the department out of the water. Though I'm sure they won't think less of your work."

"Is that a challenge?" I asked.

"Maybe," she replied. "If you think you're up for it."

"Now ladies," Ethan said, leaning forward and spreading his arms between us. "Remember, this isn't a competition."

"Correct," I said. I gestured to Jane with a fork dripping with waffle. "She probably already won. I've seen her work before, and if she's touting some last-minute muse I'm damn well screwed."

"I wouldn't say that. But yeah, my work's pretty much amazing. Just a few finishing touches and my masterpiece will be ready for the world." Her smile was wide; she must have really been pleased with her work. I don't think I'd ever seen her this enthusiastic about it before. Normally she was more humble than I.

"The question is, will the world be ready for your masterpiece?" Ethan asked.

"Always the question. But in this case, probably not."

Oliver shook his head and grabbed a grape from Ethan's tray. "You artists. I thought it was all about denouncing fame and pursuing your inner vision."

"Can it, musician," I replied with a smile. "We all have to bring our A-game to this. One weak display and the entire show looks like shit. A little competition keeps us on point."

"Exactly," Jane said. "It's all in good fun, anyway. Kaira knows I love her even if I beat her. Which I would. You know, if this were a competition. Which it should be. Because I'd win, and I like winning." She flashed me a smile.

"I'm so glad I'm not in the same showing as you," Chris interjected. "This is way too much pressure."

"Yeah, you'll give the boy performance anxiety," Ethan said.

"I highly doubt he succumbs to that," I said, kind of surprised I was coming to Chris's aid. "I mean, he performed pretty damn well last night."

Ethan chuckled and I felt myself blush as Elisa made a "mhmmm" noise.

"What?" Chris asked. "What did I miss?"

I finally caught my pun and blushed. "Oh for the love of—"

"The dance department thinks you're dating," Oliver interjected. He grinned at me. "Though now I'm starting to think the *boning* rumors were true."

"Wait, what? How would *you* know?" I asked.

He shrugged. "I have friends."

"I'm lost," Chris said.

Ethan just sat there and laughed silently. I reached over and pulled his hat over his eyes.

"*Apparently,*" I said, "a boy and a girl can't stand next to each other if they aren't dating. Which we apparently are now. And, how did you so eloquently put it, Oliver? Boning? We're doing that now too, according to some ballerinas. So maybe you should buy me a ring, just to cover all your bases."

There wasn't any real anger in my rant—joking about us dating made it okay. It made the idea seem more impractical, a little safer; if it was public domain, I didn't have to take it seriously. And neither did anyone else. Especially not Chris.

"Already covered, actually," he said. "I bought a few off of Tina. Didn't know your size so I got an array. One should fit. If not, I know how to use a belt sander." He gestured to my fingers. "I'm sure I can sand those down a size or two if the rings run small. I *did* take shop class, you know."

"Such a charmer," I replied. Though I had to look away and fight the rising blush—he'd looked me dead in the eyes when he mentioned buying a ring, and there was something in the gaze that made me think he might be serious. Maybe not about the marriage, but the rings, potentially.

Thankfully, I didn't have to try to fill in the conversation. Ethan started asking Elisa questions about *Marat/Sade* and Jane piped in about her friend's involvement with the tech department, so I was able to finish my waffles in relative peace and quiet.

It wasn't until after brunch (and a heaping bowl of ice cream) that Chris pulled me aside.

"I'm sorry," he said. We were on the path just outside the dining hall, and the snow was beginning to fall once more. Jane and Elisa and the boys were already ahead of us, running about and pretending to push one another in the snow. One good shove and those *pretends* would have consequences.

"For what?" I asked.

"For that ring joke," he replied. "I didn't really know what to say. But I know you're not dating and I didn't want you to feel awkward about it. Just . . . trying to make light of the situation."

"Nah, I get it." I started walking again, heading toward the art building. My stomach was flipping with every step, but I tried to keep it cool. "You handled it well. You're funny, kid."

We walked a little longer in silence.

"Would you . . ." he began, then trailed off. He coughed— clearly forced, but whatever—and tried again. "Maybe when you're done with your thesis tonight we could hang out? I'll just be in the painting studio finishing up work. And I have a feeling by the time you're done we'll both be ready to never look at art again."

"What did you have in mind?" I asked. This was potentially a one-eighty from the *I understand you aren't dating* thing, but I'd give him the benefit of the doubt.

"Well, Ethan said he and Oliver were going to be watching movies."

I shook my head. "No no, we don't want to interrupt that."

He raised an eyebrow—it almost disappeared under his hat.

"It's code," I said. "For when he and Oliver need *alone time*." I made sure to do air quotes.

"Oh! Well then. Um. I suppose that kills that idea."

"How about this," I said. "I'll meet you in the studio and then we can go from there. Maybe you'll treat me to frozen yogurt because I made it through my thesis without a nervous breakdown. Maybe you'll treat me to extra frozen yogurt because I *had* a nervous breakdown."

He laughed. It trailed off at the end though, and I realized we were both walking dangerous ground. Eggshells. *Had Mandy had a nervous breakdown? How long was she battling the idea of killing herself?*

"Sounds like a plan," he said. "And thank you for the heads-up about Ethan and Oliver. I might have just dropped in on them."

I laughed. "That would have been a sight worth seeing. Your expression, I mean. Not what you stumbled into. Unless you're into that."

He smiled.

"Not really my cup of tea," he said. Maybe it was unconscious, but his eyes darted to me when he said it.

"Anyway, I need to head back to my room to get some stuff.

160

I'll be in the art building until dinner, most likely. So see you around?"

He nodded. We were outside of my dorm and there was this moment, this awkward as hell second, when it felt like we should go in for a hug, but that might have been misconstrued—do we go for a cheek kiss, a nuzzle, or do we keep the space? Crows sat on the roof of the dorm, watching. Waiting. As if they, too, wanted to see if I'd break my inner promise never to fall in love again. Before the moment could linger, I did what I always did and put on the charm and slapped him on the shoulder like a bro.

"Catch you on the flip side," I said, and turned away before I could tell if he was disappointed.

The crows fluffed their feathers. They didn't speak. Neither did Chris.

It was surreal, walking back into the arts building to see Mandy's cranes gone. I half expected them to still be there, like some ghostly trick birthday candles that could never be extinguished. But no, the hall was empty, abandoned, with only a few students lingering outside the textiles room farther down. The emptiness was a presence in and of itself, a wraith crying out for recognition. It felt wrong that something else should fill this space; I didn't want to cover up her presence by inserting my own.

"I'm sorry," I whispered. I knew how it felt to be alone, to think the whole world had abandoned you. I knew what it meant to stand on the edge of your own life and peer over the precipice at the darkness thirsting for your blood.

I knew what it meant to leap.

Which was why a very, very small part of me felt okay putting up my work here, even if the rest of me felt like an interloper. Mandy might not have known how much we had in common, but I hoped that maybe . . . maybe my thesis would help heal her spirit, help put to rest any residual negativity.

Before I could get too metaphysical on myself, I put in my headphones, pulled out my portfolio of images, and got to work.

I'd settled on displaying thirteen cards in all. A strong number. Most were Major Arcana, like The Hierophant and The Wheel of Fortune, while a few were Minor—Five of Cups, Eight of Swords. I wanted to tell a story with these. I wanted to show more than my best work; I wanted to show what Islington had meant to me. I wanted this to be the culmination of my time here, both artistically and personally . . . if there even was a difference anymore.

The Eight of Swords was first. The card was a self-portrait in many ways, though I'd never admit to it in public. A girl sat on a bed with her head in her hands, eight blades piercing the cloth around her to form a cage. Very dark, all blacks and blues, and outside the window was a raven perched on a branch, an eclipsed moon behind it, and a golden key dangling from its beak. Isolation, bitterness, self-imposed distance. And yet everything needed for your own release, right within arm's reach. If only you'd look up and see it.

Next came the Ten of Swords.

I knew this card would raise a lot of shit for a lot of people. I knew some would see it as bad taste and the admin would probably think I should take it down. I didn't care. It was my shit, too, and this was how I was releasing it.

This was the first card I'd ever painted. It was how I had moved forward. It also had never been shown to anyone.

It was a close-up of two wrists, the hands upraised and a dagger resting in the palms. Across the wrists were ten slashes, five per hand. Blood dripped down the wrists and across the blade. Around the edges of the painting were pieces of notebook paper I'd collaged in. Actual entries from my actual journal, the pen smudged from tears and glue, all noting how alone I felt. How tired I was of being different. Of feeling abandoned.

The card's meaning was pretty fucking obvious: Defeat. Death. Loss of hope.

I put those cards in sequence, right at the entrance. If I was going to tell a story with my thesis, I was going to do it honestly. And luckily, from there, the cards got a little more uplifting in their tale. Islington had been my turning point; well, one of many turning points. At least the school had been for the better.

There was The Wheel of Fortune—a golden spinning wheel with a raven emblazoned on the hub and multicolored strands weaving the Milky Way—and The Star—a constellation reflected in a pool of water held within a statue's hands. The Three of Pentacles had snippets of my acceptance letter to Islington, which was mirrored in its sister card, Eight of Pentacles. The Three was all about creation and physical beauty. Eight was hard work and dedication.

It didn't seem like a project that would take very long—I was just hanging thirteen paintings, after all—but once I got all thirteen of the cards up, I began to fine tune. I moved cards around, changed height and distance and looked at them from all angles to make sure nothing looked cluttered (unless, like the cards at the beginning, I wanted it to look cluttered and chaotic). I took out a spool of silver thread and began connecting the cards, making patterns and dreamcatchers and knots. Anyone who knew how to read the cards would be able to follow a single thread and get an entirely different story from the connections. Order was everything, and I was hoping people would be able to discern different stories based on which way they viewed.

Nearly an hour passed before I was finally satisfied and done. Then came the last item: my artist's statement.

I was no creative writer. The four-paragraph essay on my project had been one of the hardest parts (and thus the one I saved until yesterday), but it detailed why I'd been drawn to the Tarot, what the cards meant to me, what I hoped the audience would gain. It was hard not to feel like the entire project was masturbatory in some way, but then again, I guess that's kind of art.

I didn't leave right away, though. Not for a while. The more I looked at the paintings, the more exposed I felt. Kids walked through and some glanced at what I'd done. Some lingered. I wanted to stand in front of them, hide the paintings from view, keep them from discussing it with their friends. It was the part of being an artist I hated the most—inviting judgment for something most people wouldn't be comfortable sharing themselves. This was a deeper part of me than my skin or makeup or clothes; this was my core. But it was also just paint on paper, and I needed to keep that in mind, especially when I got my faculty critique.

You are not the art you create. You are the life lived outside of it.

Thankfully, those who lingered were few; for the most part, my classmates kept their eyes averted as they headed toward whatever studio they would be spending the next few hours in. I wanted to give them all candy for playing coy, just as I wanted to jump up and down and tell them to look.

Man, being an artist brought out a lot of crazy.

Before I could get too self-conscious, I turned down the hall and headed to the painting studio. Chris might not be done with his work and I might not have been ready for more ice cream, but that didn't mean I wasn't going to bug him. I needed someone to distract me from what I'd just done.

I hummed to myself as I trudged up the stairs to the second-floor studio, feeling lighter by the second and also strangely heavy. I was finished with my thesis. Islington would teach me no more. From here on out it was smooth sailing. Just a few more months of class and then finals and then I'd be done. Graduated. Soon I'd hear back from colleges and the rest of my life would kick into gear. The idea ripped my heart in two just as much as it excited me. My thesis was the turning point. Everything at Islington had been building up to this one showcase. Now, everything was building up to the end. It felt like I should do something big to celebrate, like there should have been fireworks the moment I'd hung up my statement. But no, just a stupid song in my head and the lingering notion that I still had a folklore essay to write by Wednesday.

The joys of being trained to feel there was always work to be done. This place was turning me into Sisyphus—the rock just never reached the top of that damned hill. That's why I had to find the minor victories and celebrations.

I was just turning the corner to the studio when I heard the scream. My heart thudded to a halt and my legs kicked into gear. I ran around the corner to find Helen kneeling outside of the studio with her phone shaking in one hand and coffee from a shattered mug forming a halo around her.

"What's wrong?" I asked. I skidded beside her and put my hand on the studio door, but she yanked it away.

"Don't go in there. Just don't."

She focused back on her phone, her words barely discernible through the tears clawing their way to the surface.

"Yes, the arts building at Islington," she said. "There's been another suicide."

I gasped. *No, no.* Chris was supposed to be in there. I fell to my knees, bits of ceramics digging numbly through my jeans.

"You should go," Helen said. "Before the cops get here. They'd want to question you."

"Who?" I asked. I couldn't get Chris's face out of my mind. *He wouldn't. He couldn't have.*

Helen's answer was a stake to the heart.

"Jane."

CHAPTER TWELVE

I felt like a sleepwalker when Helen finally convinced me to leave. *This has nothing to do with you,* she repeated. It felt like a lie, even if she didn't know it. I didn't want to leave her there. She was shaking and couldn't stop the tears in her eyes and she kept looking at the door like she wanted to break in and double-check on Jane or run away and never look back. I wanted to feel like I was doing something when it was clear there was nothing to do; I wanted to make her feel safe. Or something. But she finally told me if I didn't leave she'd fail me, and I knew she was joking and I knew she was just trying to keep me protected from whatever godawful truth rested beyond that black door, but I forced myself to my feet and left, down the back stairs and out the back entrance. Before the cops or my mind could catch up to me.

Once outside, I squeezed my eyes shut and tilted my head back to face the coming snow. I wanted to scream. I wanted to cry. Most of all, I wanted to wake up. I wanted it to be a bad dream and when it was over I'd start the day again and everything would be okay. But I wasn't waking up. There wasn't anything to wake up from. I wasn't stuck in a nightmare, I was living one, the one I'd been trying so hard to escape. *Death will follow you.*

I couldn't tell if those words were Munin's, or mine. It wasn't until my feet began to go numb that I realized I needed to move. Escape. I just had nowhere to run. I'd already gone as far as I thought I could.

My feet led me to the woods, down one of the side paths that was covered in snow and only traversed by a handful of footprints. I didn't register the cold as my feet sank into the snow, as the woods closed around me and wrapped me in silence. My head was still screaming. My thoughts burned. Jane had killed herself. Death was following, but I swore that this time, I had nothing to do with it.

This isn't happening, I whispered on repeat, maybe inside my head, maybe out loud. I was too lost to actually know or care. Jane's apparition was everywhere I turned, her words whispering through the branches. Jane, Jane, happy bubbly Jane. She wouldn't have killed herself. She couldn't have. It didn't make sense.

It didn't make sense. But in my head, it was trying to piece itself together, and I couldn't live with how the image was shaping itself.

I stopped in a small clearing maybe ten feet wide, the snow deep and the trees circling me tall and black and bare. Everything out here was white and gray and black. Frozen. Static. Save for the flickers of Jane's ghost at the corners of my imagination.

Save for the raven that squawked from his branch high above.

"Why are you doing this to me?" I yelled. "Jane was innocent! She had nothing to do with any of this!"

The raven just puffed its wings and looked at me with its onyx eye.

Death will follow you. Until you face what you've done.

"Kaira?" Footsteps from behind me. The bird cawed and flew away. I turned and nearly broke down on the spot. Chris. The brief flash from before, the seconds I thought he had killed himself, pierced through my mind and through my heart like a bullet.

"What are you doing here?" Chris asked.

I opened my mouth to answer. A sob came out instead. He was at my side in an instant.

"It's okay," he said, wrapping his arms around me. He held me close and let me sob onto his shoulder. I couldn't speak. I could barely hold myself up. I wanted to be strong. I wanted not to show him this—the side of me he could never see, the weakness, the fear. I wanted more than anything else to sink into the earth and vanish. Chris's arms prevented that. He was the anchor holding me to this world.

Finally, with a furious wrench of self-loathing, I stopped the tears and forced myself upright and took a step back.

"What are *you* doing here?" I asked. There was probably more rage in that statement than he deserved, but my anger needed to go somewhere, and my hatred for my own shortcomings was already at its peak.

He noticed. His eyebrows furrowed and he leaned back a tiny amount.

"I saw you run into the woods," he said. "And I saw ambulances and police cars by the art building. I thought . . . I don't know. I just knew I had to follow you."

I took a deep breath. *He's not your enemy, Kaira. He's trying to be your friend.*

My frustration, though, wasn't with him. It was with me. It was for just how relieved I was to see him standing there. Chris was still alive, and for some reason, that meant more than I could understand.

"What did you hear?" I asked.

"Nothing," he said. "I just got off the phone with my parents and was going to the studio when I saw you leaving. Here I am."

My next words were lifeless, twin spent bullets dropping to the ground.

"Jane's dead."

He didn't answer at first. He stared at me like maybe I was making some twisted joke, like maybe Jane was about to jump from the trees and yell *gotcha!* But nothing moved save for the snow drifting down through the branches. Everything was silent. Silent and stark and dead.

"What do you mean she's dead?" he finally asked. "She was just at brunch. She said she was going to the studio to get started without me. She said we were going to race to finish our paintings and . . ."

"I mean she's dead," I replied, cutting him off. I didn't want to hear about their plans—I didn't want to start comprehending all the things she would never actually do. Anguish turned to anger in a heartbeat, a flare so hot it burned like venom. "What about that don't you understand?"

"Jesus Kaira. Why the hell are you acting like this? I'm just trying to figure out what happened."

I hated him for how calm he was about this, like he could take the world ending with ease. And I hated how much I couldn't mirror him. Not again. Not again.

"I don't know," I said, my words growing more frantic by the second, because in the back of my mind I heard Brad whisper over and over that I'd brought this on myself. "I finished my thesis and walked to the studio and Helen was outside saying I shouldn't go in, because someone committed suicide, and then she said it was Jane and *why would she*—?" Tears welled up and I choked, tried to find the rest of my words.

"Kaira," he said softly.

He reached out and took my hand, his skin sending sparks through my veins. I jerked back and fell flat on my ass in the snow. He reached down to help me stand but I backed up.

"No, no, I'm fine." I pushed myself to my feet and kept space between us. "Just . . . don't touch me. Not right now."

"I'm . . ." He paused and looked at me. Really looked at me, as if he was trying to see past the bullshit and fear. Whatever he found, he didn't let it show. Or maybe, like me, what he saw was enough to make him stop trying to look deeper. "I'm sorry."

He sounded hurt. He sounded like he truly meant it. And every time I blinked I saw Brad's eyes, staring at me. I saw the blood covering the snow, and I knew I couldn't let myself be his comfort. I couldn't be anyone's comfort. For their own safety.

I looked away. Everything twisted inside of me. *Jane is dead. Jane is dead. Jane is dead.*

And Brad's voice, thick and bloody and ricocheting: *It's all your fault.*

I trained my words to go flat, emotionless, wrapped my heart in snow to keep the fire from bursting through me.

"I need to be alone," I said

"I don't think you do. I think you need someone to help you."

The fire broke free, the rage of everything I'd been trying to hold in. All the hatred I had for myself, all aimed at him.

"What the hell do you know about what I do and do not need?" I yelled. "Why the hell are you even talking to me, Chris? You haven't said a goddamn word all year and now you're trying to be my friend? Right when all this shit's going down? I don't have time for this. I don't have room for this. So why don't you just fuck off and go back to being a stranger?"

My words hit him. Hard. Probably harder than if I had thrown a fist. But he barely flinched, and he didn't look away.

"I know you don't mean that," he said. "I know you're hurt and you're scared and I'm sorry for that. But I . . . I hope you don't actually want me to leave."

"And what if I do?" I asked. I made sure to look him right in the eyes when I said it. He was used to happy, art school Kaira. He had no clue what the other years of my life had created. "I told you I'm not interested in dating. So why are you even here?"

"Because I like you."

I deflated.

It was so honest, and it sounded so pained. Like he, too, didn't want this. Any of this. But especially not the affection.

"I'll go," he said. "I know you need to be alone. I just hope you'll come around again."

Then, without another word, he turned and left. The usual bounce was gone from his step; he walked with his head lowered and shoulders hunched.

Chris vanished into the undergrowth and I watched him leave. I wanted to chase after him, to apologize. Because I didn't want to hurt him, not when he was trying to protect me. But that was the problem—I was trying to protect him. And that meant he couldn't be anywhere close.

A shadow darted through the trees, and before I could act or scream it landed on my shoulder with a puff of cold air that smelled of static and the grave. I froze.

The raven perched on my shoulder, its talons gently digging into my coat. I didn't dare to move or breathe, didn't dare turn my head—I could feel its eye trained on me. And I could see that its iris wasn't black. It was as milky white as the moon. It didn't move and it didn't speak. It just stared at me, reminding me that he was always watching.

"What the hell is going on?" I whispered.

But Munin didn't answer. The raven ruffled its feathers and flew off, cawing as loud as the secrets I thought I'd buried deep and dead.

I was jumped the moment I stepped inside my dorm.

"Tell me it's not true," Elisa sobbed into my arms. "Tell me it's not true."

I held her close and rubbed her back and tried not to feel like an imposter. Munin had never appeared like that, not so brazenly. *I'm not going back*, I wanted to scream. Instead, I focused on her. On Jane. On the event I still vehemently swore to myself I had nothing to do with.

"What are they saying?" I asked.

For some reason, I felt stronger here, holding Elisa up. She weighted me down to the present, made me focus on the definite things. It was always easier to be a hero for someone else. Being your own savior was the hard part.

"They're saying she killed herself," Elisa sobbed. She barely got the words out. "She wouldn't do that, Kaira. She wouldn't kill herself. Not without saying something. Not without reaching out."

"I know. I know, it doesn't make any sense." Again, that small tell of a lie. *It doesn't make sense, and that's why I feel responsible.*

"We just saw her. We sat with her at lunch and she was happy."

I bit my lip. I knew the words to say, but that didn't make saying them any easier.

"Sometimes it's easy to hide behind smiles. Some people are really, really good at it."

"But why? Why would she do it? She wasn't depressed. She was my friend, Kaira, and she never said anything about it."

"Secrets like that are hard to share," I said. "Who knows how much stress she was under?"

"I did. We told each other everything. *Everything.*"

I sighed. "I know. And I don't understand it either."

Elisa took a deep, sobbing breath and pulled back. Her eyes were reddened and haloed with smudged mascara. She looked like an angel in mourning.

"What are we going to do now?" she asked.

"I don't know," I replied, thinking of Munin perched on my shoulder. I'd never felt more honest in my life.

Our second school assembly was called that night. Right at sign-in, when we'd normally be sequestered to our dorms, we trudged out in the snow and back into the theatre we'd huddled in one week ago.

I sat in the back once more, Elisa on one side and Ethan and Oliver on the other. I spotted Chris up front, with some other boys from his dorm. He didn't look my way. Not once. I hated admitting to myself how much it hurt. *Why did you push him away?*

Why did you want him closer?

Ms. Kenton took to the stage again. The place was already in transition for Elisa's play, with gray platforms and chains and swathes of fabric. Our president looked like a shadow among the ruins of the set, a ghost.

I didn't listen to a word she said. I couldn't focus on her, just the back of Chris's head and the shadows leaking into the corners of the room like ravens through the trees. I picked out a few words—like "solidarity" and "mourning" and "support groups"—but there was no point listening to her talk about how suicide wasn't the answer, that there were people here who loved us and wanted us to flourish and were always there to listen.

"Are you okay?" Ethan whispered into my ear.

I jolted to the side, nearly knocking into Elisa.

I didn't risk speaking, so I shrugged and nodded and kept my eyes on Ms. Kenton, who was now saying that please, everyone, life was precious. Let's not forget that.

Ethan took my hand as we left the theatre and wandered back through the thickening snow. I ignored the crows lined up on the streetlamps. I ignored Chris, who walked a little farther ahead of me. It felt like I was a character in a video game controlled by someone else. And I was perfectly okay with that. I didn't want to be responsible. I didn't want to be here.

But that was the problem with boarding school. There wasn't anywhere else to go.

"Promise me," Elisa said in the darkness. "Promise me you'll never leave me. Not like that."

"I promise," I whispered back.

Elisa mumbled something else. It sounded like a prayer to Jane, her words begging forgiveness for not being there. I turned over and buried my head under the comforter. I didn't like listening in.

The tea from Mom warmed me, slipping me in and out of my heavy consciousness. Mugwort and chamomile, peppermint and rose hips. To calm and strengthen the dreaming mind, to promote deep sleep. I prayed to the gods it would work.

I squeezed the crystal in my hand. I didn't want to talk to him. Not tonight. Not yet.

I'm not ready to go back. I'm not ready for you to take me.

When sleep finally came, it wasn't the lull of the tide or slipping under into dream. It was the flap of raven wings and the scent of burnt ash.

176

CHAPTER THIRTEEN

I woke up the next morning to a blessed lack of dreams and a few texts from Ethan. I hope you're okay, this shit's getting cray and I can't believe I just rhymed okay and cray. I'm gayer than I thought— don't tell Oliver. And finally, We need to get out of here.

A grin broke across my face in spite of myself. Leave it to Ethan to be able to cheer me up, even when things were about as shitty as they could be.

If you ever say "cray" again I'll de-friend you, I typed back. Also, yes please. I need out.

T'Chai Nanni wouldn't be open until later in the afternoon, and I couldn't imagine spending any time in the studio or this room or wandering like a ghost through the paths of the woods. Islington was a prison today, and I needed freedom. Not that anything in town sounded idyllic. I just knew I couldn't sit still. There was no way this day was going to be anything other than a wash.

Elisa was already gone, which wasn't surprising. I looked

over to her side of the room, to the photos of her and Jane on vacation together, the road trips and smiles. Jane had slept in our room a few times for movie nights, and we'd stayed up way too late watching crappy horror movies and eating junk food and trying not to squeal with laughter at the bad special effects lest an RA come in and, well, sit down and watch with us. It felt like there was a hole in my gut, one punched out by Jane's ghost. But the sadness wasn't there. Instead, I just felt empty.

The phone buzzed with Ethan's response.

I see you missed breakfast. I nearly did as well. Let's get donuts and vanish.

I typed back a quick yes please. Meet in thirty?

I wanted to call my mom. I wanted her to tell me what was going on and how to make it better. But I didn't want to worry her. The last thing she needed was to think there was some weird suicide pact thing going on around campus. Instead, I slid from bed and into the bathroom for a shower. I doubted the heat would melt the numbness inside, but it was a better course of action than staring at the wall until Ethan showed up to whisk me away.

The water offered no solace. I hadn't expected it to. I turned off the faucet and toweled off and stared into the mirror. It took all of my self-control to keep the images down, the empty bathroom and my blood on the tiles.

I knew how it felt to stand on the edge and leap. I knew what came after the free fall.

Jane's and Mandy's deaths brought it all back into focus.

When I finally slipped into clean-ish clothes, I felt no better than when I woke up. Jane was gone. Jane was gone. Why did we remain?

I hated to admit that this hurt worse than Mandy, just as I hated to admit that I was too numb to truly feel anything but distanced from it all. Maybe that was just how I coped.

I needed Ethan to root me back down. I had my parents, sure, but he was the one who was here to show he cared, and that I mattered. I didn't want to make this about me, but . . . two suicides was hitting too close to home.

Especially since I still couldn't figure out how or why Munin was involved.

Before I could get too lost in my head, I walked down to the lobby to wait for Ethan.

Maria was behind the counter again. She was clearly in distress—her usual fancy dress and wicked rockabilly hair was replaced by a sweater and track pants, her hair hanging in a limp frizz down her back.

"How you doing?" she asked when she saw me.

"Managing. You?"

"Managing." She gave me a weak smile. "They don't really train you for this sort of thing, you know? You girls are my best friends and family here."

"I know," I said. "It's . . ."

"Yeah."

We sat in silence for a bit. Then I wandered over to my cubby, where a tiny strip of paper was waiting for me.

Kaira,

I'd like to speak with you soon. Saw your thesis and felt now would be a good time to reach out. I'll be free all day. Take care.

Jonathan A.

Of course he saw my thesis—he would have seen it when searching out Helen. And of course he would be concerned.

"Hey Winters," Ethan said. I turned and stuffed the note in my pocket.

I hugged him in response. He smelled of faded cologne and boy soap and black tea. Just the scent of him helped root me back down, pull me back into my body. Ethan was a constant. Ethan would always be a constant.

"You doing okay?" he asked, still pressed tight against me. His voice was rough.

"Not really."

"Me neither. Let's go."

I signed out with Maria and followed Ethan into the dismal morning light. Gray sky, the ground covered in fresh snow. And on the streetlamp across from my dorm, a raven sat watching. Chills broke over me; I ignored them just as I ignored the bird.

"How's Oliver taking it?" I asked as we trudged away.

"He's okay. They weren't as close as we were."

I nodded. No matter what, it was still a blow to everyone

here. There was no way to live on a campus this small and not be affected by the death.

"I still can't believe she's gone," he said after a while. Only a handful of students were out right now, wandering between dorms and studios. No music came from the practice rooms, though, which made the place feel abandoned. Islington always had a soundtrack.

"I can't either," I replied. We reached his car and he took out the keys. "How's Elisa?"

"Not good," I replied. "I haven't seen her at all today."

"She was at breakfast talking to Cassie and some others. I think they were going to do some sort of vigil for her."

I nodded. Even just being in his car felt strange. The scenery was the same, but the cast was different. He and I were no longer playing the right parts. So what were the right parts? When had our lives gotten so dark?

"Where do you want to go?"

"You mentioned donuts."

"Yeah. Yeah, I did. Donuts and coffee and wandering? I don't really feel like sitting still."

"Perfect."

With the shudder of his engine, we rolled out of the parking lot and onto the street. I glanced out the window at the raven watching from the roof of the cafeteria. It watched us the entire way.

"This isn't how I expected to spend my last few months of Islington," Ethan muttered. We walked slowly through downtown. It was like the entire world had picked up on the mood from school—only a handful of people were out, and those that were huddled under heavy coats and hoods and didn't bother to say hello or pause to window shop. Ethan and I clutched our donuts and mochas and did much the same.

"I don't think anyone expected it," I said. "Especially since neither of them said anything."

He paused, and when he spoke again, there was a tentative note to his voice.

"I saw your thesis," he said.

Fear rolled in my gut.

"Yeah?"

"Yeah. This morning. After breakfast. You never showed me the Ten of Swords before."

He stopped walking when he said it. We stood outside a yarn shop with a cheery display of a knit squid and I nearly laughed. Not exactly where I thought I'd tell him about my life before Islington.

"Why didn't you tell me?" he asked. He sounded more than a little hurt.

I looked down at my boots.

"It didn't seem necessary," I said. "That was the old me."

"When?" he asked.

"Sophomore year," I said. "After . . . well, after homecoming."

The pieces clicked for him.

"Jesus Kaira. I'm sorry."

"It's the past."

"But it's still relevant. Especially with . . . you know."

I nodded.

"I just wish you would have let me be there for you, is all." He reached out and put a hand on my arm. Unlike when Chris did it, there wasn't a hallucination. Just the warmth of his touch and the words that spilled from his lips in a slow stream.

"Before I came out, I tried to kill myself," he admitted. I jerked my gaze back to him. He continued before I could ask. "Never got very far, you know. But I was scared—I couldn't tell anyone and all I saw at school were kids getting beaten up or called faggots even if they had girlfriends. This was in *middle school.* And one day I was home alone and I'd just watched some gay porn and I felt so shitty about myself. So trapped, because I was doing this thing and I didn't want to do it or like it but I couldn't stop. So I went to the kitchen and got a garbage bag and went back to my room. Wrote out a note and everything. But I couldn't do it." He laughed, which sounded more like a sob, and looked at the squid in the window. "I never told anyone that. Not even Oliver. After I started choking I ripped off the bag and threw it away and burned the note. The next day I applied to come here because it was the only escape I could manage. It felt like my only way out." When he looked back at me, there were tears in his eyes. "The last two weeks I've woken up every morning feeling like I'm suffocating on that fucking bag. And I hate myself because I want to feel worse for Jane and Mandy, but all I can think of is how glad I am that I chickened out last minute."

He started to cry then, and I pulled him close and let my own tears fall unchecked.

"I love you, Kaira," he whispered. "You mean the world to me."

"I love you too, Ethan."

"No more secrets, okay?" he asked. "I don't want to lose you."

"I promise," I lied.

Because even though I felt his pain, even though this only cemented our bond, there were parts of my life I couldn't tell him. If I did, I'd lose him.

He couldn't know that I hadn't chickened out at the last minute. That I died the night I cut myself.

He couldn't know that it was the raven that brought me back.

CHAPTER FOURTEEN

We went back to campus a few hours later, a bag of art supplies and silly gifts from the dollar store in hand. Shopping therapy wasn't my usual balm, but it worked as well as anything else. Especially because most of this was for other people.

Ethan dropped me off in front of my dorm, leaned over in his seat to hug me good-bye and make me promise we'd have a pizza party in the Writers' House later tonight. Of course I agreed, and he said he'd invite Oliver and I should invite Elisa and maybe Chris, which was the first time he'd said the *C* word all day. The look I gave him must have been answer enough.

"Just Elisa then," he replied, and I nodded and left.

But Elisa wasn't in when I got up to our room. Not in an ominous *oh no, she's missing* sort of way, but in the usual *she's probably out with friends or rehearsing* way. So I wrote her a note saying where and when the pizza would be and left it on her pillow, alongside a tiny pink stegosaurus and a chocolate bar (dark, of course).

I sighed and sat down on my bed. As usual, there were a dozen things I could be doing right now, most of them involving homework. That was the one thing about this school I loved as much as I hated—the work never stopped. Ever. No rest for the wicked. And no time to mourn.

That's when I remembered Jonathan's note in my pocket. Another sigh. I should probably go see him. I knew that if I waited too long, he'd send Helen after me. Not that I really wanted to defend my thesis to someone right now—especially someone not even *in* the arts department—but he was my adviser and had the final say in my career here. Hell, he could probably prevent me from graduating if he wanted to. Not that I thought he *would* do something like that, but it was a possibility. So I slipped back into my boots and rebuttoned my coat and headed back out into the cold.

Dealing with this was not something I wanted to be doing. But I wanted to be dealing with my inner demons even less.

Even though it was only three, the sky was darkening with storms. Seriously, was it ever going to stop snowing?

I was halfway to the academics concourse when I saw him, bouncing his way down the path toward me. Chris.

He caught sight of me and paused. Thankfully, he didn't do the awkward thing of turning around. He halted for a second and then kept walking. So I did the same.

"Hey," he said with a lackluster wave.

"Hey," I replied.

"Where you off to?"

"Jonathan's office. He wants to talk. About my thesis."

"Ah." He looked at his feet. "I saw your work. It's impressive."

"Thanks," I replied. I couldn't think of any way this conversation could feel more awkward.

"About yesterday."

"Yeah?"

"Are you feeling any better?"

It wasn't the question I expected.

"Sort of. Went off campus with Ethan for a bit. It helped."

"Good. I was worried about you. Never seen you that angry."

Well, you barely know me, I wanted to say.

"Yeah, I'm sorry about that," I said instead. "I didn't mean to direct that at you. You were just in the wrong place at the wrong time."

He gave me a sad grin. "Can we still be friends?"

I nodded. He held out his hand. I hesitated for a second, then took it. No vision, but I did hear a crow caw in the background.

"Still friends," I said. "Anyway, better be off. Don't want Jonathan to think I'm avoiding him." Which I *had* been doing, but he didn't need to know that.

"Sure. See you at dinner?"

Damnit.

"Actually, doing pizza with the boys. You can join if you want. Five p.m., Writers' House."

His eyebrows lifted in surprise. "Really?"

"Yeah, of course. C'ya then."

And it was then I realized we were still holding hands. I let go quickly and hurried the rest of the way to the concourse—just slow enough to not look like I was running—and didn't look back.

"Kaira, come in," Jonathan said.

I hovered in the door for a second, glancing around his office. I'd been in here many times, and in many ways it was the office I'd like to have if I ever had a job that, you know, actually required me to have an office. The walls were covered in posters of old woodcut paintings from mythic texts—the Bhagavad Gita, Beowulf, the Norse Eddas, even Tolkien. Books were piled in the corners against concrete statues of fauns and gods, the tiny space brimming with history and strangeness.

"Hey Jonathan," I said. I stepped in and settled myself on the chair across from his desk. The offices weren't luxurious by any stretch of the imagination—the chair and desk looked like they were from some fifties Ikea—but he'd made the place a little more homey. "You wanted to see me?"

"I did, yeah." He was even more casual than I was used to seeing him—jeans and a T-shirt—which meant his tattoos were all bared. I couldn't take my eyes off his sleeve—gods and mortals battled it out, all surrounded by a great, twining serpent. "I thought you might want to talk about your thesis."

"I'm not depressed, if that's what you're asking."

"No, no." He held up his hands. "Not that at all. The arts were developed to help mortals peer into the shadows. I don't think there's anything wrong or unsettling with your project."

"So why did you want to see me? I just kind of thought it

had to do with Jane's . . ." I couldn't say the word "death" or "suicide." It lodged in my throat, and all I could picture was Ethan suffocating himself with tears in his eyes. I shook the image away.

He sighed and seemed to choose his next words carefully.

"I suppose it has to do with that, somewhat. I *am* your adviser, and that means I'm also here if you need any emotional support. I wanted you to drop by today so we could talk. If you need or want to, that is."

"I think I'm okay," I said. "I'm kind of talked out about the whole thing."

"I don't blame you," he said. "It's been . . . a very rough few weeks."

We sat there in silence for a few moments, and I couldn't tell if it was comfortable or uncomfortable. When he spoke again, it felt like a small release of pressure.

"So tell me about your project," he said. "I read your thesis statement but I want it from your own lips. Why the Tarot?"

I shrugged.

"My mom gave me a deck my freshman year and I've been pretty into it ever since. It helps put my life into a bigger pattern, you know?"

He nodded. It wasn't one of those dismissive nods, either; he looked like he understood. More importantly, he looked like he was interested in learning more.

"Is that why you took my class?"

"I guess, yeah. I've always liked fairytales and folklore."

"But to you it's not just fairytales and folklore," he said with a grin. "I mean, the Tarot draws upon all these old myths. In order to truly believe in the cards, you have to believe there's something manipulating them."

I shrugged. I didn't like talking faith to anyone, not even my mom. I definitely wasn't about to discuss it with a teacher. "I guess," I admitted.

There was no way I was going to tell him about the dreams or events that *actually* inspired the paintings. No way in hell.

"I don't know if you remember my mentioning the tutorial group," he said. "Especially with everything else, I can't imagine it would be foremost on your mind. But they meet every other week. I'd love for you to join—I think you'd find it highly educational."

Right. The stupid study group. And I didn't have the excuse of being busy with my thesis anymore, either.

"What's it for?"

"Independent study, mostly. It's not a lot of extra work, but we explore many of the topics we only brush over in class. The relationships between cross-cultural deities, the origin of rituals, that sort of thing. I wanted to give students a safe place to explore the more esoteric aspects of what I can cover in the curriculum. Even Islington has its limits to what I can teach." He grinned, as if confiding a secret. "I figured you might be interested, what with your own ties to the occult.

"You don't have to say yes right now. Just know the offer's on the table. I think you'd find it very helpful for your future work, especially if you continue that Tarot project."

"Thanks," I said. "But I don't know if I'll have the time."

"No pressure. We're meeting again tomorrow afternoon. I

was thinking of canceling, in light of things, but then figured that work is a decent enough distraction in and of itself. Might help get your mind off things and—how did you phrase it?—put your life into a bigger picture."

"Thanks," I said. He had a point. The only way I was going to get through this was by distracting myself, and a new workload would do just that. Especially one that didn't involve art. I had a feeling I wouldn't be able to spend any more time in the painting studio than absolutely necessary. "I'll see if I can make it. Was there anything else?"

He shook his head. "Nope, just wanted to check in."

"Okay. See you later then."

He nodded. "Have a good night."

I left and closed the door behind me, hurrying out into the cold. A raven sat on the fence outside, head cocked and waiting.

"What are you staring at?" I whispered. The bird shuffled its wings and took off. "Fat lot of help you are," I muttered, and made my way back to the Writers' House to work until pizza came.

The five of us lounged in the main foyer of the building. The gas fireplace was lit and fending off the snow buzzing about outside, and the House was pretty much empty. No one wanted to brave the weather to be out here, and I didn't blame them. If I hadn't gotten here before true dark hit, even pizza would have been a tough draw.

Oliver and Ethan sat on one of the faux leather sofas, Elisa and me on the opposite. Chris was on the floor, cross-legged, right by the pizza box. There was a warmth here that I hadn't expected to feel, not after all the shit of the last few days. But maybe that was what cemented this together—all that loss made us grip what we *did* have even tighter. Especially since it wasn't going to last.

Still, I couldn't help but feel like there was an empty space, a seat at the dinner table left empty. Jane wasn't here. And neither was her ghost.

"Have any of you guys gone to the painting studio?" Elisa asked. It felt like the first time she'd spoken all night.

If not for the pizza already stuffed in my mouth, I might have lost my appetite. I glanced to the boys. Their faces all showed the exact same blank stare.

"Nope," Ethan said first. The rest of us shook our heads.

"Why?" I asked. This felt like dangerous territory. Less walking on eggshells and more dodging landmines. Elisa and Jane were besties—anything related to Jane's suicide couldn't be good.

"Because it's locked up," she said. She was staring out the large picture windows flanking the fireplace while she spoke, her voice quiet, almost entranced.

"I suppose that makes sense," Chris ventured. "I mean, it's still kind of a crime scene, isn't it?"

I shrugged. I had no idea how things like this normally went down.

"I heard they don't think it was suicide," she said after a moment. This made everyone go still.

"What do you mean?" Oliver asked.

"I mean she didn't leave a note. Just like Mandy. And like

Mandy, she had no reason to kill herself. She was just . . . dead. Right before her thesis went up."

"So, what, natural causes?"

She shrugged. "I don't know. But none of it makes any sense. It doesn't feel right."

I didn't want her words to creep down my spine, but they did. They lodged against my ribs and bored through my heart and made it impossible to breathe. It was one thing for me to think there was something strange going on. It was another for my best friend to voice it.

"Maybe it was a condition?" Chris asked quietly. "Like a heart problem. The rest could be coincidence."

Elisa went back to eating, staring into the fire with a detached look to her, like she was staring far away, at something no one else could see.

"I think she was murdered," Elisa said after a few moments of silence. "I think they both were."

CHAPTER FIFTEEN

I woke up cold, and it didn't take long to realize why. I'd kicked my sheets off some time in the night—not that it was morning by any stretch of the imagination. It was still pitch black outside, the light from the streetlamp making everything muted and dreamlike. Whatever dream was filtering in my mind vanished as my heart tilted. It felt like my bed was filled with sand. *What the hell?*

I pushed myself to sitting. Only then did I realize I was leaving dark stains in the trail of my fingerprints. Charcoal. I held my hands up to the filtered light.

"What . . . ?"

Then I leaned over the edge of my bed. The ice that ran through me at that moment made frostbite seem like a sunburn.

My sketchbook was open in a pool of lamplight, a new drawing facing me like a curse. I must have done it in my sleep; that was the only way to explain it. Jane lay sprawled on the stark white paper, her black-inked body face-up, staring at me. Her

194

hands stretched above her head and her legs were straight out under her hips. And around her, in a thick line, was a black circle. Just like . . .

No no no.

Words were scrawled between her hands, in a handwriting that wasn't mine:

The Tree Will Burn

I wanted to scream.

She was coming back.

CHAPTER SIXTEEN

I couldn't sleep after that. Of course I couldn't. I sat there in bed and fought the two wolves inside of me—one that wanted to destroy the sketch, the other that wanted to preserve it. For what? Evidence? Proof that I was or was not crazy? I had drawn Jane in my sleep, had written words in someone else's handwriting. How was that anything beyond insane? Especially since the circle . . .

But no. It was just stress. Stress and tragedy and not enough sleep and probably too much sugar. This had nothing to do with Brad. There was no way in hell they were related.

The painting studio is locked up, Elisa had said. There was something someone wanted to hide.

Which meant there was probably still some sort of evidence there, not that I was comfortable calling anything related to the death of my friend "evidence."

"You're being ridiculous," I muttered. But I couldn't help it. Every time I blinked I saw Brad's eyes. Saw the feathers in the darkness. So I kept my eyes open. *If you think of it, you give it power.*

There were many reasons I sent myself to Islington. The distraction of constant work was definitely one of them. In this moment, however, I wished I wasn't here. I wished I was anywhere else, really. Somewhere I could run around and force the memories from my head. I wanted to go out and run to the forest and scream the frustration away. But I couldn't. I couldn't call or talk to anyone and I couldn't leave the fucking dorm room, which meant I was trapped with my thoughts and three hours to kill until sunrise.

Maybe I should delete any reference to death from my vocabulary, metaphorical or no.

I was going to drive myself insane, and if I did anything on the computer I'd wake Elisa up. I didn't want to have to explain my insomnia to her—not because she'd pry, but because I knew she wouldn't, and I wanted so badly for someone to root just a little deeper. I wanted to have to share these secrets. If I kept them all in, I was going to explode.

Don't think about it. You're stressed and it's making you crack and that's it. That's it. This has nothing to do with you and nothing to do with Brad. Mandy and Jane were suicides. Brad was just an accident.

But I couldn't convince myself of that. Munin was back. People were dying. And my dreams . . .

I didn't want to go there. I didn't want to explore it. I couldn't change anything—I couldn't bring anyone back. All I could do was keep my head down and try to stay calm, to keep myself out of it. Soon I would graduate and this would all be behind me and I could—what?—run somewhere else?

You can't run forever, a voice whispered in the shadows of my mind. *It has already begun.*

I wanted to scream back that nothing had begun. I was stressed. That was it. I was stressed and other people were stressed and that caused bad things to happen. That was it. I wasn't going to open the door looming in front of me. I wasn't going to invite Munin back in.

Not when I knew what that would entail.

As a last resort, I opened a book and took out my tiny flashlight. American Civ. Nothing put me to sleep faster than American history. And I had an essay due Friday.

My next moment of consciousness was Elisa throwing a pillow at my face.

"Rise and shine, pooper," she said. Not nearly with her usual conviction though. She sounded as tired as I felt. "How'd you sleep?"

I grumbled and kept my eyes closed. She sat down beside me.

"I'll take that as insomnia," she said, tapping on the book. "Unless you're looking for a new pillow."

"Couldn't sleep."

"Are you turning your bed into a work of art now too?"

I opened one eye. Charcoal was smeared into my sheets (which were normally a very cute toy cowboy print) and probably blurred my face like some garish mascara. At least I'd hidden the sketchbook back in the drawer where it belonged. Elisa would have freaked if she saw it.

"Late-night inspiration," I lied, and pushed myself to sitting.

Now that it was light, I was able to see just how much charcoal I'd gotten everywhere. My bed looked like a firepit. Only slight exaggeration.

"Well, maybe make that your last. Unless you want to get vinyl sheets, which I think would require special explaining to the RA."

I tried to smile. The fact that she was attempting a sense of humor after everything was heartening.

Technically speaking, we should have been in class today, but we'd been given another day to mourn, which meant another day of finishing homework and trying to do everything *but* think about what had happened.

"What time is it?" I asked.

"Seven thirty. Breakfast."

I groaned. I wasn't hungry in the slightest. My stomach roiled from leftover dreams and my mouth tasted like charcoal—probably because I accidentally ate some in my sleep. Elisa seemed to catch my train of thought, or maybe my expression when I licked my lips, because she grinned and rustled my hair.

"You should probably rinse off first. You look like a panda."

"Thanks friend," I said as sarcastically as I could.

I stood and started toward the bathroom, but her next words stopped me.

"Hey, Kaira?"

I turned. "Yeah?"

"Do you remember anything about last night?"

"Besides the part where I didn't sleep?"

She nodded.

"No," I said slowly. "Why?"

"Because you woke me up. Maybe around three. You were thrashing and screaming."

My skin went cold. Was that before or after the ghost sketching?

"Yeah?"

She nodded. Her face looked paler than usual. Scared. Her black dress and leggings didn't help.

"Yeah," she said. "You kept saying *it's dying*."

"I . . ." But I didn't know what to say. I didn't remember screaming that. The image from my sketch burned into my brain: "The Tree Will Burn." But what the hell did that even mean? And how were my friends involved in all of this? That was the world of gods and demons, and that world didn't blend with mine. Not any longer. "I'm sorry. Bad dreams I guess. Sorry if it woke you up."

She shrugged and looked out the window. As usual, the windowsill outside was a churned mess of snow and bird prints.

"It's okay. Nightmares are to be expected. I haven't slept well either." When she looked back to me, her face was carefully composed, a smile that was only believable because she was an actor. And only unbelievable to me because I was her roommate. "It's just a sign of the times."

Although Elisa and I walked through the snow to breakfast together, she didn't join us at the table.

"I gotta go console Cassie," she said as she hugged me good-bye. Cassie and Jane had been roommates, along with being best friends. I couldn't imagine what the girl was going through. I didn't want to imagine it.

I went to the table where Ethan and Oliver already sat and felt something inside of me shatter at the sight. The big round table looked so . . . empty. The boys must have noticed it too. Ethan gave me a sad eyebrow raise and gestured to the seat beside him. I took it. From here, I was facing one of the windows overlooking Islington. Normally, it was a gorgeous view—the snow-covered trees, the rolling lawn. Today it just felt stark. It was better than facing the cold of the cafeteria, though.

"How's it going?" I asked.

"As expected," Ethan replied. Oliver yawned.

"Haven't slept for shit," Oliver said. He took a long drink of coffee. "What about you?"

His yawn made me yawn, and it took a moment for me to answer. "Roughly the same." I sighed and picked up a piece of bacon. I'd been mulling this next snippet of conversation for most of the shower and walk over. I still wasn't certain how it would sound. "Have you guys thought any more about what Elisa said?"

"Clarify," Ethan said.

"You know what I mean. About it not being suicide."

They exchanged a glance.

"Yeah, we've thought about it," Oliver said. He was using his *I'm trying to be soothing without being a dick* voice, which was really only a tiny amount less annoying. He dropped his voice to a whisper, barely loud enough for me to hear. "It doesn't make any sense though. If Jane was killed, why aren't there any cops on patrol?"

"Then why is the studio locked?"

Ethan looked at me like I was incredibly stupid.

"Suicide isn't always clean," he replied flatly.

I looked back to my tray. I suppose that wasn't something I'd considered. But I wasn't giving up this train of thought. Something was off—very off—and if there was a link between these deaths and Brad, if there was something supernatural going on . . . I pushed the thought down. I wasn't playing with those powers.

"I want to see it," I whispered. "I want to see the studio."

"It's still locked," Ethan replied. "Or didn't you get the message? The studio will be closed for the rest of the week. They're having class in the spare crit room now."

"There are other ways," I replied. I gave Ethan my most conspiratorial, knowing look. "Maybe we should go stargazing."

"What's stargazing?" But it wasn't Oliver or Ethan who asked. It was Chris.

He stood beside me with a tray in his hands and a tired look on his face.

Gods damnit.

I was about to lie when Ethan continued for me.

"It's when Kaira and I slip up to the roof of the arts building to smoke and people watch," Ethan said. He turned his gaze to me. I couldn't read his expression, but I knew he was saying this in an attempt to divert my plan. "Which she thinks we should do to see inside the painting studio."

Chris sat down beside me. Hard.

"Why would you want to do that?" he asked.

"I don't know," Ethan said. "Kaira hasn't illuminated us on that part yet."

I gave him my best *burst into flames* glare and then turned to Chris. Obviously I couldn't tell them that I wanted to see if the crime scene matched up with what I'd sketched. They'd think I was insane. Worse, I didn't know what I'd say if they actually *did* match up—that was a box even Pandora wouldn't want to open.

"Because," I said carefully, "I think they're hiding something. And I don't like having information withheld."

"Count me in," Chris said, popping a tater tot into his mouth.

"Wait, what? Who said you were invited?" The questions left my lips before I could catch them.

"Jane was my friend too," he said. He glanced around and lowered his voice before continuing. "Besides, I was the last person to see her, apparently. I've already been questioned by the cops and security and even my parents. I think I deserve to know what actually happened and why I'm a suspect."

His statement sent every red flag in my arsenal high into the air.

"Excuse me?" I don't know why his comment hurt me as much as it made me question his trustworthiness. "You were the last person to see her? And what do you mean, *suspect*?"

"Hell if I know," he said. "And yes, we hung out for a bit after brunch. That's why I didn't go straight to the studio. She reminded me that I needed to call home." He pointed a piece of bacon at me. His normally elfish smile vanished. "Stop looking at me like that. I had nothing to do with it, no matter what the cause of her death was. I have five different alibis and a phone log to prove I was in my room at the time of her death."

I deflated back into my chair.

"You don't need to be roped into this," I said.

"I already am. I want to know what happened to her. Whatever's going on, something isn't right here." He looked to the boys, both of whom were completely transfixed on his and my conversation. "I think we can all agree that neither Mandy nor Jane had any reason to kill themselves. The only possible cause is stress over their theses, but that doesn't make sense because they were already *done* with the projects. Something else is linking them and I want to know what. Before it happens again."

His statement was met with silence.

"Wow," Ethan said after awhile. "I feel like I should give you a standing ovation."

"Shut up," Chris muttered, chucking a tot at him. "This isn't funny."

"You're right," I said. "What we're about to do is pretty against the rules. If we're caught, we'll be suspended. Or worse."

Chris just grinned. "Please, I was an only child. I'm the *master* of slinking around unnoticed."

I rolled my eyes.

"When are we doing this?" Ethan asked.

"Dinner," I replied quickly. That was the one part of the plan I had down—the actual logistics were easy. It was convincing my cohorts that I'd thought would be the hard part. "When it's dark and everyone's distracted."

"Legit," Ethan said. He looked to Oliver. "You in?"

Oliver sighed. "I have trio practice at five thirty. If I miss it they'll be pissed."

"Seriously?" Ethan asked.

"Seriously. Besides, you've all seen horror movies. The black guy always dies first."

"Since when was this a horror movie?" I asked.

Oliver looked me dead in the eye. "Since our friends started dying."

We agreed on a plan of attack and parted ways after breakfast. I headed back to my room to change into something that wasn't pajamas, and the boys went off to do whatever boy things they had to do. Elisa was already in the room, lying on her bed with her legs crossed and a book in hand. It was surprising to see her there, working. I kind of expected her to still be in mourning.

"How was Cassie?" I asked.

"Managing," she replied. She looked over the book at me. "How were the boys?"

I shrugged. Saying *planning to spy on Jane's death scene* seemed a little too blunt. "Managing," I said instead.

My plans for today were pretty straightforward: Since we had an unexpected day off, I was going to spend most of my time working. I'd probably focus on finishing some small silversmithing pieces for the coming week, what with the painting studio closed. I just wanted to be alone. I didn't want to talk about art or Jane or gods or anything else; I wanted to get shit done, bury myself in my work and hope that I found my way out on the other side. No tutorial with Jonathan. No hanging out with friends. Which meant starting in on the American Civ reading—I'd hold off on art until later, as a treat. It would be a day of solitary productivity. I needed it.

Which is why, when my room phone rang and I answered, I was surprised at how happy I was to hear Chris on the other end.

"How are you?" he asked.

"Fine," I lied. "*Where* are you?"

"Lobby," he said. And sure enough, I heard some girls giggle on the other end of the line. "What are you doing today?"

"Working."

"Sounds fun." Once more the line was interrupted with giggling. "Hey, do you wanna come down and talk? They're watching something in the lounge and it's pretty hard to hear."

What do we have to talk about? I wanted to ask. But then, like a light switch, the idea of doing more work just to distract myself seemed unbearable. Didn't I deserve a break? Chris knew nothing about me or my past, which meant we could have some nice idle conversations about music or movies or whatever normal kids talked about.

I needed the normalcy. Probably more than I needed a good grade in silversmithing.

"Um, yeah, sure." So much for being smooth.

"Bring your coat," was all he said.

"Okay, down in five."

"Awesome. Gives me just enough time to get enthralled with this show. . . ."

"Who was that?" Elisa asked when I put down the phone.

"Chris," I said. And she did the obligatory *OooOoo*. "Shut up," I said, throwing an old sock at her.

She just giggled and went back to her reading. I ran around the room, putting on my boots and grabbing my keys and coat and wallet and oh hell I should have just put it in a purse but too late now and then went for the door.

"Have fuu-unnn," Elisa taunted.

"You're incorrigible," I replied.

"I don't know what that means!" she called as the door shut behind me. I just smiled.

Chris was waiting in the lobby, sitting on one of the tall stools and staring at the wall. The RA on duty must have been watching a movie in the lounge with the girls, as there was no one behind the desk. I paused coming down the stairs, taking a brief moment to do one of those stalker-y once-overs of him. With his duster and boots, he kind of looked like a longhaired David Tennant, or some gearless steampunk aficionado, minus obligatory goggles. I could just imagine painting him standing on the edge of a canyon, everything red and ocher, a dirigible silhouetted in the setting sun.

He turned and caught my stare. His face lit into a smile. And as much as I hated to admit it, that smile made me smile back. I continued down the steps like I hadn't just been staring.

"Hey," he said, hopping off the seat.

"Are you stalking me now?" I asked.

His smiled dropped.

"I mean, we *did* just see each other like twenty minutes ago," I continued.

"I know. But I got back to my room and realized that being alone was very boring. So I thought I'd hang out with you."

I pushed down the bubble of happiness that I was the first person to come to mind.

"Okay then. What's the plan, Stan?"

He shook his head. "You're the only person I've ever met who talks like that."

"Like what?"

"Like you," he said. He chuckled. "Anyway, I didn't really have any ideas. Maybe a movie or . . . ?"

I buttoned up my peacoat. Sitting down with him to watch a movie ventured into dangerous romantic territory. I needed to keep this light. Friendly. *Normal.* And perhaps most importantly, I needed to keep moving.

"We'll do what we always do at art school. We'll walk."

We wandered down the lane, past the art building, away from the lake. The woods and Writers' House were both ahead, neither as inviting as they used to be.

"Probably not as exciting as what you're used to back west," I said. I wouldn't lie; a small part of me was a little jealous of him for getting an urban childhood. My own small-town upbringing had been far from exciting and far from inclusive. At least, if I'd grown up in a bigger city, I might have had more opportunity to . . . *what? Find more kids like you? That's not really a thing, you know—not many kids talk to birds.*

"I only lived in Seattle a few years," he replied, pulling me out of my thoughts.

"Oh yeah?"

He nodded. "My parents move around a lot. Before that it was Vermont. Then Massachusetts. Then Wisconsin. Before that was . . ." He paused and shook his head. "Needless to say, it made settling in difficult, but I've sort of gotten used to being a guest in other people's lives."

I couldn't tell if he was being morose or if this was him opening up. Guess it didn't really matter either way.

We passed the concert hall. Music drifted from many of the practice rooms—snippets of Bach, strings of jazz, even a hint of funk. I wondered if Oliver was in there, practicing his way to eventual fame. At least the place wasn't silent like before. This was a sign that Islington was moving forward. Slowly, but surely.

"What brought you to Seattle?" I asked.

"Same thing that brought my parents to Detroit. Work. Honestly, I think they just kept changing locations so they won't have to focus on . . ." His words caught, and he looked away, which pretty much said everything he couldn't say. "On other things."

He shook his head. "Sorry. Don't mean to be a Debbie Downer."

I laughed. "Clearly you've been hanging out with me too much. Pretty certain I'm the only person under eighty who uses that phrase anymore."

He chuckled too, and when his gaze darted to mine I felt a new, not altogether uncomfortable knot form in my stomach.

"Okay then, my anachronistic friend. My turn for the questions. Why painting?"

"What do you mean?" I asked.

We were passing by the Writers' House, and I almost nudged him in, but I knew the moment I stopped walking was the moment I started thinking about other things. Especially in there; it felt like Elisa's questions were haunting that space. If we walked in, I'd be able to think of nothing beyond the question I didn't know if I wanted answered: Had Jane and Mandy actually killed themselves?

"I mean what got you into it?" he asked. "Every artist has a story."

"True," I said, guiding him toward one of the forest trails. Even though I was still a little on edge over being alone with a guy, being on campus made me feel safer. This was *my* territory. I could tell we were both skirting Jane's death and our night's plans. It felt like being an actor in a play, only I was also part of the audience, watching it all with detached interest. "I like painting because it's so mutable. Everything about it changes. A shift in light or shadow might mean you need to remix all your colors. One stray brushstroke can alter the whole composition. It's like people . . . or life, if you want to get really deep and pretentious. It's different every day.

"Besides, figure painting means I get to stare at naked old man penis, and who doesn't love that?"

He laughed so loud, I honestly think he surprised himself.

"What about you? What got you into painting?"

"Parents," he said. He sobered immediately.

"Ah. Not old man penis then. Let me guess: brush in your hands before you could talk sort of thing?"

He shook his head.

"Not quite. I started painting about five years ago, the first time they almost got a divorce. They separated for a few months—over my birthday, no less—and that was how I coped. We'd just moved to Vermont and I didn't know anyone, so I signed myself up for a painting class at a nearby studio. It was my therapy."

"That's . . ." *Horrible? Poetic?*

"Yeah." He sighed. "I dunno. It's kind of like you said—painting always changes, but it let me change my world. If I was lonely I could paint a bunch of people. If I hated the snow I could paint a beach. And it also meant I got to play with colors, which was pretty cool, since I'd spent most of my life afraid of them."

"Afraid of colors?"

"I'm colorblind," he said. He gave me a small grin. "Kids made fun of me a lot when I was really little, when I drew the grass the wrong color or made people blue, but the painting world kind of embraced it. It was nice having something I'd always seen as a shortfall heralded as innovative."

"I hadn't ever really noticed. And I definitely don't think I've ever been heralded for anything."

He chuckled. "Overstatement. I was always a loner, so there wasn't much heralding in my world either."

"So is that your cross to bear?" I asked. I don't know why I was pushing it, but I'd always liked learning people's secrets. It made them seem more human. And if I focused on this—on Chris, who was very human and very normal—I could stop focusing on Jane and Brad and the parallels my unconscious mind wouldn't stop drawing. "You're the misunderstood colorblind artist?"

"Not quite," he said.

"Well then, what's your deep dark secret?"

"Not yet," he said.

"What do you mean?"

"I mean, not yet." His voice became firm, though not exactly angry. I knew that tone—it was precisely the same one I used when someone was prodding into my past a little too much.

"Gotcha," I said.

We walked deeper into the woods, the only sound our footsteps on the gravel and the occasional gust of wind through the bare trees. When we reached the lake we stopped and stared out, our breath coming in silent little puffs. It was comfortable. In a way, it felt like all the times I'd come out here with Ethan— the closeness, the openness. I don't know how the hell Chris managed to make me forget all the shit going on and everything we were going to do tonight. Being with him just felt natural.

The moment I realized that, though, I felt my walls inch up. The crows watching from the trees weren't helping. *He isn't Brad. This isn't all an act. I don't need you to protect me from him.*

Unless he's the one who needs to be protected from me . . .

Immediately I stepped to the side and forced down whatever feelings of comfort I'd had.

"Whoa, what just happened?" he asked.

"What do you mean?"

"I mean you just went really cold. Did I say something to offend you?"

"No. It's just . . ."

"Just?"

"This whole thing doesn't make any sense. I shouldn't, I mean . . . you shouldn't fall for me."

He chuckled humorlessly and started walking again, trudging a new path through the snow.

"Don't worry, you already told me a dozen times we weren't going to date. I'm not a masochist."

"It wasn't a dozen."

"Maybe not verbally."

I glared at him. He put his hands up.

"I get it, really. It's okay. But I'm trying to get to know you and you keep pushing me away."

"It's safer that way. Trust me. You don't want to get to know me."

He took me by the shoulders. He did that eye thing, that *you will look me in the eyes and see I'm really listening* thing.

"I do," he said. "What do I have to do to make you trust me?"

"It's not that I don't trust you," I said, looking down. The fact that I wasn't lying made it harder to stomach—I shouldn't trust him. But it was me that I had to keep at arm's length. "It's just . . . there are parts of my life I don't talk about. Can't talk about. And that makes being my friend hard."

My dreamtime sketch flashed through my mind—Jane sprawled and staring, charcoal splattered like blood across the page. *If you knew half of the things that make me who I am . . .*

"We all have secrets, Kaira. We all have things that make us feel fucked up. But those are the things that make us human."

He took a deep breath.

"Fine. We'll do this. I had a little sister," he said. "Her name was Bri."

Was? Had? He didn't give me time to ask. He also didn't let

213

go of my shoulders, though his grip was gentle. His eyes never left mine.

"She was a year younger than me. She loved me, and I loved her. We did everything together—built forts, played games, went on adventures. We were living in Maine. Little town on the ocean." He glanced away and bit his lip, letting his hands slip from my shoulders to his pockets. He looked unbelievably sad, and I wanted so badly to make it go away. "I don't know why my parents let us go on our own. I was only six. But I think they were tied up in work or just tired of us pestering them. So Bri and I went to the beach. Alone."

"What happened?" I asked.

"I don't really know," he said. He brought his gaze back to me. He wasn't crying, but his eyes wavered; he looked lost. "I was building sand castles. I remember that. She was playing in the waves. I told her not to go out. I told her to stay close. One minute she was there, laughing and splashing around, the next it was silent."

"Jesus . . ."

"It's so cliché, isn't it? Swept away by the tide. They didn't find her body until a week later. I guess she was caught in some fisherman's net. Like a tiny drowned mermaid."

I put a hand on his arm. The indignation from before was gone. It was impossible to be angry. Not when he was this vulnerable.

"I still remember how quiet it was," he said. He looked away, toward the lake. "Almost like this. Like there was this great void in the world, like the weight of her soul was a tangible thing."

"I am so, so sorry," I said.

He took another deep breath and stood up a little straighter.

"Don't be," he said. "As you said, it's my cross to bear. I'm the reason my sister is dead. Every time I paint, I wonder if she'd like it. I wonder if it would make her happy."

"You can't blame yourself for that," I said. "You were just a kid."

"I can. And I do. If I had been watching her, if I'd heard her call out, if I'd done a hundred other things differently, maybe she'd still be here. Hell, maybe she'd have come to Islington with me, studied dance or writing or something. I didn't even notice her leaving, though. She's dead because of it. But it taught me a lot about life, you know? How you just have to take each moment as it comes because at any time, it could all be taken away. And it has, many times. My parents moved a few weeks after that. That's what started the fighting and the moving. As they've said, I'm the reason their relationship went downhill—they couldn't stand living with her ghost. And although they never said it, I knew they could never stop blaming me for it."

"Then your parents are assholes," I said.

He gave me a side smile. "They try."

I knew that this was the moment I should open up and tell him about Brad. *Everything* about Brad, and what had happened after. There was a large part of me that wanted to believe Chris and I could bridge this gap and move forward and maybe this time I wouldn't get hurt by a boy I wanted to care about. Maybe I wouldn't end up hurting him. But that was just a pipe dream. No one would want to be with me when they knew the truth.

Hell, not even *I* wanted to be with me much of the time, but I was kind of stuck.

"Mind if we start walking again?" I asked. "My toes are starting to go numb."

My toes were perfectly toasty in my boots. I just needed to start walking, to get somewhere closer to people and civilization because I needed an excuse *not* to talk.

"Sure thing," he said. My hand slipped from his arm, but we didn't stop touching, not entirely. "Anywhere in particular?"

"Writers' House," I suggested. "I could use some hot chocolate."

Hands just brushing, we walked out of the woods.

It felt like a metaphor. The crows watching us from the boughs didn't help.

Even though it was barely tilting into afternoon, the sky above was heavy and gray when we stepped into the Writers' House. A few students were already in the foyer, reading or typing away on computers. In the kitchen, I filled the electric kettle with water and began rummaging around in the cabinets for hot cocoa.

Something felt different between us now, and as I looked at him I realized what it was: He was no longer just a pretty face and a quirky sense of fashion. He was human. And some part of me ached to connect with that. To lay down my own fears and demons and be seen as a human too. As much as I could be.

Trouble was, I'd spent too many years in the dark, too many years pretending being alone and unwanted didn't hurt like hell. People didn't want that me, the real me, the me who stared at shadows and didn't know anything about her real family, the ones who gave her up to die. No one wanted *that* truth. So I had to create the image that I was wanted. That I was stronger.

"What are you thinking?" he asked, stepping up beside me. I ripped open the packets and poured them into the mugs. Handmade ceramics, probably from a graduate.

"About chocolate," I lied.

"Uh huh," he said.

"Why is it," I asked, pouring water in the second mug, "that I've only really known you for a few days, but feel more comfortable around you than I should?"

And why doesn't that scare me as much as it should?

I didn't expect an answer, and I didn't even really mean to ask. But now that the words lingered in the air, I knew I couldn't take them back. It felt like standing at the crossroads, waiting for direction.

"I don't know," he said after a moment. "I've been wondering the same thing."

I set the kettle down.

"I can't fall for you," I said.

"Why not?" he asked.

"Because," I whispered, suddenly aware that we were still in an open kitchen and people might be listening in. "Love is dangerous."

"That's what makes it worth it."

I turned to him then, and looked him right in the eyes. He had shown me his very human past. Maybe I needed to show him mine. Even if there was nothing human about it.

"The last time I was in love," I said, "people got hurt. Bad."

"That's a part of life," he replied.

Gods, his eyes. I couldn't stop looking into those eyes.

"No," I whispered. "This wasn't." I wanted to look away. I didn't want to say what was on my tongue, not while he was staring at me with so much intent.

"What happened?" he asked.

"I was hurt," I replied. A flicker of truth. "And the guy . . . he died. His name was Brad. The first and only guy I ever dated. And he died."

He died because he hurt you, some shadowed voice in me whispered.

He died because he deserved it.

CHAPTER SEVENTEEN

Chris didn't push the subject, probably because I pushed a mug of hot chocolate into his hand before he had the chance. He didn't say anything while I walked away, just followed me up the stairs, past the painting of a giant orchid, and into a little back alcove where Ethan and I set up shop when we weren't doing art or out fishing.

The room back here was often unused, just a couple of loveseats beside the window and a bookshelf containing the works of a few hundred poets I'd never heard of and would probably never read. That said, I had made a dent in the first shelf—poetry was a fantastic way to distract myself from my real homework. Especially when it was borderline erotic.

Another perk of Islington: no stupid committees banning books. Here, they knew that knowledge really was power, and that we were all mature enough to read about the things we'd already been thinking since puberty.

I pulled out a collection of Anne Sexton poems and flopped

down on one of the chairs, setting my mug on the coffee table between them. Chris sat across from me as I opened the book and pretended to read.

"You're not going to tell me what happened, are you?" he said after a while. I looked up from my book.

"I don't tell anyone what happened," I said.

"Not even Ethan?"

"Especially not Ethan."

He took a sip from his hot chocolate, his eyes dipping to his mug for just a moment. I took that second to breathe and compose myself.

"Why not?" he asked.

"Because I just don't like talking about my past, okay? It's not fun."

"But it's still bothering you," he said. "And you didn't answer the question."

"Ethan wouldn't look at me the same, that's why. And neither would you."

"I told you about my sister," he said.

"That's not how this works. This isn't a *you tell me your secrets, I'll tell you mine* equal exchange." Shit, that came out harsher than I meant. But he was circling around one of my biggest buttons, and I didn't know what I'd do if or when he hit it. I took a deep breath, inhaling the cocoa fumes and wishing they'd calm me down. I should have gone for chamomile tea. "Sorry," I said. "I don't mean to be a bitch. I really do feel bad about your sister."

"No, no, don't do that," he said. He leaned forward, holding his cup in both hands. "This isn't about me." His voice took on that soft tone, the one guys get when they're trying to be comforting. Trouble was, he pulled it off perfectly.

I leaned back farther in the chair and angled myself to look out the window. A crow watched us from the power line out front. It flapped its wings. My walls crept up higher. *Who are you protecting?* I wanted to scream. *Who are you trying to warn?*

"I don't even know why we're having this conversation. I barely know you."

"Maybe because you know you can trust me."

"It's not me I'm worried about."

He sighed.

"I'm not trying to pry. I'm just trying to figure out how to keep you from hurting."

I glanced out the window. The crow perching there ruffled its feathers.

"It's not your place to protect me," I said. "I'm sorry, Chris. I just can't do this right now."

And I was sorry. I really, really was. I hadn't been lying in the kitchen—he was the one straight guy I'd been around who didn't make my skin crawl. He was genuine and cute and talented and he didn't push when he wasn't supposed to. And all of that made it so much worse. He and Jane and Mandy and now the fucking crows; it was too much.

I just wanted a normal senior year. I wanted to graduate and go to college with my best friend and pretend the other shit didn't exist. No occult whisperings, no murders, and no crows.

"It's also not your place to protect me," he said after a while. I glanced back at him. I'd forgotten I'd even said anything.

I didn't retort though. I knew from the set of his eyes that we'd just go around in circles if I opened my mouth again. Instead, I turned back to the book in my hands and tried to lose myself in poetry.

It worked, for the most part. Chris started reading his own book and we sat there in silence. Not that I could focus on poems. My brain was spinning at a sickening pace and the entire time I was keenly aware of just how far away Chris was from me. His presence was like static, impossible to see and impossible to ignore.

Maybe he wasn't like Brad. Maybe he never would lift a finger to try to hurt me. Maybe he wouldn't push me to do something I didn't want. Hell, maybe we could date and everything would be fine, just like the books and movies I once thought I could live. The fact was, it didn't matter. I was tainted goods. And not because of what Brad had done to me.

I was damned for what I'd done to him in return.

We stayed in that little alcove for a few more hours, both of us reading poetry in silence, occasionally sharing our favorite lines. The heaviness between us dissipated as the snow outside accumulated. It wasn't that I was falling for him or warming up to his presence; I was just too tired to keep my walls up. Chris didn't try to force me to talk. For that, I was grateful. When I stopped freaking out about it, he was actually pretty easy to be around. Which, I suppose, was the problem in the first place.

Somehow we both missed the fact that lunch had come and gone. After a while my stomach's rumblings were too loud to ignore any longer.

"Hungry?" he asked.

"Pretty certain my stomach is eating itself," I said with a small grin. "Ready to brave the cold?"

"Sure thing," he said. He pushed himself to standing and held out a hand to help me up. I took it. Something hit the window, causing both of us to jump. It sounded like a snowball, but I caught a glimpse of black feathers. I dropped his hand immediately.

I'm not falling for him, I muttered to Munin. *You can lay off on the warnings.*

I turned my attention back to the room, back to a moment free of ravens.

"You're sure about this," I said. "About tonight?"

"What about it?"

"You know exactly what." Even though we were alone, I wasn't about to say anything aloud about Jane or sneaking around.

"I'm sure," he said. "She was my friend. I want to know what happened. And I think Elisa was right—there's something the school isn't telling us. I think we deserve to know the truth."

The truth. Such a difficult premise. If he ever found out about me, would he think I'd lied about my past? Or would he see that my greatest truth was in trying to protect him?

"Okay then," I said. I forced myself back into witty banter

mode; it was a coping mechanism that kept me from going under. "Just remember it was your choice when the FBI takes you in for questioning."

He laughed. "Trust me, the FBI is nothing compared to my parents."

We stepped into the Dark Note and Chris ordered a round of cheese-stuffed breadsticks, two vanilla frozen yogurt shakes, and a veggie burger with fries.

"Is that all for you?" I asked as Ike rang up the total.

"Nope. We're sharing this. I expect a total *Lady and the Tramp* moment when we eat one of those breadsticks."

I couldn't help it; all the stress of the last few days and the last few hours in particular just . . . cracked. I burst out laughing and couldn't stop myself until I started snorting, and had to cover my mouth with my hand.

"Wow, I didn't realize I was that funny," Chris said.

"You're not," I said. "And thanks."

He handed me a milkshake and picked up the tray of deliciously greasy food.

"You're welcome. And also, ouch."

I nudged him with my shoulder as we walked over to a little table by the window. Outside, a couple of underclassmen—and a few seniors—were knee deep in a snowball fight.

"It's weird," I said, watching the kids duck and throw and generally reinforce the idea that art kids aren't good at sports.

"What? Their technique? Because you're one hundred percent correct."

"No, this." I gestured to the caf and the store with its couple of students looking at books and hoodies and the kids outside playing war. "It's like there's this gut-deep human need to gloss things over and move on."

"I don't think it's glossing things over," he said. "I think it's honoring the dead. I mean, what better way to celebrate the life they lived than live a life yourself?"

I glanced at him.

"'What have you done with the garden that was entrusted to you?'" he asked.

"What?"

"Antonio Machado," he said. He winked. "What, you think you're the only one who reads poetry?"

I grinned, half tempted to ask him to recite the rest of it, when the door opened and Ethan and Oliver walked in.

"*There* you are!" Ethan called out, bounding over. "See, Oliver? I told you my stomach always knows best."

"You just wanted cheese sticks," Oliver muttered, only a few steps behind his boy.

They were both bedecked in full winter apparel: puffy snowpants and coats, beanies, scarves, and—

"Are you wearing matching mittens?" I asked.

Ethan just grinned and held up his hands. Yup. Big purple mittens.

"You two are adorable," Chris said, shaking his head. "That's the problem with gay couples: We straighties just don't stand a chance in terms of matching adorableness."

"Truth," I said, gesticulating the point with a breadstick. "I mean, have you seen Neil Patrick Harris and his family? Their Halloween costumes put us all to shame."

Ethan snagged a few fries while I was talking.

"You better pay for those," I said.

"I'm sure Chris takes credit."

"What are you two lovebirds up to, anyway?" Oliver asked.

Oliver sat down and Ethan went for another fry. I slapped his hand and he gave me an exaggerated pout. I just stuck out my tongue and then glared at Oliver—I hadn't missed that "lovebirds" slip.

"Just chilling," Chris said. "Somewhat literally."

"I know, right?" Oliver said. "It's amazing out there."

"Finally a man who appreciates good weather," Chris said. "You deserve a fry."

"Oh sure," Ethan said. "Playing favorites now are we?"

"Yup," Chris replied. "And your boyfriend's winning." He tossed a fry at Ethan, who chuckled and threw one back. They were going to get us banned for life.

I wandered back to my room alone, leaving the boys to chat. Elisa wasn't in, which I felt bad for being a little relieved about. She would have asked me about Chris, no question, and *that* wasn't a conversation I looked forward to, mainly because I knew she wouldn't let me live it down.

It was only when taking off my coat and feeling a familiar rustle in my pocket that I remembered the note Jonathan had left for me. *Shit.* Not that I'd really intended on going to the tutorial, but I felt guilty for forgetting. It was clear it was important to

Jonathan, and I really did appreciate him as a teacher. But I just couldn't handle anything else right now. My plate overfloweth.

Besides, I was trying to stay *away* from talk of gods and the supernatural. A study group devoted to just that would be my downfall. So I grabbed a book and started my reading for American Civ. Spending the day with Chris had been a nice diversion, but it didn't actually accomplish any of the work I'd set out to do. Not that I could really focus; all I could think about was the sketchbook crammed under my bed and the sketch of Jane, and whether or not the art studio would confirm my growing fears.

When it was five, I put on my coat and left for what was easily the most stilted dinner I'd had at Islington. My stomach turned with the thought of what we were about to do and how difficult it was to act normal with Elisa at the table. I tried to focus on making idle chatter about the upcoming production of *Marat/Sade*. It didn't work—the play was filled with sex and death and revolution, which really didn't take my mind off things.

At five fifteen Ethan and Oliver excused themselves. At five twenty, Chris left to "get some work done." Which left Elisa and me alone for a few minutes while I waited for enough time to pass before I could leave without being suspicious.

"He's really cute," Elisa said. I nearly choked on my fry.

"Who?" I asked, though of course I knew who she was talking about. It's not like Islington had gotten any fresh meat in the last twenty-four hours.

"Chris," she said. "I can tell he likes you."

"Oh yeah? What gives you that opinion?" Not that there was

any doubt in my mind that he was crushing. I was just trying to play it cool.

"The way he looks at you. There's chemistry between you." There wasn't a hint of her usual joking demeanor, and all color had left her—she was in all black, and the somber clothes reflected in her voice. The way she spoke . . . it didn't sound like she was excited—it sounded like she was delivering another eulogy.

"What, are you psychic now?"

She shrugged and poked at her Caesar salad, not looking at me.

"It's pretty obvious. You guys start leaning toward each other when no one's watching." She tapped the side of her head. "But Elisa is *always* watching. Elisa always knows."

I shook my head and laughed, grateful for that one small crack in her dreary facade. I knew it was an act, but hey, that's what she was good at. That's what we *both* were good at.

"Wow, okay, I'm going to go talk to Maria about switching roommates now. Apparently mine just turned into a creeper."

She giggled slightly and took a bite of salad.

"He *is* cute," I admitted. That was the only admission she'd get, too.

"Mmhmmm." I glanced at the clock and tried to think of an excuse to leave, but I felt bad leaving her there by herself.

And then, almost like clockwork, Cassie came over. She sat down with a mug of hot chocolate and a cookie and proceeded to cry on Elisa's shoulder. I excused myself a few seconds later.

Islington had a lot of secrets. That's what happens when you put four hundred teenagers in a small area with no real escape. It wasn't just the students, though—the very grounds were steeped in their own histories. Cabins in the woods with unlocked doors where the potheads would go and smoke, practice rooms that were definitely used for more than practicing . . . come to think of it, most of Islington's secrets had to do with getting wasted or getting laid, or, if we're being honest, both at the same time. The campus was our prison, but it was also our secret benefactor: Ask nicely, and you might find your way around some of the administration's more stifling rules.

It was little surprise, then, when—halfway through spring term last year—Ethan pulled me into a closet in the ceramics studio to show me a ladder leading up to the roof. We'd spent many late nights out there, bundled in thick coats and watching the stars turn. We'd even seen the aurora once, and in that moment I figured that if heaven existed, that's what it looked like.

Chris and Ethan were already there when I arrived. With everyone at dinner, the studio was empty: Not a single throwing wheel was taken, and the silent air was chilled and smelled of clay. I tried to push down the idea of Mandy's ghost lingering in the corners, working eternally on the project she never got to truly debut. It didn't work.

"About time," Ethan said, giving the splattered clock on the wall a knowing look. Everything in this room was coated with clay, some of it probably from the early days of Islington.

"I'm two minutes late," I said. "Elisa was making small talk."

"Whatever, boss," Ethan replied. Chris just chuckled to himself, watching us with amusement.

"Shut up," I told him, and pushed past them toward the back room.

The closet stored all the old equipment and clay: Potter's wheels were stacked together beside rain barrels filled with water and hidden clay. A single bare bulb hung from the ceiling, but I didn't bother clicking it on. Chris closed the door behind us and I flicked on my tiny keychain flashlight, a must-have when living in the woods.

There was a metal ladder in the far wall, hiding behind a few cardboard boxes. Ethan moved toward it and shuffled the boxes aside, trying to be quiet but ultimately failing.

"You sound like a drunk rat," I muttered. I kept an ear near the door, straining to hear if anyone was coming in to finish work.

Ethan just grumbled something under his breath. Then, after another shuffle, said, "Got it."

"Ladies first," I said, gesturing to the now-clear ladder. Ethan rolled his eyes and began climbing. He pushed open the small door at the top and climbed the rest of the way out. Then he leaned over and whispered "clear," before disappearing again.

I looked at Chris.

"He's taking this *Mission Impossible* thing way too seriously," I whispered. "Of course it's clear. It's the fucking roof."

Chris chuckled, which made me feel warm; I shoved the feeling aside and gestured him toward the ladder.

"After you," I said.

He winked.

"Enjoy the view," he replied. I smacked him on the shoulder. But that didn't mean I didn't, in fact, enjoy the view when he climbed. His ass looked quite nice in those jeans. From an artistic perspective, of course. He had good musculature.

Before I could start feeling like a perv, I grabbed the first rung and climbed up after him, making sure I didn't look up until he was on the roof.

The view of the sky from up here was gorgeous, but it didn't really give any perspective on the campus; the art building was only two stories tall, and the surrounding pines and dorms were much higher. The flat roof was relatively cleared of snow, thanks to the heating running through it that kept everything from accumulating.

Ethan and Chris were crouched low. There wasn't much out here in terms of light pollution, and night was already closing in thick, but the last thing we needed was for security to notice shadows moving about on the rooftop.

"Tell me why we're here again?" Ethan asked.

I hesitated. They were risking their educations to be up here with me, but I couldn't tell them the full truth. If either of them knew about the drawing or the dream, they'd call me insane and cart me off to the school counselor.

"I just want to see it," I said. "I want to know what happened."

"The body will already be gone," Chris said. He caught himself and swallowed hard. "Sorry. I mean Jane. She won't be there."

"I know," I said. "But I still want to see. If there's a reason they're locking it up, I want to know."

"This really is like Scooby Doo," Ethan muttered.

"Can it, Scooby," I said. Then I shuffled along the roof, tracing the hallways below in my mind until I reached the painting studio, Ethan muttering the entire time that he was clearly Shaggy in this equation.

Light streamed from the skylight, and I gave a quick thanks to whatever gods were listening that someone had left the lights on—I hadn't even considered that before. Ethan and Chris were right behind me, silent as ghosts, save for the occasional kick of pebbles across the slabs.

I took a deep breath, then crouched only a few feet away from the edge of the skylight. For some reason, standing there, waiting to look at a scene I feared I'd already seen in my journal, I felt naked. Exposed. Like the whole cosmos was breathing down my neck, waiting for me to discover some dark secret. I tried to shake it off as nerves but couldn't lose the feeling. What if there was blood, or if Jane *was* still in there for some reason, staring right up at me? This was the moment that would tell me if my fears were confirmed, or if this was all some big delusion. Was I ready for that truth?

Ethan put his hand on my shoulder. I nearly jumped out of my skin.

"You ready for this?" he asked. He didn't ask if I wanted to leave, though I knew he was thinking it.

"Yeah," I said. I'd have to face this some time. Class would go on. In a few days, I'd be back in that studio, painting and pretending a body hadn't rested at the foot of my easel. The thought made my skin crawl.

I moved to the edge of the window and looked down.

A thick ring of black paint encircled the space within

the easels. It stared up at me like an eye, like a portal to Hell itself, the void within blank and white and crawling with memory. No body. Of course there was no body. But there were notecards on the ground at strategic locations, no doubt pointing out evidence of some sort. Seeing it brought a sick feeling to my chest, a tightening of revulsion like the cogs of some terrible torture device. My vision tilted to the side and I stumbled back.

"Whoa," Chris said, his arms catching me before I could fall on my ass. "Careful there."

I glanced back at him, my heart thudding a thousand times a minute.

"Thanks," I said. I pushed myself out of his arms. "Vertigo." Which was a lie. I wasn't scared of heights. I was just fucking terrified. I took a slow breath and went back to the skylight.

"Do you think she moved it?" Ethan muttered. "The still life. Do you think she moved it before she died?"

"Must have," Chris answered. "Nothing else has been touched."

For a while we just crouched there, staring down at where our classmate and friend had lost her life not a day before. My heart didn't slow down. The circle burned into my mind, along with the words scrawled along the top.

The Tree Will Burn

It was one thing to worry that you'd had a premonition about something. It was another entirely to realize that premonition had been correct. My pulse was heavy and fast in my veins, my breath a beast I couldn't control. I was linked to these deaths after all. And that circle . . .

Maybe I hadn't run far enough away. The ghosts of my past were still here. And they weren't just haunting me—they were striking out.

"It wasn't her," I said after a moment.

"What do you mean?" Chris asked. Ethan made a noise in his throat, like he was agreeing with me but wasn't certain why.

I couldn't take my eyes off the black circle.

"Look at the paint," I said. "The circle is hers—the flourishes at the edges are exactly like she'd do. But that's not her handwriting." *I've seen those words before, hidden in the pages of my notebook.* But this wasn't my doing, just as it wasn't my handwriting.

"She was going to kill herself, Kaira. I don't think she was worried about perfect cursive."

"No, Elisa was right. She didn't kill herself."

"So who killed her?" Ethan asked.

Chris sat back. I was still transfixed by the circle and the words above it. I could see the ghost of Jane, almost, splayed out against the white, her hair a fan around her head and her eyes open in confusion.

Who killed you? I whispered inside.

She didn't answer, of course, but the sudden gust of wind sent chills down my spine.

"I don't know," I finally replied. "But there's no blood. It doesn't look like there was a struggle. But there's no way she killed herself."

"That doesn't sound possible," Chris said. "If she didn't kill herself and it wasn't a murder, why would she draw a circle and just drop down dead inside it? And who would write that and then not report the body?"

I didn't say anything. Helen was the one who found her, but she was innocent. Helen wouldn't hurt a fly.

Someone or some*thing* else had been in that room. But whether they'd forced Jane to draw the circle or done it themselves, I had no idea. All I knew was it wasn't a suicide. And it wasn't a simple murder. This was something beyond mortal doing. I knew this. I'd seen it before.

Only this time, I wasn't the one who'd accidentally called down the gods.

CHAPTER EIGHTEEN

We parted ways after coming down from the roof. The ceramics studio was empty and the whole of the arts building felt like a tomb. I think we were all reeling from the weight of our discovery; we needed to process. And we artsy types often processed best on our own.

Ethan left us outside the building to go wait for Oliver's practice to finish, and Chris walked me back to my dorm before giving me an awkward hug and returning to his. There was something so distanced about that parting, yet also heavy with closeness. We'd shared something big, and that both bound the three of us together and forced walls between the spaces. I knew, as I watched Chris walk down the road to Rembrandt, that things between us would never be the same again. And seeing as things with Chris had only just begun, I had no clue what that would spell for the rest of our . . . friendship.

But I knew one thing: These suicides weren't natural.

They weren't human. And I knew precisely who to talk to to figure it out. It was time to talk to Munin.

"How was dinner?" Maria asked from behind the desk.

I had to intentionally keep myself from getting defensive or wondering if she somehow knew what I'd been up to.

"Pretty good," I said. "Cookies for dessert."

"As always," she said. Then another girl came in from one of the halls and asked something about the Internet, so I took the opportunity to bail.

I wandered up to my room where Elisa was hard at work on calculus and, feeling guilty for not actually getting any work done, pulled out my own academic homework. It was the last thing I wanted to do, but getting wrapped up in essays meant I didn't have room to think about Jane or the circle or the strange correlation to Brad's death. Or what I was going to do about all of it.

I knew the risk. I knew what toying with the gods would do.

But if someone was meddling in things they shouldn't, I needed to figure out how to stop them. Before they made a few deaths look like mercy.

Elisa left around nine to go sleep over with Cassie. She kissed me on top of the head when she went and handed me the last cookie from our old package.

"For luck," she said with a grin, then walked out, already in her panda pajamas.

I did work for a little while longer. A part of me considered calling Ethan, but I figured he'd be busy with Oliver. Then I considered calling Chris, which was stupid because I barely knew the guy. Still, the fact that I even considered it made me feel strange. I knew I couldn't fall for him, not without spelling disaster. But a part of me—the part of me that remembered how his hand felt brushing mine, or how his eyes looked past all my walls—wanted to. It wanted to very, very badly.

I pulled out my notebook and a pencil that wasn't charcoal and left it on the shelf. Just in case my dreaming mind decided to divulge any more information. My brain was a cesspool as I lay there in the dark, staring at the shadows stretching along the walls. Jane and Mandy were both dead, and there was no way any of this was a coincidence. But how it was related to me . . .

The gods require blood.

The thought flickered through my mind, but for the life of me, I couldn't remember where I'd heard it.

Brad deserved it and you know it, hissed my inner voice. *He raped you. He would have done it again, too. Maybe to you, maybe to someone else.*

"No one deserves to die," I whispered to the darkness. Outside the window, a raven fluttered past.

But in your eyes, in that moment, he did. Munin's voice rang in my head like a judge's gavel. I couldn't tell if he was mocking or praising me for it.

I squeezed my eyes shut to block out the bird, but the darkness behind my eyelids was home to a far worse scene. Munin was the bastard bird of memory; his magic was far more cruel than mine. He wouldn't let me forget. Ever. And as the darkness behind my eyes closed in, the memory of the night I'd lost myself filtered back.

I was curled on the tiles of the bathroom, orange light filtering through the window. Steam clung to my naked, raw skin, made my lungs rasp. I'd spent a good thirty minutes under the scalding water, trying to get clean, trying to burn away Brad's fingertips and kisses, the scent and taste and stick of him.

It hadn't worked.

So I rocked there against the cool, slick tiles, trying to find numbness. Trying to find a place outside of myself, a place Brad couldn't violate. A place I was safe.

But I knew—I would never be safe. I would never be whole or clean again. Brad was just another reminder that I was unloved and unworthy. My friends didn't give a shit. My real parents had given me up when I was born. Even though I had a new family, they couldn't put me back together; I was broken from the start. No one could love something that was broken.

The reality was a bell that pushed the shadows away: Nothing in my life would change. I would always be Kaira the outcast, the girl who never fit in and never felt safe. Nothing I did would change it. I was damned, marked from the very start.

The only thing I could do was end it.

As I grabbed the hair shears from the vanity, I cursed Brad under my breath.

"Who's weak now?"

He told me I'd never be strong enough to get rid of him, that I'd always come crawling back, that this was all my fault. So I would make sure I never got the chance to screw up again.

I would never crawl back. And I would never let someone else hurt me.

I cut long and deep. I barely felt the blade pierce my wrist; steel slid through flesh, gentle almost, a stark contrast to how Brad had entered me. The only similarity was the tears. I couldn't stop crying. By the third slice my face was as wet as my forearms. But I didn't want to risk recovery. I didn't want to show that weakness, the hope that maybe someone would rescue me. No one would rescue me. I wasn't worth rescuing. Not after what he'd done.

My hands shook. I forced myself to stay standing. The room swam around the edges, shadows shifting, sinking, sucking me under.

"This is for you," I hissed. I stared into my eyes in the mirror as I said it, unsure if I was talking to Brad or myself. I had been weak. I'd let him do this to me. And now I'd never be weak again.

The scissors dropped from my useless fingers after the sixth cut. I braced myself against the sink, let the blood swirl down the drain. I didn't want Mom and Dad to have to clean up too much.

I kept staring at myself as the room inked out. Watched my eyes as they shuddered, as my whole body trembled. And when I couldn't stand any longer, when I felt my knees collapse and the floor rush up to hold me, I kept watching the mirror. Because the mirror wasn't showing my eyes anymore. A girl reflected back. A girl with purple eyes and raven's hair, her pale flesh glowing like a moon.

The room churned with darkness and feathers, shadows seeping into everything.

"Are you Death?" I asked. The girl was no longer in the mirror, but beside me. A large raven with white eyes perched on her shoulder. Who was larger, the raven or the girl?

"Yes," the girl replied. "But not yours."

I laughed then, because I was dying. Or I was dead. And this was ridiculous because death was supposed to be scary, not a naked teenage girl with a bird on her shoulder.

"Why?" she asked.

She didn't need to say more. I knew everything she meant in that word.

"Because he hurt me," I said. I still couldn't move. My blood pooled around me and my limbs were numb. Finally. Numbness felt like heaven. And still we talked there, on the tiles of the bathroom, as the world floated orange and red and black.

"This is your revenge?" she asked. "To give in?"

"What else could I do?"

She smiled.

"What would you do? If you could do anything? Be anything?"

"I'd kill him." The words fell from my lips like bullets. I knew, the moment I said it, that the deed was as good as done.

"As you will, so shall it be," she said. "His death will be in your honor."

"What's it matter?" I muttered. The room was spinning now. I tumbled down the whirlpool, a stupid grin slashed on my face. "I don't have any honor; I'm already dead."

"Your time has not yet come," came a voice, deep and

resonant like the movements of the shadows in the darkest depths of the ocean. It wasn't the girl. It was the bird. "Your death will serve a greater purpose than this. When the gods battle, you will be their sword and shield. You were born for greater things."

I laughed. This was hilarious. I was dying, and these hallucinations were every dream of grandeur I'd ever had. Too bad they were lies. The girl leaned down and placed one hand on each of my wrists, right over the cuts. Her hands weren't cool like porcelain. They burned.

"Blood for blood," she said, her smile widening. "An exchange. A gift."

"Remember what we have done for you," Munin said. I knew his name in a flash of insight. We all knew his name. We just never remembered. "When the time comes, when we come calling, remember this exchange. Remember this power."

Her hands were fire. They burned into my skin, rode my bones and veins like an electric current, searing my heart, my lungs, my brain. It was ecstasy.

"Who are you?" I asked her.

She didn't answer.

She clenched tighter. My wrists shattered. Vision turned white. Everything burned white and black and I was there, floating above Brad as he wandered drunkenly through the school's football field. A light coat of snow frosted the ground, everything beautiful and pastoral and perfect. He was humming to himself. I felt inside his heart; he was ecstatic. He felt like a god.

He stopped when he saw the girl. The naked girl with skin white as snow, a raven on her shoulder.

"What's . . . what's a fine piece of ass like you doing out here?" he slurred, grinning. He shambled forward, already excited. She was naked and alone and he was on fire. He'd fucked one girl already. This was his night.

She didn't say anything. Instead, she sauntered toward him, and wait, hadn't there been a bird on her shoulder earlier? He shook his head and fell to his knees. She didn't turn away from his drunkenness. She walked right up to him and knelt down, forced him to sitting. She straddled him, and it was then he realized she wasn't fully naked. She had gloves. Red gloves. And they were dripping.

Her lips found his in an instant and his heart swelled with heat. She smelled like cinder and dirt and she leaned into him, pressed him to the ground with the sheer weight of her lips and torso. He closed his eyes. He couldn't think beyond the friction of their skin, the steady beat of his blood.

He didn't see her reach above his head to trace a thick, bloody line into the snow, arching her arms out to the sides like wings, dragging my blood in a halo around them both. So much blood. How had I lost so much blood?

She bit his lower lip and tugged, causing him to gasp.

"In humility I offer this sacrifice," she whispered heavily into his ear. He squirmed, his eyes closed. Fuck, he wanted her. He wanted her more than anything he had ever wanted in his life. And he would have her. "May his soul nourish the great Yggdrasil. Through his suffering, may the Tree grow."

She slid her hands to his chest and arched her back, looked straight up into the sky. Straight at me.

"May his life pave the way for the Great Battle. May his sacrifice give you strength."

Then she plunged her bloodied hands into his chest. I felt her fingers claw around his heart, stop the blood in his veins. I felt the scream die short in his lungs as his soul was sucked down, down into the roots of the Underworld. His death was swift. Painless. But his death, I knew, was just the beginning of his punishment.

She stood smoothly. No wound in his chest. Her hands still bloody.

"For you, Kaira," she said. "This is all for you."

Then, from the shadows, the great raven Munin flew toward her, fast as an arrow. He pierced through her chest and pain pierced through mine as both she and the bird and the football field exploded in a torrent of feathers and smoke.

I opened my eyes and was back in my dorm room. The raven still sat on the windowsill. He didn't need to show me the rest; every day was a testament to the power Munin had wielded. I rubbed my wrists. The skin was smooth, never kissed by a blade. I'd woken the next morning in my bed—no blood in the bathroom, no cuts on my skin. A bad dream. Until Mom told me Brad had been found dead on the football field.

"Why is this happening?" I whispered to the bird. To Munin's messenger. I pushed myself to sitting. "Why is he back?"

The bird didn't answer, but it didn't fly off. It cocked its head toward the pillow.

And I knew then what it wanted. I reached under and grabbed the crystal Mom had sent me. It was hot to the touch, and the crow flapped its wings the moment it saw it.

I held it out to the bird.

"Is this what you want?" I asked. "You want me to dream again."

The raven cawed.

"Can I stop it?" I asked. "From happening again?" I thought of Ethan and Elisa and Oliver. And Chris. "Can I keep them safe?"

The bird shuffled. I pushed myself to standing and walked over to the window, my legs unsteady with the memory of memory, the weight of my past dragging my heels. I didn't want to reclaim anything. If I did, I'd have to admit that I was the one who killed Brad, that I'd wielded some great and terrible power against him.

And I'd have to admit to myself that I hadn't felt bad about it. Not once. Terrified, maybe, but only of myself. I was just as cold and ruthless as the violet-eyed girl, and that's why no one could love me. I wasn't safe.

I opened the window and held out my hand, the raven only inches from my skin, its black beak poised over my wrist. I waited for it to strike, to lash open my flesh and take back the blood that shouldn't still be pumping through my veins.

Instead, it looked up at me with those dead black eyes and waited for the question still lodged at the back of my throat, the one I'd been fearing since I woke up to see Jane's body drawn in my hand.

"Are you the one doing this?" I whispered. "Am I?"

Munin's reply was fast and sharp.

No.

Then the raven plucked the crystal from my hand and took off, disappearing into the darkness.

I watched it fly off, my blood as cold as the snow. This had nothing to do with me then—this wasn't my past or curse catching up. This wasn't some strange karmic retribution. But that meant it was someone else. Someone else was killing my friends. And if it wasn't the gods I knew, I couldn't imagine being able to stop it from happening again.

CHAPTER NINETEEN

Dreams tumble

Yggdrasil's roots stretch from floor to ceiling

break past desks and chairs

and there is Jonathan, drawing circles on the chalkboard

and there are the owls, sitting silent in their chairs, watching.

Waiting.

"You've come back," she says

and I turn to see the violet-eyed girl.

She stands among shadows and ravens,

her blade drips blood.

"I thought you had turned away."

"I need to know," I whisper.

"I need to know what is happening."

The girl presses a hand

to a gnarled root.

Ravens twine under treeflesh.

"The end times come," she whispers.

247

"Our battle with the Aesir comes,

but another . . .

another god stirs,

one who should not waken."

"But my friends. Why are they dying"

"Because the gods require blood.

And this god starves."

"But why them?"

She turns, and the raven on her shoulder tilts his head.

Munin watches us. Waiting. His beak drips crimson.

"They were chosen,

as you were chosen."

"Chosen for what?"

"To serve."

Shadows stretch and through the gaps

I see a battlefield, bodies prone and bleeding,

ravens harvesting.

"The owls are screaming," she says,

tilting her head to the sky.

Blood drips against her porcelain skin.

"And the ravens have gone silent."

"How do I stop it? How do I keep them safe?"

She steps closer and in her violet eyes I see the void.

"No one is safe. Not from what is yet to come."

Her blade kisses my skin,

the tip drags against my neck.

"This is not how things were meant to be.

We must stop
this new god.
Before he throws off the balance.
Before he kills again."
"You saved me once. How do I save my friends?"
She doesn't smile.
But I swear that Munin does.
"By giving yourself to me. Be my vessel.
Together, we will fight him.
When he is gone, our battle with the Aesir may begin."
Roots twist tighter around us,
bind my arms and legs.
"Vessel?"
Her blade presses deeper,
draws shadows from my neck.
"We gave you your life," Munin says.
"Now, it is time to give it back."

CHAPTER TWENTY

Class resumed as normal the next day. I nearly slept through breakfast without Elisa there to wake me up, but at least when I did drag myself from bed there weren't any new scribbles in the notebook. My dreams were like a bad aftertaste in my mouth; I remembered only snippets of them, but I didn't want to know the details, not really. All I knew was that the thought of them made my pulse race, made me feel like I was living on borrowed time. Like everyone was. Every time I blinked I saw that damn circle, the one surrounding Jane and Brad and most likely Mandy. Every time the darkness closed in, I saw the violet-eyed girl with her hands in Chris's chest, offering him to the World Tree. Swearing that this was my power.

But in this case, it wasn't my power. If this was the same thing as what happened to me, a life for a life, then other kids were dying and being saved and having scapegoats go in their place. Was that even something I could stop? Maybe no one was summoning the gods—maybe the gods were coming here of their own accord. Meddling.

Another god stirs. . . . Chills raced across my skin at the thought. It didn't make sense—none of it did—but did it even matter? Did the gods ever make sense to mortals? I had to save my friends. That was it. Understanding the gods' motivations could wait.

The boys were already at breakfast when I arrived, and there was an odd sort of tension between us when I sat down. Elisa and Oliver were deep in conversation about something in their shared French class, but Chris and Ethan just sat there, stirring coffee or picking at scrambled eggs and staring out the great picture windows at the frozen lake beyond. My stomach twisted. I wasn't an actor, but I knew I had to be cheerful, witty Kaira. It was the only way forward. But I really didn't think I had it in me today. Not with my carefully constructed walls between myth and mortality dissolving.

"How goes?" I asked, setting my tray down beside Ethan. He glanced over at me and shrugged.

Chris, at least, was a little more talkative.

"Sleepy," he said. His jaw cracked with a yawn. "Bad dreams."

"Me too," Elisa replied. "Though maybe it was from sleeping on the floor."

"I have a funny feeling everyone's having bad dreams," I said.

"Yeah," Ethan said. He gave me a look that clearly said *especially after what we saw*. I knew he and I needed to talk. The painting studio discovery was probably more of a shock for him and Chris than it was for me, for different reasons. But he'd be more inclined to think there was a killer on the loose, rather than something mystical. I almost laughed; the fact that I was more comfortable with this being supernatural in nature rather than a psychopath was crazy.

"We should do something tonight," Chris said. "You know, movie night or something."

"We could rent a movie from the library," Elisa ventured.

"Or go off campus," Ethan said. His expression lit up—he was a Sagittarius, and I knew he was always eager to get on the road, even for small trips. "There's a really great comedy playing at the cinema."

Of course he was the type of boy to say "cinema" rather than "movie theatre."

I had no doubt the next few nights would be spent doing everything we could to get off campus. Something about Islington had changed—it no longer felt like a bastion of safety as it had before. It was starting to feel like a tomb.

We spent a few minutes talking about movies and homework and upcoming concerts. I couldn't focus on the conversation. It took everything I had to move my fork to my mouth and swallow. There was a voice screaming in the back of my mind, a goddess ranting about power and duty. The crows that kept sweeping past the windows didn't help. With every black shadow that crossed my gaze, her voice grew stronger.

"You okay?"

I shook my head and forced my attention back. Back to the cafeteria, back to my friends, and away from the oil of feathers and pressure of power. Chris looked at me with serious eyes; something about that expression helped root me down and force the voices away. When I was focused on him, the rest of the crazy world went silent.

I realized he'd asked me a question.

"Sorry," I said, glancing down to my plate. "Just a bit distracted."

He placed a hand over mine and squeezed my fingers. I didn't flinch like I usually would have. I was just too damn tired to care.

"I understand," he said. And it sounded like he actually might. That was dangerous. "Do you need to talk?"

I shrugged. "I'm okay. Just a lot on my mind."

"That's a lot of *justs*," he replied. "I gotta head to class, but let me know if you need anything, okay? I'm here for you."

I looked in his eyes again and felt the weight of his words. *I'm here for you.* I didn't want to admit how many years I'd yearned for someone to tell me that and mean it. Ethan and my mom, sure . . . but this was different. This made my heart ache with the promise of something I couldn't let myself desire. Then Brad's face flashed behind my eyes—him in the bathroom and him dead on the field—and I drew my hand back to my lap.

"Thanks," I said. "I'll be fine."

"Of course," he replied. I could tell he was hurt by my withdrawal. It was better that way, though. There wasn't a point in falling for me. You couldn't date someone with a bloody past and no future.

I watched him walk away. Apparently I wasn't the only one.

"He's really sweet," Elisa said. I turned around and realized she and I were the only ones at the table. Had Ethan and Oliver said good-bye without my noticing?

"He is," I replied.

"I thought you said you weren't dating."

"I'm not . . ." I couldn't finish the sentence. Everything I wanted to say felt like a lie.

She studied me for a moment. We'd spent so much of our friendship being smart-asses. There wasn't room for that anymore. Everyone's life had been colored by the events of the last few weeks. In this new hue, none of us could act the same.

"I think you should do it," she said. "Fall hard and fast and don't think twice about getting hurt. Life's short, Kaira. Life's way too short. You gotta take the good when you can and that boy is about as good as it gets. I say this as your friend: If anyone's worth the hassle of falling in love, it's Chris."

I opened my mouth, but nothing came out. A week ago I would have told her it was stupid. I would have gotten pissed and said I couldn't date and how dare she tell me I should fall for a guy because I was independent and didn't need something as stupid as love. But now her words struck chords in me that drowned out the resentment.

Despite the fact that we had ten minutes before class, I didn't want to move. I didn't want this moment to end—it felt important, like this was the first breath after a long silence. Chris vanished through the door, but I could still sense him, still feel his hand over mine. And in spite of everything, he was the one thing in my world that felt right. For some insane, impossible reason, the wrongness of wanting to date Chris paled in comparison to the wrongness of everything else.

"Go for it," she whispered. "Before he's gone."

She sniffed as tears filled her eyes. I knew she saw Jane every time she blinked. I stood and walked over to wrap her in a hug, and she cried in my arms for a few minutes. Then, with the sniff and shiver of an actress putting on a mask, she collected her things and led us out of the cafeteria toward Jonathan's class.

I spent all of Folklore thinking of Jane. It was impossible to think of anything else with Jonathan talking about the Vikings invoking their gods for battle or Egyptians calling down their deities for fertile harvests. So much of humanity's past involved conspiring with the gods. When had we lost that thread?

I barely even registered when class ended.

"Doing okay, Kaira?" Jonathan asked. He stepped over to my desk while the rest of the class filtered out.

"Yeah," I replied.

"You sure? You seemed pretty out of it all of class." He gave me a grin. "I'm not that boring, am I?"

I tried to laugh and failed, fumbling with my notebook in the process. It fell in a flurry of papers. He reached down and picked it up for me, his eyebrows furrowing.

Shit.

It was open to the page I'd scribbled in my dreams.

"What's this?" he asked.

I snatched it from his hand and flipped it closed.

"Brain dump," I said.

"That looked like Jane," he replied. "Are you *sure* you're okay?"

I wondered then if he had seen the crime scene as well.

Helen would have called him, would have wanted support. If he drew any correlation between my sketch and the scene though, he didn't admit it.

"Fine. I mean, as good as I can be."

He nodded, not breaking his gaze.

"I was kind of disappointed you weren't at the tutorial yesterday," he finally said.

"Sorry," I said, but I wasn't really. I had too much on my plate to feel guilt over missing a study hall.

"It's okay," he said. "I understand you're busy. But I do wish you'd drop by." He looked to the notebook in my hand. "I think it would be good for you. What we're studying. The support of your peers. I think you might find it helpful in navigating life right now."

I shrugged. The room felt heavy and close, way too close, and I wanted to get out of there immediately.

"Maybe next week," I said.

"Actually, we're having another meeting tonight. Yesterday wasn't a good day for anyone, so I figured I'd reschedule. We'll be meeting after dinner."

"I . . ."

"I hope to see you there," he said. He gave me a knowing look. "I've been talking to a few members of the arts faculty, and there's been some dissent over your thesis. I thought it might be smart to prepare you for their critique tomorrow."

Tomorrow. I closed my eyes and tried to keep myself from freaking out. My critique was tomorrow. How the *hell* had I forgotten that?

If the professors already hated it, tomorrow was going to be a bitch. Why did I even care? With everything else going on, I might not even *make* it to the critique.

"Yeah, sure. I'll try to be there."

"I'd like you to do a little better than *try*, Kaira. I know there's a lot going on, but this is the culmination of your career here. I want to make sure you're able to defend yourself properly tomorrow."

"Thanks," I said, because there didn't seem to be much else to say. "Anyway, I guess I'll see you later on tonight."

"Looking forward to it," he said. I turned to leave. "And Kaira?"

His words froze me. I knew that tone—it was like every cliffhanger in every drama ever. He was about to drop a bomb.

"Yes?"

"Be careful who you show that to. They're still not sure what happened to Jane, and I'd hate for you to get involved in this mess."

I swallowed hard and nodded.

It wasn't until I was halfway down the hall that I realized what he'd been implying. He must have seen inside the studio. He knew I'd drawn her exactly as she'd been found. And I had a terrible feeling he knew what it entailed.

"Kaira!"

Chris's voice cut across the commons. I paused outside my dorm and turned to see him jogging toward me. I'd spent the last hour and a half in the silversmithing studio for class, and my stomach was grumbling.

"What's up?" I asked, walking toward him to close the space between us. I was acutely aware of the way he smiled when he neared, but the smile slipped after a second.

"Not much." Clearly a lie. "Are you busy?"

"Not really." Another lie, because if I didn't eat soon I would become hangry, and that was not a place I wanted to be today.

"Cool. Wanna walk?"

"Sure."

Without another word, he took my hand in his and started leading me toward the Writers' House. The fact that I didn't let go surprised me more than it should have.

After a few seconds of silence, he chuckled.

"What's so funny?" I asked.

He squeezed my hand. "This. You're not immediately telling me to back off."

I sighed dramatically. "What can I say? You've tired me out. I've given in to your animal appeal."

"Really?"

"Something like that," I admitted. "What's up anyway?"

He bit his lip and tore his gaze away, looking out to the forest. Even though it was noon, the sky was heavy and gray, making dark shadows in the undergrowth.

"I wanted to talk . . . about last night."

Of course. My stomach plunged to my feet.

"What about it?"

He sighed, squeezed my hand again. *Stop enjoying that sensation.*

"It . . . it looked familiar."

258

He was too busy staring at the trees to notice the terrified look I shot at him. I had to carefully compose my face and voice before answering.

"What do you mean, 'looked familiar'?"

He shook his head like he was fighting off some inner monologue—a tick I knew all too well—and glanced at me.

"I mean, it's come up before. After my sister died." He sighed and tilted his head back to the clouds and stared up like he wanted to scream or wake from a nightmare. "I can't even believe I'm telling you this. You'll think I'm crazy."

"Doubtful."

"Promise?"

"Mostly."

He laughed without humor and looked everywhere but me. A clear sign this was killing him.

"After she died . . . I started having these nightmares. They were pretty much all the same, but I could never remember them entirely. The one thing I did remember was finding her in the sand, just after the tide. It was so. Fucking. Vivid. Her lying there with her hair in a halo and starfish and clams twined about her like constellations. It sounds beautiful when I say it like that but it was horrifying. Her face was so white, her lips so pale, staring up at the sky with pearls for eyes. And around her was this circle drawn in the sand, and no matter how many waves lapped against her, the circle stayed.

"The psychiatrists said it was just stress imagery. My subconscious' way of finding resolution or some bullshit like that. That's why I never told them about the rest."

"The rest?" I asked. I hadn't realized we'd stopped walking until then. He stood before me, still looking at the woods, both of my hands somehow now in his and the silence around us deeper than a tomb.

"I haven't told anyone. How could I tell anyone? But this is all so insane. . . ." He looked at me. Tears welled and froze at the corners of his eyes. "The week before we went to the beach I was playing in the front yard. Just kicking the ball around. The ball flew out into the street and I ran after it because I was young and stupid and didn't see the car. It didn't see me either."

He shuddered.

"I remember how it felt. When it hit me. It was like falling in a dream, that thud when you hit the bottom and then wake up. It struck me head-on. I felt the impact. And there was a shock, like I was hit with a lightning bolt, and then I was standing on the street like nothing had happened. The car didn't even stop. Like it never happened. But I know it did. I *felt* it." He pressed our hands to his heart. "I felt my chest explode from impact. And then I was fine."

A tear fell down his cheek. I half expected it to turn into a snowflake as it caught in the stubble on his chin.

"I thought I'd made it up. Daydreams or something. Nearly forgot about it after my sister died. Until the nightmares. Every time. Every single fucking time, right before I woke up, I heard a voice. *Your debt has nearly been paid* it said. And I knew she died because of me. My sister died because I was supposed to live. And now it's happening again."

CHAPTER TWENTY-ONE

We stared at each other for a moment, letting the weight of his statement sink in. When he broke his gaze, the moment snapped, shattering to the ground like ice.

"What the hell is going on?" he whispered.

"I don't know," I lied.

"Am I insane?"

"No." I let go of his hand and rested my palm on his shoulder. He stiffened under the touch, then nuzzled my hand with his chin. It sent sparks racing across my skin, but now was definitely not the time for romance. *Do I tell him? Do I tell him the truth about Brad?*

He sighed and looked at me. "I can't believe I'm telling you this. I barely know you and now you're going to think I'm crazy."

"I don't think you're crazy," I replied. "Actually . . . that actually makes you sound more sane."

"Impossible."

I didn't want to go there. There was no way in hell I wanted to tell him about Brad and what happened after. But as we stood there in the snow, I felt like my life was at a terrible crossroads. I'd been doing all I could to avoid the gods ever since they gave me life in exchange for Brad's. I thought I was an anomaly, some sort of freak. But here was Chris, standing before me looking naked and vulnerable, and I knew I couldn't pass this off. Rule number one: Never ignore an omen.

"Do you mind if we keep walking?" I asked. He nodded.

I don't know why I took his hand then. It felt fitting, a motion of solidarity rather than romance. There weren't any sparks when our palms touched, and if he was taken aback by my sudden advance he didn't show it. I think he felt it too, the importance of this. The strangeness. Whatever we were, we weren't just two stupid teenagers fighting off a crush.

Guess it was time to figure out what that "something else" was.

"Remember when I told you I couldn't date?" I asked. He nodded. "Well, I think it's time you heard the full story."

We made it down to the lake before stopping and staring out at the frozen expanse while I finished my story. I'd never told anyone about the suicide or the girl or Munin. Not even my mom. And yet the words came out easily around Chris. Not because I was exceptionally comfortable around him, but because, somehow, he'd experienced the same thing.

"What the hell is this debt?" he muttered when I finished.

"A life for a life," I replied. "We were spared, so someone had to go in our place."

"At least you got to choose yours."

My anger was harsh and instantaneous, a flare I'd been holding back for years.

"Don't you dare," I hissed. "I didn't want him to die. Not really. I was hurt and scared and stupid. Don't you ever, *ever* accuse me of that."

"I'm sorry," he said. "It's just . . ." But before he could put his foot in his mouth again, he shook his head and whispered. "Never mind. I'm sorry. But whatever's going on, we have to stop it." He laughed. "This sounds so insane, you know that, right? We're talking about gods here. Like, real-life mythical figures with magical powers meddling in human affairs. Killing people. It doesn't make sense."

"A few hundred years ago, it wouldn't sound so insane." I thought of Jonathan's lessons on how gods and man used to walk side by side. And remembered I still had to meet with him at the stupid tutorial. *How am I supposed to pretend everything's normal after this?*

"But this isn't a few hundred years ago. This is now. In an art school. And our friends are paying whatever debt is out there. We need to stop it."

I shuddered as, above us, the crows cawed out angrily.

"You don't stop the gods," I said gravely. "Neither of us asked to be saved. Neither of us asked for this. We aren't special. We're just lucky."

Again, I knew it was a partial lie. I was being saved for *something*. To fight. But I wasn't a fighter and neither was he.

"I don't like that logic," Chris said.

"I don't have any other logic to give," I said. "We're not heroes, Chris. We're kids. Whatever is going on is beyond us. We get involved, we get killed. It's that simple."

In the back of my mind, I knew this wasn't over. Not yet. There wasn't any settling in and waiting for it to pass. Dreams filtered back into my thoughts. *The end times come.* That's what the girl had said. This wasn't a series of deaths. This was the beginnings of a war. And if I gave over, if I became the violet-eyed girl's vessel, I'd be on the front line. The crows above cawed again, and a new fear struck through me: Would Chris even be fighting on the same side as me? The girl kept mentioning the Aesir, and if Chris . . . I shook my head. No. No. No matter what, I wasn't becoming embroiled in this—whatever war this was, it wasn't mine. And it wasn't his. This wasn't our fight.

Chris stared at me for a while. I looked away. I couldn't tell what sort of judgment he was passing. What I was suggesting was ludicrous. And yet . . .

"You're not running away screaming," I ventured, trying to make my voice light.

"Not yet," he said. He grinned. Then it slipped. "This is . . . this is all a lot to process. I mean, a few weeks ago all I could think of was graduating and maybe getting your attention. Now there's . . . all this. What do we do now?"

I shrugged.

"We stay the fuck out of it." I glanced to the crows. "Nothing good comes from messing with the gods. Nothing. This isn't a battle we can fight."

"So, what? We just hope no one else gets hurt?"

"I don't know if there's anything else we *can* do," I said. I hated myself for it. "These are gods, Chris. You can't fight a god.

And neither of us summoned them or whatever when we were saved. I think this might be out of our control."

"Bullshit," he whispered. "I know you don't mean that. You're not the type to just give in; it's not fair to anyone."

"Fair?" My voice was too loud, borderline hysterical, but I forced it back to submission. "*Fair?* What about this is *fair*, Chris? Our friends dying? You and I getting spared? I've spent every single day of my life thinking that I was alive not because I was special, but because I was willing to do something terrible to survive. How the hell is that fair?"

But he was right. We both knew he was right. I just hated that he was perceptive enough to notice.

"You know what I'm talking about," he said quietly. "What if Ethan was next? Or Oliver? Or Elisa. Hell, what if it was you or me? None of us are safe, Kaira, even if it is out of our control."

"We can't do this, Chris. We can't interfere; we have a debt. We're here because we're vessels. They keep mentioning a war and how we have to fight. But it's not us doing the fighting. We were spared because the gods need bodies to inhabit if they're going to battle each other. The moment we open up to them, the moment we let our guard down, bam. We're no longer Chris and Kaira. We're hosts. And I'm not ready to give up this life. Not just yet. And neither should you."

"But if this is happening to others . . ." he began.

"It means there are more gods on the playing field. I don't know what's going on, Chris, but they're preparing for a war. And I have a terrible feeling you and I aren't the only ones who are being prepped as cannon fodder."

CHAPTER TWENTY-TWO

I expected conversation to be stilted after that; I mean, it's not like talking about gods taking over our bodies and killing our friends was an everyday conversation. But the moment we left the woods and headed into the cafeteria, we slipped back into our old modes. We barely talked, but if we did, it was about classwork. Since we'd missed most of lunch, the cafeteria was largely empty, and the table we normally shared with Ethan and the rest was abandoned. We ate fast and pretty much in silence, and not one part of me gave a shit about the rumors I knew would be circulating after we'd spent this much time together. Let people think we were dating; it clearly didn't matter anymore.

And yet, every time I glanced at him I wondered if maybe those rumors wouldn't be unfounded. I mean, we'd definitely rocketed past the whole teen-angst-romance thing. This wasn't a crush. We were bound by something I couldn't place, something I didn't necessarily want to be a part of, and it didn't matter that he was cute or intense or sensitive. He had a secret similar to mine, and that meant we would always be in the other's orbit. For better or worse.

When we finally got up to leave, it felt like committing a crime. Like we shouldn't be parting ways—we needed to stick together. Which was stupid, because I was just heading to class and would be seeing him after . . .

Shit.

"I can't go to the movie tonight," I said as we left the cafeteria.

"What? Why not?"

"I have a tutorial." I couldn't have sounded less excited if I tried.

"Skip it," he said. "You're a senior."

"I can't." Which was true. And it had nothing to do with learning academics. Jonathan knew something about all of this, I was certain. If there was any way to figure out what was going on without actually losing myself in the process, it was through him. A part of me wanted to tell Chris about the sketch and Jonathan's reaction, but I didn't want him to get too hopeful. Not when lives were on the line. "I have to talk to Jonathan about my thesis tomorrow. Apparently some professors are upset over the subject matter."

Which I knew was a lie. I mean, maybe they *were* upset, but I knew it wasn't the real reason Jonathan insisted on me coming to meet with him. He wasn't the only one used to telling half-truths through lies.

"Sucks," Chris said. He looked to his feet, then to me. "What are we going to do now?"

It was a question he'd already asked a dozen times, but I knew he wasn't just talking about the deaths. He was asking about *us*.

"I don't really know," I said. "But we're in this together. We'll figure it out."

Maybe not the most convincing of statements, but it was the best I could do under pressure.

"Thank you," he said. "For, you know, not thinking I was crazy."

"I don't think I'd ever be in that position."

"Yeah, but. It feels good. To have a friend who knows."

I nodded. I hadn't really allowed myself to notice it, but he was right. Now that I'd told him everything, I felt a little freer. A little less alone. Things weren't any less crazy or confusing, but at least I wasn't navigating them on my own.

I wasn't certain how I was going to make it through the rest of the school year like this. I couldn't focus at all in American Civ—not that this was a huge departure from normalcy, in all honesty—and spent the entire hour drawing ravens and circles in my notebook. How was I supposed to focus when every movement, every second, felt like careening toward the end? Even the world outside seemed to mirror my thought process. The sky was prematurely dark, clouds roiling like sulfuric soup. And everywhere, the crows. They perched on gutters and trees and car hoods, all watching, all waiting.

They were my protectors. I knew that, in the far corners of my soul. They were my watch. So why were they all here en masse? It made my skin crawl.

After class, I headed straight toward the painting studio to get work done. Or, well, the studio we were using while the other got . . . cleaned. I made sure to go through a different entrance to the arts building—I had zero desire to see my Tarot cards up in the hall. They were my one foray into the mystical world, the one safe zone I had between mundane and magical. Now, even they seemed like too much. I didn't want to be reminded of the night everything had changed, the night Munin and the violet-eyed girl came in and fucked everything up for good.

The studio was smaller than most, down one of the side hallways in the sculpture wing. And it wasn't empty. Ethan sat at one of the stools, staring down a still life that was eerily similar to the one we'd begun. They must have picked up the table and moved it down here in one go, though the lighting was a little off from the original setup.

He had his headphones on and didn't look up when I entered. Not until I sat down beside him and began setting up my own paints.

"Hey," he said. His voice had that distant, tentative tone of one needing to talk about something, but being terrified of what the conversation would actually reveal.

"Hey," I replied. I looked over; he wore two long-sleeve shirts layered atop each other and jeans caked with paint and Celtic runes. There were dark shadows under his eyes, and the red knit hat over his scraggly hair told me he hadn't showered. He only wore that hat when he was feeling particularly gross.

"How are you?" he asked.

"I'm okay. You?"

He nodded like that was answer enough and glanced to the still life.

"I didn't sleep at all last night," he said.

"I could tell."

He closed his eyes and pressed a palm to his head, like he was trying to push out the dreams or memories or whatever was plaguing him. I put a hand on his shoulder. He actually flinched under the touch, then leaned into it.

"I kept dreaming about it. About her." A small shudder wracked through him.

"Yeah?"

"Yeah."

He peered through his fingers.

"I don't know if I can do this anymore," he whispered. His voice sounded so small.

"What do you mean?"

He closed his eyes again.

"This. Moving on. Pretending everything's okay when nothing's okay. Pretending I can sleep at night."

"What are you dreaming?"

"Don't really remember. I just know I wake up feeling like I'm suffocating. I'm lucky I haven't screamed myself awake. Feels like I could be, sometimes."

I sighed and leaned over to wrap him in a hug.

"It's stress," I whispered. "It'll go away soon."

"But it won't. Because they aren't coming back." He took a deep breath, his whole body shaking. "I keep thinking about what we saw. And I swear, every time I blink I see that damn circle. And I can just imagine her lying in there, stretched out like that DaVinci picture. It's horrible. It makes me feel so . . . I don't know. Wrong inside. Tainted."

"Like you saw something you weren't supposed to see?" I ventured.

He nodded. "It's just a fucking *circle*. But I keep seeing it and drawing it and I feel like . . . what if these weren't suicides? What if they were murders or something? And what if that's just the calling card? What if it means I'm next?"

My heart thudded to a violent stop.

What if he's next?

Suddenly, the boy in my arms was a very real, very fleeting thing. I couldn't save him. Not without killing myself. But if he *was* next, if I could save him . . .

"You're not next," I said. Was I trying to comfort him, or me? "There's nothing sinister going on and you know that. You're just stressed with your thesis and tired and this is all compounding. You're going to be okay."

"But what if I'm not?"

"Ethan," I said levelly, "you're going to be fine. I promise. You're going to graduate with flying colors and get into college with Oliver and me and we're going to grow old and get a mansion with separate wings and die in our rocking chairs, just like we planned."

He chuckled silently. "I don't remember planning any of that."

"I took liberties."

As always, comforting him was easier than comforting myself. Especially because I knew I was lying through my teeth.

"It's always before a thesis," he said. He leaned back from my hug and looked at me with reddened eyes. "The deaths. Always the night a thesis goes up. And mine goes up next week."

"You're not going to die."

"You don't know that."

"I do," I said. "You're not allowed to die. I won't let you."

He took a breath to compose himself and looked back to his painting.

"You make it sound like you have some sort of sway with the reaper there."

I looked out the window, to where more crows were gathering.

"Maybe I do," I muttered.

Ethan and the rest were going off campus to grab food before the movie, which meant I was left to my own devices after our time in the studio together. I'd finished most of the still life, but really, what did it matter anymore? Hell, I couldn't even be too worried about my thesis response tomorrow. It seemed like every moment that passed, my chances of making it through Islington grew smaller. I couldn't even say I was freaking out about it—it seemed inevitable, and I felt resigned. After all, I'd been living on borrowed time. At least this way, hopefully, I could make my life mean something.

I sat at dinner on my own, in a far corner of the cafeteria, vainly picking at my salad (Chinese night again, which pretty much meant everything was inedible) and staring out the window. The sky was already black as night, lit by a few lamps in the distance. It felt like the first night in ages where it wasn't snowing, yet the lights were constantly twinkling and shifting, thanks to the crows that darted in and out of the shadows. It made my appetite dwindle even more effectively than the scent of bad stir-fry and moist eggrolls.

What was weird was the dichotomy of it all. The cafeteria was warm and muggy and homey. It should have been welcoming. The occasional laughter and constant drone of conversation should have made me feel like I was part of something. I was an artist at Islington Arts Academy. I was on the road to self-discovery, to becoming a better artist. But as I sat there by the windows, watching the crows, I realized I was none of that. I wasn't a normal teenager. I wasn't even an abnormal teenage artist. I was something else entirely, and I couldn't fit in here if I tried.

It reminded me way too much of how I'd felt back at home, even before Brad entered my life—the days sitting in the lunchroom on my own, the nights doing homework in silence. My heart twisted like a rusted cog, shredding my lungs and making it hard to breathe. Maybe I hadn't escaped my past after all. Maybe I hadn't changed. Maybe I was still the loner girl who couldn't really fit in.

I shook my head and forced myself to standing. I was just tired. Stressed. And it had been a long, long time since I'd had a meal without Ethan or Oliver to keep me company.

Another twist in my chest. If Ethan was hurt next . . .

I quickly bused my tray and hurried out into the cold before the warmth could suffocate me.

Jonathan's tutorial was meeting after dinner, I knew that much. But I didn't head toward the academics concourse right away. I couldn't get the image of Ethan sprawled in a circle from my head. I turned instead and walked down toward the lake, following the snow-dusted, lamplit trail through the woods. No one was out here. The trees rose silent and white all around me, boughs heavy with snow and silent crows. Chills raced up and down my arms as I crept deeper and deeper into the woods, trying to keep to the path and feeling with every step like I was about to fall into a horror movie. One where the girl gets her eyes gouged out by crows and then haunts the woods for eternity.

I didn't stop walking until I neared the lake. A few evening fishermen were out there, their huts glowing like yurts in a snow-swept mountain pass, all of them completely oblivious to the darkness gathering around them. It should have felt like I wasn't alone, like there were still people out there living normal lives, people I could connect with or emulate. But here, on the shore, I *was* alone. Alone, save for the crows.

But they were the ones I was out here to find.

"Okay," I whispered, my breath clouding before me, "I want to talk."

In response, a single raven flew down from the branches behind me, landing in the snow five feet away. It peered up with blank onyx eyes. Not Munin, then. But I knew he could still hear me.

"I want you to keep Ethan safe," I said. "From whatever's happening. He seems to think he's going to die next and I won't let that happen."

The bird cocked its head, but that was it.

"This is crazy." I shook my head and looked around, positive there would be some kid out here watching and laughing. No one was out, however. Just me and the birds. "I don't even know why I'm out here."

What will you bargain with?

The voice came from nowhere, deep and resonant and vibrating against my bones. Munin. Suddenly, this stopped feeling like a stupid fantasy or delusion. This was real. And this was life and death.

"I'm not bargaining with you," I said. "You want me alive. I want Ethan alive. I think you can fill in the blanks."

It is not in my realm to save him, the raven said.

"You're a god," I hissed. "Or something close to it. You can keep him safe."

You can keep him safe. Not I.

"How? This doesn't have anything to do with me—I never summoned you; you came to me. I can't prevent you—"

You were different.

His words stopped my tirade in its tracks.

"What do you mean, I was different?"

You we came to by choice. These are not interventions. These are sacrifices.

My blood went cold as the bird stared up at me, motionless.

"Sacrifices? But who would do that? Why?"

To bring the end, Munin said.

Then he flew off. Behind me, the trees erupted in caws and spiraling birds.

I didn't stay by the shore. The moment the bird flew off, I jogged back up the slick path toward the academics concourse, crows swarming around me like angry bees from a hive. They cawed and circled and swept past me in a fury of shadow and talon, grazing my skin but never actually touching. Their screams were terrifying.

As was the complete silence that followed the moment I left the forest.

I paused on the path just outside the woods and looked back. No crows thrashing in the trees, no flurry of feathers. Just silent white pines and the empty shadows waiting within.

"What the fuck?" I whispered to no one.

Maybe I *was* going crazy. Maybe that would be for the best.

I headed straight to Jonathan's classroom. The silence was almost suffocating. Why wasn't anyone out here having snowball fights or singing show tunes? Why did tonight of all nights feel like I lived in a mausoleum?

My stomach was in knots when I knocked on the classroom door.

"Kaira," Jonathan said when he opened the door. He smiled.

"Hey, sorry I'm late. Got a bit distracted."

"It's fine. You're right on time. Come on in, we were just about to get started."

He held the door open for me and I stepped past him, taking in the room. My heart thudded in my ears, and if not for him standing behind me, I would have turned and left.

The desks were all pushed against the walls, and a few of my classmates—five in all—lounged against them. There was Tina, the silversmith girl who did all of the rings. And Kai, whose thesis completely blew the rest of his work out of the water.

And there, in the center of the room, was a black circle painted in ink.

"Excellent, friends," Jonathan said behind me, the door audibly locking shut. "Now we can begin."

CHAPTER TWENTY-THREE

"What the hell is this?" I asked.

Jonathan put a hand on my shoulder and guided me into the room. I was too shocked to put up a fight.

"This is our independent study," he said calmly.

"But what—"

"I told you, this is where we explore the more arcane aspects of what I teach in class. It's one thing to read about communing with the gods. It's quite another to take part in the ancient practice."

"It's you?" I asked. "You're the one killing people?"

Jonathan didn't speak, though. It was Tina who came forward. Tina, with her reddish-brown ringlets and smoky eye shadow and plethora of handmade jewelry.

"We're not killing anyone," she said. "Those deaths were just suicides."

And I knew, then, just from her voice, that she thought she was telling the truth. She hadn't seen the circle around Jane or

Mandy. She had no idea there was a correlation with the black ring in the center of the room and the bodies that were beginning to litter this campus.

I looked to Jonathan, who raised an eyebrow very calmly and gestured for me to sit down. I didn't. I couldn't move.

"What are you doing?" I asked him.

"Upholding tradition," he replied. He nodded to the kids assembled. "Since the dawn of time, man has been intrinsically linked to his gods. As I've said in class over and over again, man viewed the gods as true entities, ones who could be entreated or invoked, feared or loved. Only in the last few centuries has that practice moved away from common thought. Now the gods of old are seen as myths, and the gods many worship today exist behind veils and walls of liturgical hierarchy. Here, in this room, we go back to the basics. We explore what it means to be truly human, and to truly connect with the divine."

My stomach churned and it took all I had to keep standing and not just collapse to my knees.

He squeezed my shoulder. "I know what you think," he said. "I know the correlation you're drawing—I saw your sketch, and I know you think what we're doing is a part of it. But I assure you, it's not. We are intent on not harming anyone. In fact, the main purpose of this group is to grow and flourish as artists."

"What are you talking about?"

"The muses," Tina said. She stepped closer to me. Was it my imagination that her eyes were wild, or did she truly seem a little touched? "Think about it. All the great artists made a huge

278

deal about calling down the muses. I mean, look at Homer! He started his epics with an invocation."

"So, what? You're calling down the muses to be better artists?"

"Exactly," Tina said.

"That's . . ."

"Insane?" Jonathan asked. "Look a little deeper, Kaira. I think we both know it's far from insane. We've all seen your thesis—we know that you understand the truth. The arcane is everywhere, waiting to be invoked to further the progress of art. That's why I asked you to join us. You're already connected to that world—you already see the potential and inspiration within the occult."

"But people are dying," I began, but he cut me off.

"Suicides happen," he said flatly. "They are tragedies, but they happen. What we do here has nothing to do with blood."

"But Jane? And Mandy? Were they part of this?"

It was the first time Jonathan actually looked uncomfortable by my questions. He looked to the others.

"Just Mandy," he replied after a moment. "But she was not a suitable vessel. She wasn't strong enough to withstand the powers of a god. But look around you. Look at the work your fellow students have achieved, without harm, without pain. You have that strength within you. If you opened yourself to the power, you could achieve anything."

Without harm, without pain . . . *The gods require blood.* Maybe the kids doing the summoning hadn't been hurt, but the gods demanded a price. *Someone* had paid. And that someone was Jane. Who would it be the next time?

"Nothing is free," I said, forcing down the image of Munin perched on my sink, my blood pooled around me. "What about Jane? How was she involved?"

"She wasn't," Jonathan said. "I already told you—it was a suicide. A tragedy."

"Then why the hell was there a ring around her body?" I asked. I glared around the room. "Was it one of you? Did you sacrifice her?"

Jonathan put a hand on my shoulder. "You need to calm down, Kaira. Jane was not involved in this, and no one here was involved in her death. We aren't trying to harm others—we are trying to further art."

"Then explain the ring," I demanded. "Why was it there? Why was she a sacrifice?"

Jonathan said nothing.

"Why don't you just join us for tonight?" he finally said. "Leave your misconceptions at the door for another hour and we'll show you there's nothing at all diabolical here. We are merely exploring ancient rituals and integrating them into a modern practice. It's no different from praying before a recital or giving thanks for a good show."

"Then why the locked door?" I asked.

"Magic has always been scrutinized. What the world doesn't understand, it fears, and we have no room for fear or hatred here. This is a place of learning. Of connection."

I wanted to hate him. I wanted to scream. But the trouble was, everything he said made sense, and that made it worse. I grew up with a pagan mother—I'd helped with rituals and solstices, made her charms and teas. I believed what he said—the gods were there to be invoked, and many were the beneficial sort. But as Munin had warned, there were more gods than there were stars in the sky. And not all of them wanted humanity to flourish.

"Who are you invoking?" I asked.

Jonathan just smiled.

"Not all gods are named," he said. "Come, we don't have much time. Kaira, if you'd stand over here."

"No."

He paused and looked at me.

"No?"

"I'm not doing this." I gestured to the circle on the floor. "This is wrong. You're playing with something you shouldn't, and yeah, maybe a few of you haven't gotten hurt, but others have. People are *dead*, Jonathan. My friends. They're dead, and I know it's because of what you're doing here. You're invoking *something*, and whatever it is demands payment. Maybe not your life, but the life of someone else. You don't just get free magic. You need to stop, before someone else gets hurt."

Jonathan studied me for a long moment.

"Kaira, I wasn't expecting this from you. Surely you see you're being irrational?"

"This can't go on," I replied. I looked around the room, to Tina and Kai and the other musicians and artists I knew only by face. "You guys . . . you're toying with something you shouldn't be messing with. Kids are dying. And they're dying because of you."

"I think you should leave," Jonathan said. "Normally, I wouldn't have invited someone in like this, not without a more thorough screening. I'd thought you were a little more open-minded than the rest, but seeing as you're already leading a witch hunt . . ."

He turned and walked toward the door. I didn't move.

Why didn't they see? How could I get them to stop? I wanted to rip my hair out. This was it. This was the key. And no one seemed to give a shit.

"You guys . . . you're killing people. I know you think you aren't, but you are. I've seen it. First hand. What you're doing is wrong. You have to stop. Please." It wasn't until I reached the end that I realized there were tears in my eyes. But the kids weren't having it. Tina actually looked sad.

"I thought better of you," she said. "We're all sad about Mandy and Jane. That's partially why we're here. To connect with them. To honor them. I wish you could see that. I wish you weren't so blinded by your own fear."

I opened my mouth. I wanted to slap her.

But how could I show them I'd seen the other side? I'd toyed with these powers and felt the full backlash.

"Nothing is free," I said. "Everything you're doing has a price. And you're making other people pay it."

Jonathan's hand was on my shoulder. He led me to the door and unlocked it for me.

"I'll tell them," I said. "I'll tell them what you're doing."

"And I'll tell them you've read too many fantasies." He said it with remorse. That was the worst part—he wasn't vengeful or power hungry. He thought I was actually in the wrong. "I don't want to play these cards, Kaira, but if push comes to shove I'll have to recommend you graduate in absentia. After all, with your thesis and the stress you're under, it would be an easy connection to think you might be inclined to suffer delusions. I don't want it to come to that. So for both of our sakes, pretend you weren't here. I'm sorry to have believed in you."

Then, before I could rebut, he closed the door and locked it.

I wanted to scream. I wanted to kick and pound on the damn door until he opened it. I wanted to do anything I could to interrupt their stupid little ritual. If they went through it again, someone would get hurt. If they were invoking something darker, they might not know what was going on. They might not actually know the price other people were paying. And that ignorance was more dangerous than willful evil.

I stood there for a good fifteen minutes. I couldn't hear anything on the other side of the door and had no clue if they were waiting for me to leave or had already started. Leaving felt like admitting defeat; worse, it felt like taking responsibility. If something went wrong, if someone got hurt . . . it would be my fault. Because I hadn't stopped it.

What happened to not getting involved? What happened to graduating and going to college and living a normal life?

The questions were transparent. They didn't matter, not anymore. I had to stop this. But no one in their right mind was going to believe me. I needed someone at my side to help convince the faculty to make Jonathan leave, or to shut this down. Maybe, if I called my mom, she could do something about this. I needed her, needed someone who could actually take Jonathan down, prevent him from hurting someone else.

Or you need me. The voice wasn't Munin's. It was the violet-eyed girl, the goddess with no name. I felt her hands on the back of my neck, a gentle caress. But it wasn't just her hands. It was Brad's, as he pulled me close, as he whispered in my ear and pushed her image down.

No one will believe you about this, Brad said. *Just like why they would never believe you about me. You didn't fight against me; you won't fight against this. You will let them die, Kaira, because you will never stand up for yourself.*

I squeezed my eyes shut and leaned against the door, tried to block him out, but he was there, beside me, against me, his cologne in my nostrils and his saliva on my tongue.

Your friends will die because of you, he whispered. *And you will run away again. You are weak, Kaira. And you always will be.*

"No."

I don't know where the word came from, but it didn't feel like mine. It was a flame in my chest, the tiniest spark in the darkness, the glint of the moon on a raven's eye. Brad hovered there, in the emptiness, a shit-eating grin on his face.

The flame grew.

"I'm done hiding from you," I whispered. "I'm done hiding from what you've done."

He stepped forward, reached out to touch me. But he wasn't alone in the void of my mind. Ethan was there, and Oliver. My mother and Elisa.

And Chris.

"I'm not broken," I said.

The spark inside grew, became a rage.

"I'm not going to let anyone get hurt because I was afraid. Not again. Not by you, and not by this."

Brad laughed.

You couldn't save yourself. How are you going to save anyone else?

"I *did* save myself," I replied. There, in the darkness, the violet-eyed girl floated. Waiting for me. "And I'm not going to run away again."

I opened my eyes, the flame inside me hot, raging. I knew what I had to do.

Or rather, I knew what I couldn't do again.

I turned and pounded on the wood door over and over until someone finally opened it. It wasn't Jonathan, it was Kai.

"Kaira," he said, "What are you doing—"

I pushed past him and into the room. The kids all surrounded the circle, chanting something softly. Jonathan stood in the center of the ring with his arms raised, his head tilted back in invocation.

I didn't think or call out. I ran headfirst into the circle and swung.

Darkness.

I knew, in the far corners of my mind, that this was somewhere in between. That the circle had been a gateway of sorts. That knowledge was infinitesimal compared to the man floating in front of me. Jonathan was there in the darkness, frozen, my fist inches away from his face. But it wasn't Jonathan holding my attention. It was the force behind him. Around him. Within him. A ghostly white light that seethed in the stillness, a haze of snow and shadow that froze me to the bone.

He is coming.

Behind the spectral form of Jonathan appeared the girl. Her violet eyes were sad. Even Munin on her shoulder appeared upset.

"What is that?" I asked. My lips didn't move, but the thought carried through the silence like a shout.

"The Endbringer," she replied. "The god your professor has been summoning."

"I don't understand."

"There has always been a balance between the realms of gods and men. Heaven and Hell, Valhalla and Niflheim, Olympus and Hades—they have many names, and they have always been at war for human worship. But this . . . this god, he is not of those worlds. He was cast aside, and now, he desires revenge. With every sacrifice in his name, his power grows. And now, he tries to breach your world." She looked to Jonathan. "If he breaks free, if he upsets the balance, he will destroy us all."

The Tree Will Burn. I didn't understand what that had to do with anything, but I didn't care, not anymore. I knew what I had to do. The bastard had killed Jane. He wouldn't kill again.

"You cannot take him as you are," the girl said, following my thoughts. "You must invoke me."

"Will I die?" I asked. My voice didn't waiver as much as it should have.

"In a sense," Munin said. "But it is the only way the rest will live."

"Then I'll do it. I invoke you."

286

The girl smiled. There was so much sadness in those lips. Munin cawed and flew from her shoulder, his wings unfolding into a greater darkness as she stepped forward and the world faded to black.

"Our will be done."

CHRIS

CHAPTER TWENTY-FOUR

I don't know why I went to the academics concourse.

I told myself it was because I wanted to take a shortcut to the arts building, to check out the space for my thesis. I told myself it was because it was cold and windy and dark outside, and the warmth of the concourse made me forget all that. Mostly, though, I told myself it was *not* because of Kaira. Not because I knew she was there for a tutorial group. Not because I hadn't been able to get her off my mind all day.

It's why I ended up skipping the movie. It wasn't just the wind or the snow or the ever-present darkness. There was something in the air. Something beyond the crows clumped like snow. Something darker. And I knew, somewhere deep down, that it was because of her.

I felt stupid, but I'd had the boys and Elisa drop me off after dinner. It was a bit more of a trek for them but no one questioned the change of heart—we were all in that headspace, when nothing felt right or real. So there I wandered, slowly, down the hall, toward the arts building, and saw her farther on. She leaned against a door and there were tears streaming down her face, her fists balled tight. And she was shaking.

My heart nearly stopped.

There had been way too many tears lately. Too much death. Too much sadness.

I jogged toward her, but as I did so I watched her expression change, watched her face tighten and her fists slam into the door and then she was pounding on it, screaming at the top of her lungs. I called out her name but I know she didn't hear me. I barely heard myself through the screams of crows outside the window. Then the door opened and she ran in, and everything in my head was crows, and for some reason, with every blink I saw her. My sister. In that ring of sand. I ran faster and pushed into the room.

Everything else was a blur.

The black circle on the floor, ringed with students. Jonathan in the center, his hands upraised as Kaira leaped at him, her fist aimed straight at his face. People were yelling, the crows in my head going wild. And then, the moment her foot stepped over that damned black line, a silence. A pause. Like that great big inhale before the bomb goes off.

And then it did.

There was an explosion. Kaira's fist smashed into Jonathan as the window smashed open and then there were birds, birds everywhere. Crows and ravens, cawing and screaming and flocking toward the circle. They swarmed it, funneled around like a tornado, like a cocoon of black wings and beaks and flashes of violet light, and the kids around the circle were screaming too, trying to get away, but I was pushing forward. Forward. Pressing through the crows that slashed at my skin and pierced my eardrums and it was more than caws, it was screaming, the screams of a thousand dead and dying, the screams of the damned. I knew those screams. I heard them every time the nightmares came. Every time I heard my sister's voice.

The birds imploded, collapsed in on themselves and the circle in a whirlwind of shadows. I braced for an explosion, but it never came. Silence rang loud as a gunshot. No birds. No screaming classmates. Just Kaira and Jonathan in the center of the circle.

I fell to my knees at her side and pressed my head to her chest. No movement. No heartbeat.

Jonathan didn't move either but I was too focused on her. I picked her up in my arms. Her head dangled to the side and all I could see was my sister's face. Back in the nightmare, back on the beach.

"Kaira, please," I whispered, holding her close. "Please don't leave me. Please. Please."

Something scratched on the tile. I looked up, blinked hard. A bird. But not a crow. The falcon, its golden eyes trained on me.

"Get out of here," I hissed. "Get out of my head!"

The fucking bird. The bird that was always there, always at the edge of my dreams and vision, saying my debt was yet to be paid.

You must rejoice, the bird said. *She has banished our enemy. And now that she is dead, the Aesir will triumph in the battle to come. In our battle.* Behind him stood a boy, his skin gold, a halo of daggers crowning his head.

"It's not my battle," I said. "I'm not going to fight for you. I'd never fight against her."

I pushed the bird out of my mind and cradled Kaira close, prayed to every god I knew to bring her back, to make her okay. *I can't lose you. I can't let you go. Please, don't let her die. Take me instead.*

Kaira gasped.

"Chris?" she asked.

I looked down and stroked her hair. "It's okay," I said. "Everything's going to be okay."

"Chris, I'm scared. She's . . ."

Then her eyes closed, her entire body going stiff.

"No! No no no no!" I tried to steady her, tried to get her to calm down. Tried to ignore the sound of ravens in the distance. "Kaira, don't leave me!"

"I am not Kaira, vessel of the Aesir," she whispered. "My name is Freyja."

She opened her eyes. Violet eyes. Then she screamed and curled over, away from me, shook harder.

"Chris," she moaned. "Chris, please. Save me."

I reached out to touch her, but she screamed again, and this time the scream was echoed by a hundred ravens, their oily wings bursting from her body. They circled her, swarmed her with shadow.

And when they flew out the shattered window, Kaira was nowhere to be seen.

ACKNOWLEGMENTS

This book began as a hasty sketch of a tree and a quote in my journal at 3 a.m. in Scotland. It was one of those lines that I knew was important: *The Godchild was born in the tangled roots of the World Tree.* Since then, the story has undergone countless transformations over three continents. From that initial seed on Scottish soil to plotting on trains across the Norwegian countryside to finishing a few (completely different) drafts in Seattle, the Ravenborn Saga has lived a dynamic life. And that means there are many people to thank along the way.

First, and always, my deepest thanks to my fabulous agent, Laurie McLean, at Fuse Literary. She has been my knight in shining armor every step of the way. Without her knowledge and encouragement, this book would still just be a scribbled page in a forgotten notebook.

Next, to my editor extraordinaire, Michael Strother, and the entire Simon Pulse team, for taking a chance on me and turning this story into a true work of art.

To my mother, for helping me leave the nest before I knew what it meant to fly; I couldn't have done any of this without you. To my father, for inspiring my love of books and adventure. And to my brother, for showing me what dedication truly looks like.

To Will Taylor, for helping me fine-tune both this book and my life. And being the sparkly unicorn to my . . . opposite of sparkly unicorn. At least in terms of writing.

To Interlochen Arts Academy, for giving me a boarding school experience worth writing about.

To Adam, for groggily listening to plot points on that aforementioned Norwegian train ride (and the rest of that trip).

To my Seattle writing team—Danielle Dreger, Kristin Halbrook, and Danny Marks—for keeping me on track. Or at least caffeinating me.

And finally, to you, my dear readers, for being a constant source of inspiration.